It takes only a couple of minutes to fill the hole back up again. Once we're done patting the sand down, Coralee looks for a rock to mark the spot with while I count the paces to the beach, like I guess people who bury treasure are supposed to.

"Look!" she says. "This one's shaped kind of like a horse."

I stare at the rock, screwing up my face and squinting, but I don't see it. "Nope," I say. "Not a horse. What about that one with all the barnacles on it? That's easier to recognize."

Coralee agrees, and we haul the rock over, dropping it on top of our hiding spot.

We fall into the sand and sit for a minute, catching our breath.

When I look over at Coralee, I glimpse a spark of excitement in her eye, and suddenly her whole face lights up in its glow. "This is kind of fun, huh? Like a real adventure."

"Yeah," I say, feeling a sudden squeeze of guilt.

It's exactly the kind of real adventure that Kacey and I always wanted to have together.

The kind we'll never have.

You can't be with her. You can never be with her again.

The
Ethan
I Was
Before

Ali Standish

HARPER
An Imprint of HarperCollins Publishers

ISBN 978-0-06-243339-8

18 19 20 21 22   BRR   10 9 8 7 6 5 4 3 2
❖
First paperback edition, 2019

For Arun, who dared me to be more

࿇

Contents ❧

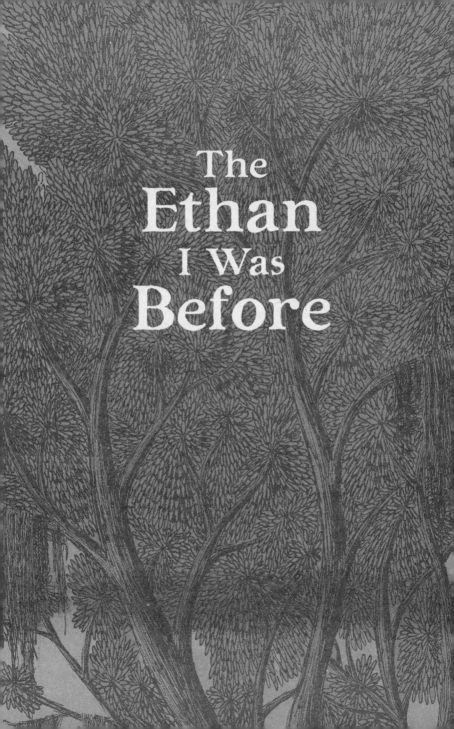

The
Ethan
I Was
Before

Prologue

⌔

Kacey's window has been dark for fifty-nine days.

It's been dark for so long that someone else might easily forget she ever even lived there. Or that she ever existed at all.

I haven't forgotten.

Tonight, like all the other nights, I wait until everyone is asleep. Then I tiptoe downstairs, slip into my coat, and creep out the front door. I climb onto the roof of our Subaru and sit there, staring.

I have stared at Kacey's window for so many nights that I no longer see the four black panes held together by the skeleton of the frame.

All I see is a dark hollow where there used to be light.

But tonight, when I step out onto the porch, something is different.

Tonight, there is a car in Kacey's driveway.

Kacey's window has been dark for fifty-nine days.

But now a light flashes on, and a yellow glow seeps into the night.

I pull my breath in so fast that the frigid air burns the back of my throat.

I hold it there.

Before I can stop myself, my feet slam against the pavement, and I'm running across the street and into the Reids' yard. My gloveless fingers fumble on the ground until I find a suitably large pebble. I position myself underneath Kacey's window and swing the stone up into the air, hitting the top left pane.

For a second, nothing happens.

Then a shadow slides up the wall, and a face appears in the window.

I feel Kacey's name rise up from the place where it stays, deep in my chest.

But then I get a better look at the face above, and her name lodges in my throat.

The drawn complexion and mussed hair belong to Mrs. Reid, Kacey's mother.

I duck down into the shadow of the Reids' hedge, next to their front stoop, hoping that she didn't have time to spot me. I crouch with my face resting against the scratching branches until I feel sure she isn't looking anymore.

My eyes flicker to the stoop, where a crisp, white square of paper rests against the bricks.

Before I have time to think about it, I snatch the letter up.

Then I sprint back to my own driveway and drop onto the porch stairs. I look at what's in my hands.

Not a letter. A bill.

I glance at the return address. I know what the words mean, but they don't make any sense.

The earth begins to seesaw.

Stupid, stupid, stupid. Throwing rocks at her window like I expected her to be up there. But of course she isn't.

I know where she is now.

I'm still trying to catch my breath from my dash across the Reids' yard. But I am suddenly filled with the urge to run until I am sure I will never see this place or that window ever again. Like swimming so far out to sea you know you won't have the energy to make it back to shore.

Once my feet start moving, I can't seem to make them stop.

I have to get to Kacey.

What I Know about Myself

1. My name is Ethan Truitt.

2. I am twelve years and four months old.

3. I have been in the car for fifteen hours, four minutes, and thirty-two seconds.

4. Which is probably why my left butt cheek has gone numb.

5. My older brother, Roddie, who is snoring next to me, hates me.

6. Sometimes I hate me too. Because I know I am responsible for everything that happened in Boston.

7. That's why the Ethan I was before is gone.

Palm Knot

❧

ACCORDING TO THE CITY limits sign we see when we drive into town, Palm Knot, Georgia, is the "Hidden Jewel of the So th." Mom says that it *used* to be the "Hidden Jewel of the South" before the wind and ocean air swept away the paint from the *u*.

When I think of jewels (not often), I think of bright, sharp, polished things. But driving through Palm Knot, everything I see is kind of drooping and faded and flat. More like an ocean pebble that's been washed smooth over a lot of years.

As we turn onto Main Street, my butt cheek starts to cramp up again.

I've been leaning against the car door for the past few hours, trying to keep as much distance as I can between me and Roddie.

But now I shift my weight and accidentally bump my knee into his.

The rattle of his breath suddenly stops; his eyes flash open and he jerks his leg away from mine as if he's afraid I might be carrying some highly contagious disease. He looks at me in disgust. He doesn't say anything, but I can read the words flashing through his eyes. *Watch it, freak.*

I don't flinch. I'm used to this now. Roddie hasn't spoken to me since the day I tried to run away. For the third time.

That first night, when I found the bill that Mrs. Reid must have dropped on her way into the house, I only made it to South Station before a police officer stopped me. Apparently, a twelve-year-old hanging around the bus station alone in the middle of the night is suspicious.

But the second time I ran, I was smarter about it. I looked up the bus times in advance, I made it to the station for a midafternoon bus, and I got on behind a middle-aged woman who could have been mistaken for my mother. And it worked.

That time, I almost got to Kacey.

Almost.

That's why I knew I had to try one more time. I waited for my chance, for the first opportunity when Mom and Dad would leave me home with just Roddie. And then I ran again.

I only got halfway down the block before someone jerked my shoulder back, making me trip over my own feet and fall to the pavement.

6

Roddie was right about everything he said that day. I know that now.

But I don't have to tell him that.

"You boys awake back there?" Mom calls from the front seat.

Roddie grunts and pulls his Boston College hat down lower over his eyes.

"Doing okay, Ethan?"

Mom has started saying my name the way she placed the teetering stacks of her best china into boxes back in Boston. Carefully. Slowly. Like she's afraid of breaking something fragile and precious.

I nod.

"We're almost home," she says.

Roddie glares out the window. "This place isn't home. It's a dump."

He has a point. The porches of the houses all sag like giant hammocks. Trees grow crooked and clawlike out of the sandy soil. The narrow roads are rough and lumpy, and even the ocean water looks clouded and gray, like the bay is filled with lead.

"Your grandpa Ike needs us here, Roddie," Mom says, turning around to face us. "We need you to stay positive, please. This is a fresh start for all of us."

Roddie's eyes narrow into little pools of ice, and he aims a kick at the console between the two front seats. "Stop lying!

We don't even know Grandpa Ike. He's your own father and you barely even *talk* about him."

"Roddie!" Dad barks. "Don't start again. That's enough. Just—enough. It's been a long drive."

But Roddie's right about this, too.

Mom and Dad announced we were moving here the day after my third attempt at running away. They said we all needed a change of scenery. I guess it shouldn't have come as such a surprise. This is the only place they *could* move us to get me away from Boston, since Grandpa Scott lives just a few streets down from our old house and it's not like Mom and Dad could afford to just buy a new place somewhere.

They've been telling anyone who will listen that we're moving to Palm Knot so we can "help" Grandpa Ike, who's "getting up there in years." I pretend to believe them, but I know they're lying.

We didn't move so we could help Grandpa Ike.

We moved because of what I did to Kacey.

Grandpa Ike

❧

FIVE MINUTES LATER, DAD swerves onto a gravel road, and we pass a few houses in varied states of dilapidation before pulling up in front of a boxy, wood-sided house at the end of the street. It's not the most run-down place on the street, but it's not the nicest one, either. There's a rusty truck parked out front, and the garden beds are overflowing with brown tufts of withering weeds.

Mom gasps and covers her mouth with her palm. "Look at the place," she says. "He's let it go to ruin."

"Then it's a good thing we came!" Dad says, forcing cheer into his voice. "Everybody out."

I unhook my seat belt and thrust the door open, desperate to stretch my muscles and feel fresh air.

But as soon as I'm out of the car, the humidity wraps

around me like a wet fleece blanket, so thick I can barely breathe. An insect drone swells up from the gnarled wall of marsh trees that surrounds us.

Mom stands in the gloomy shade of the house, squinting up at it and shaking her head. Maybe it's just the effect of the shadows, but her eyes look gray and stormy.

I hear a croaking noise and look toward the wooden porch to see a door open and the silhouette of a man emerging. Grandpa Ike. He doesn't come down to greet us. He just stands there, hands in his pockets, staring.

"Hello, Ike," Mom says. She greets him with all the enthusiasm of someone who's just opened their door to find a greasy salesman waiting on the stoop.

Grandpa Ike says nothing.

"Great," Roddie mutters. "So he's a lurker."

Mom hisses something back at him.

Dad watches closely as Roddie and I each grab two suitcases from the trunk. Mom and Dad have been careful to keep an eye out whenever Roddie and I are together, ever since they found us in the street that day, Roddie pinning me against a parked car while blood dripped onto the pavement from my scraped knees.

Reluctantly, I shuffle up to the porch, where most of the white paint has chipped away to reveal the bare skin of the wood. Then I'm standing face-to-face with Grandpa Ike.

He's tall—over six feet—and solid, like someone built

him from a stack of bricks. His eyes and beard are the same silvery-gray color, and he has a smear of mustard in the corner of his mouth.

"'Lo, Ethan," he says. He looks me straight in the eye for a few seconds before lifting a duffel bag easily from my shoulder and leading me inside. "Your room's upstairs."

Grandpa Ike's house is very different from our house back in Boston.

For one thing, it's old.

Our house in Boston was old too, but it didn't seem like it. It had clean showerheads that sprayed hot water, and shiny marble counters and digital appliances in the kitchen.

It only takes me a couple of hours to figure out that Grandpa Ike's house—I mean *my* house—has none of those things. The shower spurts out lukewarm water, the kitchen counters are stained green and brown, and every few minutes the fridge makes a noise like someone with a cold clearing their throat. *Huu-hukk! Huu-hukk!*

There are also boxes everywhere, stacked behind the washing machine, wilting on the back porch, peeking out from under the beds. Most of the garage is taken up by an ancient hunk of metal on wheels that Grandpa Ike calls the Fixer-Upper.

After we unpack the car, Mom bakes a frozen pizza and

hands out slices on paper plates. Grandpa Ike says he's already eaten but sits in near silence at the table with us, looking on while we wolf down our dinner.

I'm glad that he doesn't seem interested in telling me how much I've grown or forcing me to answer questions about my best subject or my favorite sports.

"Can I be excused?" I ask after ten long minutes.

"Did you eat enough?"

"I had two pieces, Mom."

"Okay, well, let me come with you and make up your bed."

"I can handle it." I throw my plate in the trash can and retreat upstairs before she can object.

My new room is actually okay. It's a lot bigger than the old one, and it even has a window seat, where I sit for a long time, staring. The window looks out on a marsh, where moonlight shimmers on the black water winding through the reeds, giving it shiny scales.

I'm just about to go to bed when I hear a rapping at the door.

"Come in."

Grandpa Ike swings the door open and stands in the hall. "Settling in okay?"

"Sure, I guess," I say, standing awkwardly by my bed.

"Well, all right, then." Grandpa Ike nods and squints

around the bare room. "Planning to decorate?"

"Not really."

"What's the point, eh?" he replies. "You've got all the necessities." His eyes fall on the chest of drawers stuffed into the corner of my room. I follow his gaze and notice that a photograph has been placed on it.

Grandpa Ike clears his throat. "Well, good night. I'm next door if you need me."

Roddie's room is on one side of mine, so Grandpa Ike's must be on the other. Behind the door that's been kept shut since we got here.

"Good night," I say, relieved that there is not going to be a pep talk, no I'm-always-here-if-you-need-anything speech that all adults feel required to give me these days.

Suddenly, I hear a scratching sound coming from the ceiling.

Grandpa Ike shrugs.

"Only mice," he says. "Nothing to worry about. Unless it's squirrels. Then you've got a big problem. Anyway, sleep well."

Just then, Roddie's speakers thrum to life, the bass of his music vibrating against our shared wall.

Grandpa Ike looks at me, one eyebrow raised. "Or not."

I decide I am going to like Grandpa Ike.

Main Street

❧

ON MY FIRST MORNING in Palm Knot, Dad shakes me awake at eight o'clock. I squint when I open my eyes, because the sun is blazing through my window. I hear a loud humming, which I think is in my head for a minute before I realize it's just the buzz of insects down in the marsh.

"Time to get up," Dad says. "Mom made breakfast, and then we're off to the hardware store."

"Why do I have to go?" I groan.

"Because I need your help," Dad says.

Another lie.

As if going on a quest to the hardware store will somehow make me feel any better.

But I get up and get dressed, because it takes less effort than fighting with him. Mom ends up coming too, so she can

14

make sure Dad and I get "the heavy-duty cleaning stuff" and "the humane kind of mouse traps."

Grandpa Ike's truck is already gone from the driveway by the time we leave.

As we twist back up the gravel road, Mom points to each house and tells us who lives there. My new neighbors are:

1. The Bondurants, who are now actually just the Bondurant. Mr. Bondurant lives alone in a rusty trailer next to the house he used to live in with Mrs. Bondurant, who Mom says left him for his own brother.
2. The Millsaps, whose house is painted purple and green. They have two little kids and keep goats and chickens in their backyard. This morning, Mrs. Millsap brought Mom canned peach preserves and a basket of fresh tomatoes from her garden.
3. The Preyers, who I haven't seen yet because they go to Cape Cod from April to September.
4. An old rotted house—the biggest of any on the road—that used to belong to a family called the Blackwoods but is now empty. Unless there are ghosts who live there, which seems likely.

Palm Knot isn't the kind of town tourists flock to for vacation. It would be more accurate to call it a pit stop than a town, a strip of shops and a stretch of cracked highway built into the crook of the bay. "The old Texaco station halfway between Savannah and Jacksonville," Mom says as we cross over the inlet bridge. "That's what tourists call Palm Knot."

The bay sprawls out to our right. Almost all the buildings are clustered on the other side of the road. "It's on the left, Dave!" says Mom, pointing to the first brick building we pass, with a sign in front that reads *Mack's Hardware Store*.

But Dad has already driven past it, and we have to turn around in the parking lot of the Pink Palm Motel.

On the far side of the motel, there's a restaurant called the Beachy Keen Fish House. Nearer to us, next to the parking lot, is a bean-shaped pool. Even though it's only the beginning of April—when the kids in Boston are just hanging up their snow coats for spring—steam rises off the turquoise water. The pool is already crowded with kids who all seem to know each other, judging by how they splash and roughhouse together.

I like swimming, and diving especially. But this pool is nothing like the one Kacey and I used to go to in Boston, the only one nearby that still had a high dive board.

"Mr. Ernie always lets the local kids swim, since he never has any paying guests anyway," Mom says, following my gaze. "I used to play there all the time. Do you want me to take you later?"

I think of the press of alien faces that would greet me if

I showed up at the pool. The eager crush of questions about where I'm from and what Boston is like and when I'm starting school.

I watch as the kids line up on one side of the pool for a race. It looks like fun.

"No," I say.

Flowers line the outside of Mack's Hardware Store, and wind chimes hang above the door, clanging against each other in the breeze. Two identical tabby cats lie side by side on the welcome mat, so anyone who wants to come into the store has to clamber over them.

I follow Mom and Dad inside and trail behind them, stopping every once in a while so they can debate the pros and cons of organic glass cleaner and what the probability is that Grandpa Ike has a working lawn mower.

The air in the shop hangs heavy and moist, and everything smells like earth. Like we're standing in a giant coffin. My stomach begins to churn, and I suddenly feel a choking that makes me want to claw at my throat.

"Mom? Can I wait outside?"

Mom fumbles with the screwdriver in her hands, and it clatters to the ground. She casts a bleak look in Dad's direction as she bends to pick it up. "I don't know, Ethan," she says. "I don't think it's a good idea for you to—"

"I'll stay right outside," I say. "I want to, um, pet the cats."

Okay. So sometimes I lie, too.

"Maybe your dad should come—"

"I'll stay where you can see me through the windows. Promise."

"Where I can see you," she echoes, looking flustered as she reaches into the basket and pulls out the wood polish Dad put in, scanning the shelves for a different kind. "We won't be long."

As I make a break for the exit, a dreadlocked woman behind the shop counter, who is fanning herself with a square of sandpaper, points to a colorful jar in front of her. "Taffy?" she asks.

I shake my head and yank the door open, hurdle over the cats, and heave myself out into the seething heat, where I inhale deep gulps of salty air. It's hotter out here than it was in the store, but at least a breeze rakes in from the ocean.

I pull my sweatshirt up over my head and knuckle it into a ball. No one told me it would be so much hotter here.

I look over my shoulder, on a hunch, and see Mom staring at me through the window. She waves at me before ducking behind a display of toilet-cleaning supplies.

I guess even here, a place with no buses and no trains—no way for me to get to Kacey—they're afraid I'll try to run again.

I sit down on the edge of the hot curb and stare across the

road at the murky bay, which as far as I can tell has no official name. The no-name bay has no beach, either, just waves lapping against a ridge of rocks that separates the ocean from Main Street. A few boats bob on the lazy ocean swells.

Maybe they think I'll steal one of those and try to sail back up the coast.

And maybe the Ethan I was before that day Roddie tackled me onto the pavement would have.

But *I* won't.

My gaze wanders to the Sand Pit, the only building on the other side of the street. I know it's a grocery store, since Mom pointed it out on the way into town. But there are also hopeful advertisements in the windows for snorkel sets and shark-tooth necklaces, and blow-up pool toys line the sidewalk outside. A woman comes out and holds the door open for two little kids. A boy and a girl, both licking ice-cream cones.

Suddenly the girl trips on a crack in the sidewalk, and her cone goes flying. The boy is quick to help, lifting her up and offering her his cone to stop her tears. She wipes her eyes and beams at him.

Hurt boomerangs unexpectedly through me, and I look away.

I'm not lying when I say Mom and Dad don't have to worry about me trying to run again.

Back in Boston, I ran because I wanted to find Kacey.

19

If I could find her, then I could make everything okay again.

But I know now that I can't.

Because where Kacey has gone, I'll never be able to find her.

Suzanne

❧

AFTER WHAT SEEMS LIKE a lifetime, Mom and Dad finally emerge from the store, carrying about twenty bulging bags each.

"Oh, Dave, we forgot to get something to get rid of that spider infestation," Mom says. "Could you—"

"All right," Dad mutters, setting his bags down on the curb next to me and shuffling back into the store.

Mom hovers over me and smooths my curly black mop of hair. "So what do you think so far of—"

"Is that Lara? Lara Pomeroy?"

I look up to see a woman with platinum-blond hair in cut-off jeans and a tank top striding toward us. Her long legs, her shoulders, and her face are all burned pink, which makes her look kind of like a giant flamingo.

"Gretta? Gretta Carroway?" Mom responds uncertainly.

"You remember!" the woman exclaims, throwing her arms around Mom. "Lara Pomeroy! I can't believe it."

"It's Truitt, now," Mom says. "My husband is inside. And this is my son Ethan."

Mom gestures for me to stand up.

"Ethan, this is Mrs. Carroway."

"Oh, it's just Ms. Carroway now," the woman drawls. "Mr. Carroway took the Greyhound to Orlando some years ago."

She holds out a manicured hand. "It's a pleasure, doll. I went to high school with your mama. And my daughter, Suzanne, is—" Ms. Carroway casts a look over her shoulder. "Suzanne! Stop gabbin' on that phone and come say hello."

A girl steps out from behind a parked car, her face half hidden by her phone. Her fingers whir across its screen.

"I don't know where her manners are," Ms. Carroway says, making a clucking sound. "Suzanne, this is—er— Edwin?"

"Ethan," Mom corrects tersely.

It's weird to think that Mom is the same age as Ms. Carroway. Her graying hair and the crinkly lines around her eyes make Mom look older.

Suzanne taps her phone one last time, probably hitting "send" before finally lowering it. My first thought is that she looks like a doll. She has neatly curled blond hair surrounding her heart-shape face, and a smudge of blue over each eye. She

22

wears a bikini top and white shorts, and there's a towel draped across her arm.

"Hi," she says, looking me over.

"Hi," I echo, flinching as I hear my voice crack.

"What grade is Ethan in?" Ms. Carroway asks.

"Seventh," Mom says. "He'll be starting over at the middle school next Monday."

"Well ain't that just somethin'! Suzanne is in seventh grade too!" Ms. Carroway titters, folding her arm around her daughter's shoulder. "She can be Evan's friend on his first day."

"It's *Ethan*," Mom says again.

"Ethan, yes. So what brings you back?" says Ms. Carroway, tapping a pointed nail against her lip. "You must have had an awful good reason to come back to this hole."

My heart stumbles in my chest. I don't like the way Ms. Carroway looks at Mom, like she knows she's hiding something. Mom makes the usual excuses.

"Dave and I, we both work from home anyway, and with Dad getting up there in age, we thought he could use some help."

"I bet. We hardly ever see him in town, you know. Not for years. Not since—"

As Mom interrupts Ms. Carroway to continue her list of fake reasons, I turn my eyes back to Suzanne, who is studying me.

"Where'd you move here from?" she asks finally.

"Boston."

"Oh. That's really cool," she says, raising her eyebrow as if impressed. "I've always lived here. We almost never get new kids. What was your old school like?"

"Um, you know," I say. "Boring."

Suzanne rolls her eyes. "*Tell* me about it. But I bet you were popular there, weren't you? I can always tell."

I don't really know how to answer this, so I look down, but Suzanne's rhinestone flip-flops are glittering so brightly in the sun, they make me wince. I squint back up at her and shrug, the only response I can muster.

"Don't worry," she says. "I'll make sure you know who to hang out with. You can sit with me at lunch, and I can show you off to everyone."

The idea of Suzanne showing me off like a new doll at show-and-tell makes me want to wrinkle my nose, but I stop myself just in time. "Okay," I say reluctantly, willing Dad to be done inside the hardware shop so we can go.

It works. Suzanne is just opening her mouth to respond when I hear Mom say, "Come on, Ethan. Dad's ready."

"Nice to meet you," Ms. Carroway says, reaching out to shake Dad's hand, even though both his hands are completely full. He gives her a tired smile and struggles to lift the bags out of his right hand. "Suzanne and I are off to the pool. Y'all are welcome to join us."

"Thanks," Mom says. "But we really have to be going."

"Later," says Suzanne, glossy lips smirking. "Don't forget. Monday."

"Yeah," I say. "Bye."

It's not until they turn and are swaying off that I realize I am shaking. Mom didn't remove her hand from my back the whole time we were talking, and now she is steering me toward the car.

"Suzanne seems nice," she says. "You talked for a long time."

Longer than I've talked to anyone my age since before the incident, she means.

"Yeah. I guess."

"Friend of yours?" Dad asks Mom.

"Horrible woman," Mom says under her breath. "Or at least she was in high school."

She glances at me. "But I'm sure her daughter's a lovely girl."

She hands me a few bags to put into the car. "Things'll be easier for you here, honey," she whispers.

I nod back, but inside I wonder.

Roddie

❧

BACK IN BOSTON, "EVERYONE" agreed that I should have some time off school to "process" the incident and the move. "Everyone" is (listed in order of importance): (1) Dr. Gorman, my therapist, (2) Mom, (3) Dad, and (4) Ms. Lawdry, my old guidance counselor.

I'm not included in "everyone," because no one asked me what I thought until after they'd already decided that I would get a week.

I'm not sure what was supposed to happen in that week, though, because by the time Mom and Dad take me to Palm Knot Middle to register on Friday, I don't feel any different than when I got here.

"Just wait there," Mom says to Roddie, pointing to a chair in the corner of the office. "I'm sure we won't be long. Then it'll be on to the high school, okay?"

Roddie shrugs and pulls his cell phone out of his pocket as he drops into the chair. "Whatever."

Mom says something to the receptionist.

"Oh, yes!" she replies. "Mr. Beasley is expecting you."

Just then, a door behind her desk opens and a heavy man in a tie and slacks emerges.

"Here he is now," the receptionist says to us, beaming like she's just performed a magic trick.

"Hey, sport!" Mr. Beasley, my new principal, twangs, clapping me on the back as if we already know each other.

There should be a rule against strangers calling you "sport." *Or* clapping you on the back.

"Mrs. Oakley tells me you were on the honor roll back in Boston," he says, nodding to the receptionist. "And did your parents tell me you like to skateboard?"

Everyone blinks at me (except for Roddie, who hasn't looked up from his phone). I pretend to be noticing Mr. Beasley's shiny black shoes, which match his shiny bald head. I've spent a lot of time noticing people's shoes recently.

"Ethan?" Dad prompts. "Mr. Beasley asked if you liked to skateboard."

"Not anymore," I mutter to Mr. Beasley's loafers, which respond by shifting backward uncomfortably.

Mr. Beasley blabbers on for another ten minutes about Palm Knot Middle until his receptionist interrupts.

"I have a phone call for you. An Adina Jessup?"

Even though I've been rude, Mr. Beasley says twice how happy he is that I'm joining the seventh grade before he takes his call. And on the way out, Mrs. Oakley gives me a super-size Snickers bar. Just because.

Because Mom and Dad told them what happened.

But I'll bet if they knew the whole story, they wouldn't be so friendly.

When no one's looking, I stuff the candy bar in a trash can.

If Mr. Beasley and Mrs. Oakley knew the *whole* story, they would probably treat me more like Roddie does.

Like now, when he shoulders open the door to the parking lot just wide enough for himself to get through, letting it slam behind him instead of pushing it open for me.

I don't know if he hates me for what I did, or because we had to move, but I think probably both.

I get it. If I were Roddie, I wouldn't have wanted to leave Boston either.

Roddie played shortstop on his old school's baseball team, the best in the league. He was supposed to be a starter next year, his junior year. Lots of scouts would be at his games, and his coaches told him he might have a chance at playing in college. Roddie's wanted to play baseball for Boston College since he was hitting plastic balls off a tee.

He used to take Kacey and me to the Red Sox games sometimes, if none of his friends could go. We always sat up in the nosebleed seats where even the big screen is only the size of your thumb, but Roddie clapped and cheered for each batter just like he was sitting right behind home plate. When something great happened, like if Ortiz hit a home run, he'd jump up out of his seat and whistle and slap me on the back and ruffle Kacey's hair.

Kacey was around so much that I guess it was kind of like Roddie had a little sister, too.

Before the incident, I was working up the courage to tell Roddie I was thinking about trying out for the middle school team and asking if he'd help me train. Kacey was helping me practice, because I wanted to get good before I brought it up. I didn't want Roddie to be worried about being seen throwing the ball around with his butterfingers kid brother.

Since he was so good at baseball, Roddie always had a lot of friends, and a lot of girls who liked him. But he only ever really cared about Grace.

They started going out last fall and spent pretty much every day together from then until the day we left. I could tell Roddie loved her because of how he used to float around the house all dopey-eyed after their dates. And then one time I was skateboarding in front of the house when he came home, humming and bouncing on his toes. "One day you'll understand, bro," he said. "You'll know what it's like to love a girl so much, you'd give your life for her." Then he grinned and winked. "Who knows? Maybe it'll be Kacey."

I punched him in the shoulder because he knew it wasn't like that between me and Kacey, and what would I want a girl-friend for anyway?

I get why my brother likes Grace so much, though. She smells like a garden and always hugs me when she sees me. Kacey liked her too. Grace showed her how to pull her hair back in some special kind of braid.

After the incident, Grace brought me chocolate-chip cookies. I didn't eat them, but it was still nice of her.

Before we go to the high school office, Roddie insists we stop at the baseball field so he can check it out.

The infield is covered in dirt instead of grass and over-grown with some kind of vine that spreads out like giant squid tentacles.

We all stand in silence, listening to the bug chorus that seems to follow us everywhere we go.

"Nobody would play on a field like this," Roddie says finally. "I bet they don't even have a team here, let alone scouts." His voice breaks. Then he spits at the rusted wire fence and kicks it with a loud *ping*, which I feel in my stomach for a long time after.

Things That Happen on my First Day of School

1. I run into a light pole in the parking lot. I guess that's the downside to staring at the ground all the time. I have to go to the bathroom and wait for my nose to stop bleeding, so then I'm late for homeroom.

2. The custodian forgot to bring an extra desk to my homeroom, so I have to sit in Ms. Silva's chair, in front of the whole class.

3. Mr. Beasley comes over the intercom to tell the entire school about the "newest addition to the Palm Knot family," who should be "welcomed by all with open arms." Everyone stares at me.

4. In PE we play soccer, and Coach Sluggs makes one of the team captains pick me first. Which is the only thing worse than getting picked last.

5. After PE, Mrs. Oakley tracks me down and tells me to follow her to the office for testing. She says this is so my teachers will have "accurate data" on my "levels of prior

knowledge." So I spend the rest of the day taking tests.

6. Except for lunch. Which I eat by myself in the cafeteria because Mrs. Oakley forgets to dismiss me in time to go with the other kids. I wonder if Suzanne is mad about not getting to show me off.

7. Mom's car is the first one waiting in the carpool line after school, and she waves hysterically as I walk toward the parking lot, causing a group of eighth graders next to me to snicker.

Getting Along

❧

"So, Ethan, how do you like your new school?" Dad asks as he chews a bite of burned roll. Mom is always burning things because she gets distracted and forgets about whatever's in the oven. Like, she'll remember an idea she has for a textbook she's editing and go running off to jot it down, or she'll decide that she has just enough time to fold the laundry before taking the nachos out of the oven.

"School's fine," I say. Then I add "pretty much" because my parents like it when I give them descriptive answers. It makes them worry less.

"Did you like your teachers?" Dad asks. "Did they seem competent?"

"How is Ethan supposed to know if his teachers are competent?" Roddie interrupts. "He's twelve."

"I asked *Ethan* a question," says Dad, straightening his glasses and shooting a stern look at Roddie. Dad is short, pale, and wiry, so he has to try very hard to look intimidating. "I'll ask about your day next."

"Don't bother," Roddie mumbles, stabbing at a green bean. He misses and stabs again.

"Stop that," snaps Mom. "Or you'll ruin the china."

The front door opens and closes, and after a few minutes, Grandpa Ike shuffles in from the kitchen. It's the first time I've seen him all day. He's not eating Mom's mac and cheese, rolls, or green beans. His plate holds a ham-and-mustard sandwich and a few salt-and-vinegar chips. The same thing he's eaten every night since we've been here.

Mom rolls her eyes and shoots Dad a look. "I made plenty of food for you, Ike."

I'm not sure why Mom calls her own father "Ike," or why he refuses to eat her food.

I don't know much about Mom and Grandpa Ike's relationship at all, except that Mom never talked about him back in Boston. I always kind of figured it was because talking about Grandpa Ike reminded Mom of Grandma Betty, which made her sad.

Instead of answering her, Grandpa Ike slides into the chair next to me. "You can't teach an old dog, right, Ethan?" he says. Then he takes a huge bite out of his sandwich as Mom scoffs.

They definitely don't get along. Maybe that's the real reason we've never been to visit before.

Roddie is still harpooning at the prey on his plate, and Dad has started tapping his fingers on the table like he's typing at a keyboard, something he does when he gets anxious. He's a coder, so he spends too much time with computers.

"Ethan?" Mom prompts. "Your father asked you a question. Did you like your teachers? What about Suzanne? Did you talk with her today?"

"That's three questions," corrects Grandpa Ike. "How is the boy supposed to answer all those questions at the table? He's trying to eat, for God's sake."

"This food is too gross to eat anyway," says Roddie. "Even the green beans are burned. I didn't know that was possible."

Mom drops her fork to her plate with a clatter. Her cheeks flush and her lips pucker. She looks like she can't decide whether to yell or cry.

"Someone else can do the dishes," she says in a dangerously quiet voice. "I'm going upstairs."

She stomps out of the dining room, and we all hear her door slam a minute later. Dad chews and taps furiously on his place mat. Roddie grabs his baseball cap, which Mom always makes him take off at the table, and jams it back on. He alternates between his Boston College hat and his Red Sox hat. Tonight it's Red Sox. Grandpa Ike polishes off the last bite of his sandwich and goes to the living room to switch on the TV.

No one is getting along.

No one is happy here.

"My teachers seem nice, Dad," I say, too late, but trying to sound enthusiastic. It's the least I can do. I shovel a large bite of crunchy pasta into my mouth. "Tell Mom I said the macaroni was good."

"Suck-up," Roddie mutters.

The Second Day
of School

DURING HOMEROOM THE NEXT day, Ms. Silva, who will also be my English and social studies teacher, asks me to stand up and introduce myself again, even though Mr. Beasley already did it for me over the intercom.

"I thought you might like to tell us a little more about yourself," she says.

She's wrong.

At least today I have a desk, near the back of the class.

I stand up, wincing when my chair makes a screeching sound as it drags across the floor. Suzanne waves her fingers at me one by one before placing her fist under her chin. "Um," I say.

"Why don't you start with your name?" Ms. Silva says gently.

"I'm Ethan," I say to my desk. I keep my eyes on the words **EDDIE WUZ HERE**, which have been carved in blocky letters into its corner. "From Boston."

I'm not looking at her, but my guess is that Ms. Silva is nodding encouragingly and smiling. Judging by her shoes, which are adorned with purple bows, she seems like the kind of teacher who would.

"Is there anything special we should know about you, Ethan? Any hobbies or fun facts?"

"Um. I don't think so."

My voice cracks slightly on the word *so*, and I hear someone whispering. I concentrate on keeping my cheeks from going pink.

"Well, I'm sure we'll get to know you better soon," says Ms. Silva. "You can sit down now."

My legs drop me gratefully back into my seat.

Ms. Silva says something about a diorama project, but my head's buzzing so I don't catch much of it.

I'm remembering what school was like before. When I had Kacey. I didn't mind talking in class back in Boston. If I said something stupid, she would just make a joke about it afterward, and we would both laugh. If my voice cracked, she would do an impression of me, and I would shove her and she would shove me back.

Everything was funny all the time.

I push those memories out of my head and go back to

staring at **EDDIE WUZ HERE**, trying to guess where Eddie is now. I wonder when he carved his name here. If he's already long gone and grown up.

Not everyone gets to grow up, says a voice inside my head. Maybe all that's left of Eddie is these letters scratched into this desk, like words etched onto a tombstone, or Kacey's name typed on that bill.

I jerk my eyes away.

After homeroom I have health instead of PE. All we do is take notes on a video about the causes of cancer. Tomorrow, a guest speaker is coming in to talk to us about the dangers of carcinogens. I guess some things are the same no matter where you go to school.

The next period is science with Mr. Charles, whose hair sprouts thin and white from his head like a dandelion tuft, but whose beard is oddly full and black. He takes my pale hand in his dark-brown one and shakes it firmly when I enter the class.

"It's nice to meet you, Ethan," he says. He talks to me like Grandpa Ike does. Like I'm a grown-up.

"I don't do assigned seats in here," he continues. "So you can take whatever is free. Here's a packet of make-up work I'd like you to do. Take your time. It's what we've done so far this unit. I'll give you one for math later today."

I take my packet and nod. By the time I turn around, the rest of the class has shuffled in, and there are two empty seats.

Suzanne nods toward one of them, next to her in the

third row. The other is behind her, next to a gawky boy with greasy hair and acne. I trudge down the aisle, heading toward Suzanne.

"You don't want to sit next to Herman," she hisses. "He stinks." She waves her hand under her wrinkled nose like she's trying to get rid of a bad odor, then giggles. Out of the corner of my eye, I see Herman's shoulders droop.

I was just about to put my stuff down in the seat next to her, but now I hesitate. Maybe Suzanne is popular, but so was Kacey, and she would never make fun of someone like that, no matter what she thought about them.

"I like the back," I say.

Suzanne squints her eyes at me and shrugs. "Whatever."

I take a seat next to Herman, who gives me a small smile. Suzanne was right. He does smell. Like stale Doritos.

I smile back at him uncertainly, and he puffs his chest up, like a human blowfish. I'm not sure if I want to encourage him. I don't know if I want the smelly kid to be my first friend at Palm Knot Middle School. I'm still not sure if I want *any* friends at all.

Or if I deserve them.

Memories

❧

WHEN WE GET HOME from school that day, I find Dad trying to push Grandpa Ike's Fixer-Upper out of the garage and onto the driveway, where huge piles of mildewing boxes are already stacked. I can see for the first time that it's a truck, even older and rustier than the one Grandpa Ike drives now. Grandpa Ike stands behind the truck bed, trying to push the car back inside the garage.

"You can't throw this out," argues Grandpa Ike. "It's my property. An antique. And besides, I'm gonna fix her up one of these days."

Roddie leans against the garage, watching. "He's right, Dad," he says. "You can't just throw it out."

Dad finally throws his hands up in defeat and stalks inside.

Before dinner, I go to my room and sit in my window seat, watching the Spanish moss blowing in the trees and the marsh tide draining out to sea. It would be peaceful except for Roddie's emo music, which thumps through the walls. He's been listening to that stuff a lot since we moved here.

After a while, I get up and bring over the framed photograph I noticed on the chest of drawers my first night here. It's a black-and-white photo of a woman I recognize as my grandma Betty. In it, she perches on a bike underneath a leafy cascade of tree branches. A bandanna is tied over her hair and her head is tilted back in laughter. One rounded corner of the photo is thick and blurry, like whoever took the picture accidentally held one finger over the camera lens.

Grandma Betty died of cancer when Mom was still a kid, so looking at pictures of her is the closest I've ever come to meeting her. Whenever Mom talks about her, she starts crying, so Roddie and I don't really ask.

I wonder if Grandpa Ike put the picture in my room on purpose or if it has been here all along. Something about the way he looked at it that first night, like he wanted me to notice it, makes me think he placed it there specifically for me.

I go back to staring out the window for a while, until a creaking floorboard makes me turn my head.

Mom is standing in the doorway, a basket of laundry tucked under her arm. She's staring at me.

"You never used to sit still like that in Boston," she says with a little sigh.

I guess she's afraid of what I'm thinking about.

Like right now, I'm imagining what Kacey and I would be doing if she were here. Probably, we would be kayaking through the marsh, daring each other to do a backflip into the water or pet an alligator.

My fingers brush the scar I have from when Kacey and I capsized our canoe last summer and she accidentally busted my chin open with her paddle. I had to have eight stitches.

Kacey always went with us on our family camping trips. The summer before fifth grade, my parents sent the two of us to get water after we got to our campsite. But when we shone our flashlights at the pump, a skunk was crouched right beside it, glaring at us. It looked at us for a minute, then turned and waddled off as fast as its stumpy legs could go, which was still pretty slow.

We should have known better than to chase it. We *did* know better. But where's the fun in that? We didn't even have to dare each other. We just hurtled through the dark after it.

Mom made Dad drive the two of us back that night. We drove the whole way with all the windows down and stopped at a grocery store so Dad could buy all the tomato soup he could find. When we got home, he filled a kiddie pool up with it, and Kacey and I both had to take tomato soup baths in the backyard to get rid of the smell—even though it was the middle of the night.

It wasn't until the next day that we both realized we must have followed that skunk right through a patch of poison ivy.

When we started school again that Monday, we stank so bad, no one would sit near us, and we scratched our legs so much that the nurse had to wrap bandages around our calves to keep us from itching. We didn't make a lot of new friends that year. But it was worth it.

Not until my cheeks start to ache do I realize that my lips have been stretched out in a stupid grin.

I drop it from my face faster than if someone slapped me.

Coralee

∾

IN HOMEROOM THE NEXT day, Suzanne purses her lips
in a pout when I mumble "Good morning," which makes
me feel a little bad about not sitting next to her yesterday.
So when we go to the gym for health class, I sit beside her
on the bleachers as we listen to a doctor talk about smok-
ing and lung cancer. While he uses a puppet to illustrate the
effects of secondhand smoke, Suzanne stealthily introduces
me to Maisie, a freckly, snub-nosed girl I've seen following
her around, and Daniel. When I finally look up from his
fat-tongued black sneakers, I recognize him as the captain
who had to pick me for his soccer team. His mouth is set in a
permanent scowl, so it's hard to tell, but I don't think he's at
all excited to meet me.

"Ethan's family moved here to take care of his grandpa,"

Suzanne whispers to them. "He's, like, dying or something, right? That's what my mom said."

"Um," I say. "No."

I decide to sit next to Herman again in science.

All the other students bring in diorama projects to science class. Herman explains that the seventh grade took a field trip to some wolf preserve nearby, and everyone had to re-create the ecosystem they saw by making a diorama.

"Don't worry," he says. "I'm sure Mr. Charles didn't expect you to do one."

"Did you really see wolves?" I ask, curious in spite of myself.

Herman nods. He smells a little better today. "Red wolves," he replies. "They're like regular wolves, but smaller and—"

"Redder?" I guess.

"Exactly," Herman agrees. "They're, like, an endangered species or something."

Mr. Charles asks for a volunteer to present first.

"I'll go," Suzanne says, raising a prim hand with purple nails.

Mr. Charles waves her up to the front of the room. Maisie whispers something that makes her giggle. Suzanne pops a bubble with her gum and clears her throat. "Eh-hem."

"Stop," Mr. Charles commands. "Gum. Spit it out."

"But it helps me concentrate!"

"Out."

Suzanne sighs and saunters over to the trash can, dropping her gum in. She sets her diorama on a table in front of the class and pulls out a thin stack of flash cards.

"As I was saying," she starts again, "this is my diorama, depicting a mother wolf and her pups. The average mother wolf will give birth in the spring to up to nine pups. She likes to nest by a stream bank, or in a dark, confined . . ."

I find myself more interested in watching the sixth graders on the jungle gym outside than listening to Suzanne prattle on in her flat voice, which makes me feel like taking a nap.

I must be close to falling asleep, because I nearly jump out of my seat when the door bursts open, slamming into the wall. Thankfully, only Herman sees me.

Suzanne stands with her mouth agape, looking at the girl who just marched in through the open door.

"Oops," says the girl, planting her feet apart and spreading her arms out with her palms up, like a starfish. "I forgot how these doors fly open. I hope I'm not interrupting."

Mr. Charles stands up. "You must be—"

"Coralee Jessup, that's me, reporting for duty. Pleased to make your acquaintance, sir."

"You're not supposed to be here!" Suzanne sputters, accidentally dropping one of her flashcards. "You're supposed to be in Atlanta!"

Ignoring her, Coralee sidesteps Suzanne to shake Mr. Charles's hand. She looks too short and scrawny to be in the seventh grade, and I wonder if she meant to walk into one of the sixth grade classes instead. Her elbows and knees jut out from her long cutoff shorts and pink T-shirt. Her hair hangs loose around her chestnut face in dozens of little braids, and a sly smile plays on her lips.

Suzanne looks from Coralee to Mr. Charles in confusion, as if she's trying to solve a difficult math problem in her head. "Why are you here?" she demands. "You don't go here anymore! You live in Atlanta now!"

Coralee turns her attention to Suzanne and arches her eyebrows. "Do I?" she says. "The evidence doesn't seem to support your hypothesis."

Next to me, Herman snorts. A couple of kids chuckle, while some whisper to each other.

"I see you know your scientific method," Mr. Charles says. "But why don't you have a seat now. Miss Carroway is in the middle of a riveting presentation, and I would hate to have it delayed further."

"Thank you, Mr. Charles," Suzanne says, her chin lifting. But the way Mr. Charles said "riveting" makes me wonder just how much he is enjoying her presentation. "As I was saying, the mother likes to make her den by a stream bank, or in a dark—"

Coralee skips across the classroom and down the aisle in

front of me. She slides into an empty seat.

"That's *my* seat!" Suzanne cries.

Coralee jumps up like she's sat on hot coals and raises her hands in the air. "I hope I didn't catch anything!" she says, causing a few more giggles to erupt around the class. Maisie looks like she's sucking lemons as her eyes follow Coralee, who scoots over to the seat next to Suzanne's, diagonally across the aisle from mine.

"Take your seat *quietly*, Miss Jessup," Mr. Charles reprimands.

Coralee gives him a silent thumbs-up and turns around to hook her backpack over her blue plastic seat. She catches my eye and stares at me for a minute.

"You're new," she observes.

"So are you," I reply.

She shakes her head. "You've got a lot to learn, new kid."

Time Travel

❧

DURING ENGLISH, SUZANNE PASSES me a note: *Lunch 2day?* ☺

Kacey used to pass me notes.

They were folded into little footballs—not squares, like Suzanne's. She would flick them to me when our teacher had turned around to write something on the board. *Pizza despues de la escuela?* if we were in Spanish class, or *R U coming 2 my soccer game today?* during math.

Suzanne's handwriting is big and loopy. Kacey had neat handwriting that could have belonged to either a boy or a girl. I can see it now, as if her tidy letters have been etched onto my brain.

I crumple the note before Ms. Silva can catch me with it, and Suzanne stares expectantly at me while the other kids finish their vocabulary warm-up. I give a half nod and muster an awkward smirk.

Ms. Silva hands out copies of a novel about time travel that I already read earlier this year in my old school. I don't say anything, though. First, because I don't want her to assign me another book. Second, because I liked the book a lot. And third, because I don't really say much these days anyway.

"Yes, Coralee?" Ms. Silva asks.

Coralee is sitting across the room, on the windowsill, with her hand in the air. Apparently no one remembered to get her a desk either.

"Ms. Silva, this book is about time travel, right?"

"That's right," Ms. Silva agrees. Her hair is swirled into a loose knot today and she wears an orange dress.

"But it says that it's historical fiction," Coralee says, holding her book up and pointing to the back. I turn my copy, which has a corner ripped off, to the back cover. Sure enough, the label in the bottom right-hand corner reads *Historical Fiction*.

The boy next to Daniel, whose name I think is John or Johnny, rolls his eyes. "What a dork," he mutters.

"What's the question, Coralee?" Ms. Silva asks patiently.

"Well, if it's about time travel, shouldn't it be classified as *science* fiction instead of historical fiction? Isn't historical fiction supposed to be realistic? So does that mean the publisher thinks that time travel is real?"

Ms. Silva puts a nail to her mouth and taps at her bottom lip. She seems to be taking Coralee's question very seriously because she doesn't respond right away.

"That's an interesting question," she says finally. "But maybe it's one that we can answer better once we're finished reading the novel. Then we can decide as a class what we think. Can you remember that question until we finish?"

Coralee grins. "Is that a challenge?"

Ms. Silva smiles back at her. "Who knows?" she says. "Maybe we'll all be time-travel believers before we're done."

I know how the book ends. It didn't make me believe in time travel.

I wish that it had.

Ways I Could Fix Things If I Could Time Travel

1. I could have convinced Kacey that we didn't need to go to that stupid party.

2. If that didn't work, I could have hammered nails into her dad's tires so he couldn't drive us there.

3. Or I could have told her I wanted to stay inside the party with all the other kids.

4. Or fallen down the stairs and broken my leg on purpose, so she'd have to go with me to the hospital.

5. Or just not dared her to do it.

6. There are a million ways I could fix things, if I had the chance.

Everybody Needs
a Friend

BACK IN BOSTON, DR. Gorman gave me a journal and told me that I should start making lists. "That might help you to make sense of your world and yourself as it exists now," she said. "The Ethan you were before may be gone, but now you have the chance to get to know the new Ethan."

I doubt that Dr. Gorman would appreciate my time-travel list. She would say that I'm "fixating." That was the word she used when I told her about staring at Kacey's window.

She was right, though. The lists do help. Sometimes I write my lists down in my journal, but other times I just make them up in my head.

Like right now in the lunch line, I'm making a list of all the foods I miss from Boston: (1) Mrs. Reid's oatmeal-no-raisin cookies—Kacey hated raisins. (2) Fenway Franks and fries.

It's distracting me from my pizza slice, which is drowning in a puddle of grease. It looks like the kind of pizza you might find a hair in.

So I don't notice until I'm almost to the register that my lunch money is no longer crumpled in the corner of my tray. I look around as I inch closer to the cashier. It's not on the metal buffet. It's not on the floor. It's not under the plate that's holding my greasy hair pizza.

That's when I hear someone laughing. When I turn around, Suzanne's friend Daniel is standing there with the thickset boy who seems to be his sidekick. They both have mean grins plastered on their faces.

Suzanne hovers behind them, biting her lip.

Only two people separate me from the register.

"Um. Did you see where my money went?" I ask Daniel.

He stops laughing and looks innocently at his friend. "I didn't see anything, Jonno," he says. "Did you?"

Jonno shakes his head and leers at me with a crooked-toothed smile.

I may not be sure if I want new friends, but I know I don't want new enemies. Having enemies means drawing attention, and that's the last thing I want.

"Look—" I start.

But before I can make a feeble attempt at convincing Daniel to give my lunch money back, Coralee marches up behind him and taps him on the shoulder.

He turns around and looks at her like she's a gnat that won't stop buzzing in his ear. "What do you want, Bite-Size?" he asks.

"Give the new kid his money back," she says. She barely comes up to his shoulder, but she rests her fists on her hips and stands with her feet firmly planted. She looks up at him like a determined little tree in the face of a hurricane.

"Why should I? No one's going to make me," Daniel says with a smirk.

"It's not like you need any extra cash," says Coralee, pointing a finger at the expensive logo on his shirt. "So what's the point? You're just terrorizing him because you think your *girlfriend* might like him more than you."

I jerk my head back automatically. Is *that* why Suzanne keeps trying to be my friend? Because she likes me?

I glance at her just long enough to see that she's blushing. Daniel stands up straighter, and some of the hilarity drains from his face. "She's not my girlfriend," he says, recovering. "And how do you know I wasn't stealing his money for *you*, Coralee? Maybe I was just trying to be nice. We all know you could use it."

I don't know Coralee, but I know Daniel has crossed a line.

"Hey," I say. "That was—"

"Kid! Let's go!"

The lunch lady is glaring at me. It's my turn to pay, so I slide my tray slowly up to the register.

Coralee's eyes narrow. "Maybe I could use it," she says. "But I don't think Mr. Beasley would be very happy if I told him you were bullying the new kid. Isn't bullying against the law now?"

"That's two dollars and fifty cents," the lunch lady wheezes. She has an angry-looking rash on one of her arms that she keeps scratching. Any appetite I had left disappears completely.

I want to mutter something about changing my mind, but just then Daniel thrusts my money back at me so that I have to grip the dollar bills against my chest. I hand them over to the lunch lady, who stops scratching long enough to take the money.

As she hands me my change, I hear Daniel say something under his breath. I can't make out everything, but I catch the word *snitch*.

"Don't listen to him," Coralee says to me. "He's just mad because he knows I could take him in a fight. And I have, too."

I pick up my tray and gaze out at table upon table of strangers.

Suzanne sidles up next to me. "Daniel and Jonno were just kidding around," she says. "It's no big deal. Just come sit at our table. Once they see you're cool, you'll be one of us."

But I don't want to be one of them.

"I'm sitting over there," says another voice. On my other side, Coralee points to a pink lunch box three tables away.

"Why don't you come sit with me?"

Coralee starts walking. I hesitate for a second. Then I shuffle away from the register, catching up to her.

"Hey," I say. "Hey, why are you being so nice to me?"

I must look confused, because she laughs and puts a hand on my back to guide me through the cafeteria. "Everyone needs a friend, new kid. Even weirdos like you."

An Invitation

~

ONCE I SIT DOWN and take a sip of milk, the room comes back into focus. I see Suzanne whispering with Maisie. She shoots a glance toward me, then looks away and tosses her hair. Across from them, with their backs to me, sit Daniel and Jonno. In the far corner, Herman and his Doritos have a table to themselves. Mr. Charles walks between the tables, watching the students. All around me, chatter and laughter swells and bubbles like an ocean tide.

And across from me, Coralee unpacks the contents of her lunch box.

She looks at me with concern through a thick layer of eyelashes. She has cartoon-character eyes.

"Are you okay?" she asks. "You look kind of freaked out."

"I'm fine," I reply.

"If you say so," she says, taking a bite of her PB&J.

"Thanks for helping me," I add. "You didn't have to do that."

"Sure I did," Coralee says with a shrug. "Daniel and Jonno are creeps. Everyone knows it. And Suzanne is— well—Suzanne. She *does* like you, you know."

"No, she doesn't," I say firmly. The last thing I want is to be dragged into some kind of love triangle.

"Then how come I overheard her in the bathroom this morning telling Maisie how cute and mysterious you are?"

I don't answer. I don't want to talk about this anymore.

But I feel like I need to make conversation, say something normal, so that Coralee won't think I'm some kind of freak. "This pizza looks disgusting," I say. "I wish I had brought my lunch."

"I always bring mine because I'm a vegetarian. And the school doesn't provide vegetarian meals. Can you believe it? Isn't that the stupidest thing you ever heard?"

I nod, but I don't really have strong feelings on whether the cafeteria serves tofu scramble or not.

"Don't you want to know why I'm a vegetarian?" she asks, blinking at me.

"I guess."

"It's because I love animals. Especially horses. Horses belong in pastures, not between hamburger buns, don't you think? Did you know some countries actually *eat* horses?

Dogs, guinea pigs, you name it. If it's a pet, somebody some-where eats it. Some places around here serve *alligator* burgers, which also makes me especially angry because I had a pet alli-gator once."

I try to keep up with Coralee, but she's talking really fast, especially considering that we're in Georgia.

"You probably don't believe me," she continues. "That's okay, a lot of people don't, but it's true. I won a baby alligator at the county fair as a prize in one of those tossing games. I named him Tiny, and we kept him in the bathtub until he got too big. Then I had to set him loose, and I never saw him again. Isn't that sad?"

"Cool," I reply finally. It's the first word I can find, and I'm surprised when more follow. "Not that you never saw him again, I mean. My mom's a vegetarian too. But I don't think she would let me keep an alligator in the tub."

"Cool," Coralee echoes. "About your mom." She flashes a smile at me. "Do you like animals?"

"I guess so."

Kacey had a pet cat named Punky growing up, but since Dad is severely allergic to fur, we never had any.

"You're probably bummed about missing the field trip to see the red wolves, too, huh?"

"Yeah," I say truthfully. "That would have been pretty fun."

"You have to feel sorry for an animal like that," Coralee

says, pausing to sip from her juice box. "An animal people care so little about that it was almost hunted to extinction without anybody speaking up for it? And they weren't even hunting it for food. Every creature should have someone looking out for it. Don't you think?"

I nod.

"You better hurry," she says, glancing at my pizza. "Lunch is almost over."

"That's okay," I say. "I'm not hungry."

Mom would never let me get away with that excuse. After the incident, all food started to taste like charcoal to me, so I stopped eating until she threatened to take me to the hospital to get a feeding tube inserted. She still likes to look at my plate and cluck her teeth to guilt me into eating every last bite.

"Did you get those packets of make-up work to do?" Coralee asks.

"Yeah," I say. "Bummer."

"Me too. Wanna work on them together after school?"

"Sure."

The moment the word comes out of my mouth, I can't believe I've said it. All day, I've been looking forward to going home and sitting by myself in the window seat. Where I can stare at the marsh and try not to think about Kacey. I wonder if I can backtrack, make an excuse to get myself out of it, but Coralee is already talking location.

"Let's go to the library," she says. "It's close by, and there's always saltwater taffy there."

"Sure," I say again, my excuses dying on my lips. "Sounds good."

The bell rings. Mr. Charles yells at us to clear our tables. As I pick up my untouched pizza, I think that it wouldn't have mattered after all if Daniel had taken my money.

On my way out of the cafeteria, Suzanne catches up to me. "It was a big mistake to sit with that girl," she says. Her voice is icy, but her cheeks are flushed.

My eyes flash toward Coralee, who's walking just a few steps ahead of me.

"I was trying to be nice, trying to help you be popular. I stuck my neck out for you. But I guess Daniel and Jonno were right. You're not meant for our lunch table."

Then she flips her hair again and stalks off, bumping Coralee's shoulder on purpose as she passes her.

Coralee turns back to look at me and cocks an eyebrow. "Guess you don't have to worry about her liking you anymore."

The Library

∽

"I DIDN'T KNOW THERE was a library here," I say.

Coralee is walking beside me, pushing her bike through the throng of kids making their way home or toward the Fish House for fries and a shake. Some of them shout greetings to her, which she returns with a grin or a wave.

"It's not an *official* library," Coralee admits. "But it's better."

"Because of the taffy?" I ask.

"Among other things."

We walk out of the school parking lot, passing a snarl of minivans.

Before we left, I called Mom from Ms. Silva's room to tell her I was going to study after school with a friend. At first she said no, but the idea that I might make an actual friend was too tantalizing for her to refuse.

"You'll be with an adult?" she asked.

Coralee, not bothering to hide the fact that she was eavesdropping, nodded at me.

"Yes, Mom," I replied, embarrassed.

"You call me as soon as you get there so I can speak with an adult."

"Okay," I said, and hung up.

"Your mom is kind of overprotective, huh?" Coralee asks as we turn onto Main Street.

"Um, yeah."

"You can tell her not to worry," she says. "Nothing bad ever happens in Palm Knot. In fact, *nothing* ever happens here, period."

"So you went to this school?" I ask. "Before?"

"Yep," she says. Now that we're out of the crowd, she hops on her bike and pedals it slowly alongside me.

"Why'd you leave?"

"Because I got a scholarship," she says. "To a boarding school in Atlanta for prodigies."

I feel my eyebrows raise. "You're a *prodigy*?" I've never met a prodigy before.

Maybe that explains why Coralee seems to have ten thoughts for every one of mine.

"It means a genius," she says.

"I know. What do you do?" I ask. "I mean, what kind of prodigy are you?"

"Violin," she says simply, pedaling in a lazy circle.

"So why are you back here?"

"I got kicked out. It's actually a funny story."

I wait for her to go on, but she just looks at me. "Can I hear it?" I say.

Apparently, those are the magic words, because once I ask, she jabbers all the way past the Texaco, the Fish House, and the Pink Palm. She's like a bird that's been waiting all night for dawn to start her morning warble.

"And so all the musicians hate the dancers, because they always act like they're so much better than us, you know?"

Across the street, I see Herman disappear into the Sand Pit, maybe to replenish his supply of Doritos.

"So anyway, we got into this prank war. And I had this idea to break into the dance studio one night with a couple buckets of water and some dish soap—"

Sweat already streams down my back and gathers in beads on my forehead. We've only walked two blocks. We pass a fallen frond from one of the palm trees lining the bay, and I want to grab it to fan myself.

But I don't because that would be weird.

"Like a giant Slip'N Slide. It was So. Much. Fun," Coralee says.

Broken white lines of tide glide into the bay and break

gently against the rock wall. Shards of light glimmer on the water, and I have to shade my eyes. It reminds me of how the sun used to reflect off the snow in Boston so bad, it could give you a sunburn on your nose if you weren't careful.

Even though it's a million degrees outside, thinking about the snow makes a shiver rattle in my chest. I try to concentrate on Coralee's story instead.

She's wheezing with laughter now. "They were slipping and sliding everywhere in their little shoes, and they started clinging to each other, which just made them all fall. Like a herd of frilly pink flamingos."

She does an impression of the dancers and starts flailing her arms back and forth while she rides her bike.

"It was like dominoes," she says, catching her breath from laughter. "All of them screaming and falling together. I didn't even *plan* that."

I can't help but smile at Coralee and the image of a herd of ballerinas falling like dominos.

Coralee gets off her bike outside Mack's Hardware Store.

"Anyway," she says, "it was worth it. Except that one girl broke her ankle. So they expelled me."

"That stinks."

"It's okay," she replies. "I didn't like Atlanta much anyway. I'm a country girl."

I stop as Coralee walks up to the door of Mack's. I remember how it felt last time I went in the store. Like I might suffocate in there.

"I thought we were going to the library," I say.

"We are," she replies. "It's inside."

She stoops down to scratch the two cats, who are lying on the doormat again. "Ethan, meet Zora and Zelda," she says. "Zelda, Zora, meet Ethan."

"We've met," I mumble, remembering my mad dash from Mack's on my first morning in Palm Knot.

Reluctantly, I follow Coralee in. It still smells like soil in the store, but I also detect whiffs of rubber and wood chips, and the air-conditioning seems to be working a bit better today.

Coralee looks around the store. "Mack?" she calls. "Mack! It's Coralee."

A large woman in overalls and with a red kerchief tied over her dreadlocked hair enters the store through a door in the back. I recognize her as the woman who offered me taffy when I was here before. She's carrying two potted plants but sets them down when she sees us, wiping away a bead of sweat from her cheek.

"Coralee?" she says. "Is that you, girl? I heard you were back in town."

"In the flesh!" Coralee chirps, skipping over to the woman and hugging her tightly. Her tiny frame almost disappears in the woman's arms.

"Ethan, come meet Mack," Coralee calls.

"Oh," I say, trying to hide my surprise. "Okay." I had

assumed Mack was a man. I walk over to shake her hand. She takes off her dirty gardening glove, revealing a hand as rough as burlap, with deep lines that run across her palm.

"I like your cats," I say.

Coralee snorts. "Don't mind Ethan. He's a little, well, new."

Mack studies me. "It's nice to meet you, Ethan," she says. "I don't suppose y'all would be interested in some saltwater taffy?"

"We'd love some," Coralee interjects before I can answer. "Do you have any green apple?"

"As a matter of fact, I do," Mack says.

"We also wanted to know if we can use the library," Coralee continues. "To do our homework."

"That's fine with me," Mack says. "As long as it's okay with Ethan's mama."

I use Mack's store phone to call Mom again. Mack gets on the line and says a few reassuring words, then hangs up. "She says she'll be by to pick you up at five."

She reaches behind the counter and hands Coralee and me each three pieces of saltwater taffy, wrapped in waxy plastic, and leads us through the back door into a dimly lit room walled from floor to ceiling with dusty books.

"Wow," I breathe, turning in a circle to see the whole room. There must be thousands of books here. By the window, a wooden desk faces the ocean. In the opposite corner, a small table is flanked by a squishy sofa and two armchairs.

"Make yourself at home, Ethan," Mack instructs.

"Is this all yours?" I ask. "It's so cool."

"I'm a bit of a collector," Mack says. "My apartment is upstairs, but I use this as my study. And occasionally I rent it out as a library. For a select few." She winks at Coralee. "Y'all get to it. And holler if you need me."

When she leaves, Coralee flops down on the sofa.

"Are you related?" I ask. "You and Mack?"

She shakes her head. "Mack took over this place from her dad when he died, but she was an English teacher before that. She taught my mom, my aunt, half the town. She's had some of these books for decades. Isn't this place great?"

"Yeah," I reply, suddenly glad that I didn't come up with a bogus excuse not to come. "It kind of is."

Driving Lessons

❧

CORALEE AND I GET through half our math packets and most of the science worksheets on weather systems before I hear Mack calling my name from the storefront.

"Ethan! Your ride is here!"

"Just a minute!" Coralee yells back.

"Do you need a ride too?" I ask. "I'm sure my mom could drop you off."

"I'm okay," she replies, stifling a yawn. "I think I'll stay here and pick out a book to read. Then I'll bike back. But thanks."

"No problem," I say, picking up my backpack and swinging it over my shoulders.

"Nice getting to know you, new kid," she says to me as I'm leaving. A mischievous smile plays on her face. "Same time tomorrow?"

"Yeah," I say. "That would be fun."

I realize that I mean it. It *will* be fun to hang out with Coralee again.

Mack tosses another taffy to me on my way out the door. "One for the road," she says. "I hope we'll be seeing more of you around these parts."

I thank her and wave, breezing through the door and looking for our Subaru. Forgetting about Zora and Zelda, I trip over them, causing one of the cats to arch her back and hiss at me.

Above their complaints, I hear a horn honk across the street and spot Grandpa Ike's rusty pickup truck.

"I didn't know you were coming to get me," I say. I pull open the door, which lets out a mighty groan.

"Your mama burned dinner again," he replies. He's wearing a red baseball cap over his thin hair, the logo so faded I can't read it at all, and a bulky leather jacket, even though it must be almost eighty degrees out.

"She's been in a mood all day," he goes on, waving his hand, "complaining about the kitchen and talking about pulling up the floors. Calling painters to come give estimates. She was too busy bellyaching to notice her casserole had been in the oven near on two hours. Whole house is filled with smoke, and who does she blame but me for not cleaning the oven. It's enough to make a man want to kill some—"

Grandpa Ike stops short. He has broken one of Dr.

Gorman's cardinal rules, which I heard her tell Mom after one of our sessions. We are not supposed to talk about death unless I bring it up.

Grandpa Ike must know he's made a mistake, because he clears his throat and offers me some sunflower seeds.

I shake my head.

"Ethan? I didn't mean—"

"It's okay," I interrupt. I don't want Grandpa Ike apologizing to me, treating me like I'll break into a hundred pieces if he says the wrong thing. "I'm fine," I add for good measure.

We're through town and passing by strawberry fields now. There are small wooden stands alongside the road for the farmers to sell their produce, but they are all empty. Grandpa Ike abruptly pulls the car onto the shoulder of the road, by one of the deserted stands.

"What are we doing?" I ask.

"Has anyone ever taught you to drive?"

"Not unless go-karts count." Kacey and I have been go-karting lots of times. "I'm only twelve. That's—"

"Two years past the time when I learned. Let's switch."

Before I can respond, Grandpa Ike has already shut the driver's-side door behind him. I unbuckle my seat belt and scoot over into the driver's seat. My stomach churns with what I think at first is fear, a feeling I'm used to.

But then warm tingles rise like sparks inside my stomach, and I realize that for the first time in a long while, I am excited.

I get the hang of the pedals pretty quick. Steering comes easily too. Not very different from go-karts. It's shifting the gears that takes some concentration. I stall out right away and then again a few yards down the road. A shiny Lexus behind us honks, and Grandpa Ike cranks down the window and extends his arm out. I'm pretty sure I know what his hand is doing.

"Don't worry," he says. "Just keep going."

My right palm is sweaty by the time I finally manage to get the truck into second gear, then third, without stalling.

"You're a natural," Grandpa Ike says as I pull over just before we reach the gravel road that dead-ends into our house. The truck shudders to a halt.

"I was going really slow," I reply. But his praise still makes me feel good. "Can we do it again sometime?"

"Course we can. There are some things a man's got to learn, and someone's got to teach him."

"Thanks," I say once we've switched places again and Grandpa Ike has steered the truck back onto the road. "That was—fun."

Grandpa Ike shrugs. "Not a word to your parents about this. But maybe you should try to convince your mama to take you to the Fish House for dinner tonight."

"Oh," I say. "Yeah, good idea."

"That way, you get to eat a fish sandwich and hush puppies instead of one of your mama's vegetarian *experiments*,

74

and I'll get an hour's peace and quiet."

"You won't come with us?"

"They don't serve ham on rye at the Fish House," he says, turning down the gravel road to our house. "And besides, I like to eat on my own."

Grandpa Ike seems to like to do a lot of things alone.

"I'm sorry Mom wants to rip up your floors," I say.

"It's not the first time your mama and I have butted heads." The folds around his mouth deepen into a grimace.

"Why don't you get along?" I ask suddenly. "Why hasn't Mom ever brought us to visit before?"

Grandpa Ike glances at me as we pull up to the house. "You're talkative tonight," he says. "I guess that's a good thing, right?"

"My therapist would probably say so," I agree, which makes Grandpa Ike chortle.

"Kids are strong," he says. "Stronger than most adults think. You'll be all right, Ethan."

He wants to change the subject, but two can play at that game.

"Thanks," I reply. "But you didn't answer my question."

"Another time, kid," he says. "Another time."

A Normal Kid

~

MOM DOESN'T TAKE ANY convincing to agree to have
dinner at the Fish House. "But not because your grandfather suggested it," she says. "Just because I don't have the
energy to cook another dinner and listen to you all complain
about it."

"Will they have the game on?" asks Roddie.

The Red Sox are playing the Marlins tonight.

"Probably," Mom says.

"Does 'probably' mean yes? Because if not, then I want to
stay here."

"This family needs time together," Dad says.

Roddie heaves a disgusted sigh.

"Car," Dad barks. "Now. Let's go."

To appease Roddie, Dad puts on the Red Sox game for the

drive to town, but the radio is too jammed with static to hear much, except that they're losing. I turn my attention out to the bay, where a lone sailboat skims across the sun-shot horizon. The color of the water is like a box of melted crayons, like something from a dream.

A dull ache stretches out in my chest. I get that feeling sometimes when I see something really beautiful or hear a funny joke or read something crazy. It makes me sad, because I know Kacey and I will never share it together.

Like how I'll never get to tell her about Grandpa Ike letting me drive his truck and hear her say, "No way! I want to try!"

It's almost funny, that everything that would make a normal person happy is what makes me feel the most sad.

Once we're seated, a manager with overgrown eyebrows, who Mom says she knew in high school, introduces himself to the rest of us as Just-Call-Me-Reese. As soon as he drops off a basket of on-the-house hush puppies and honey butter, Mom clears her throat.

"Roddie," she says, "would you like to ask Ethan anything about his day?"

Roddie shrugs. "Not really."

Mom purses her lips together.

"What about you, Ethan? Are you curious to know how your brother's settling in?"

I glance over at Roddie. He's squinting at the TV in the

corner by the bar. "I guess so," I say.

Dad nudges Roddie. "Well, son? What do you want to tell your brother about school?"

Roddie rolls his eyes. "You guys want to know about school? Fine. There's no baseball team. All the kids here care about is football. I don't have any friends because I can't understand what anyone's saying through those backwater accents. I'm studying the stuff we did in eighth grade back in Boston. Oh, and my guidance counselor put me in music class even though I don't play an instrument, because that's the only elective she could fit me into. So, in summary, everything pretty much sucks. Anything else you want to know?"

Mom's face has gone beet red, and Dad is tapping on his place mat and looking very much like he regrets asking Roddie anything.

Just-Call-Me-Reese suddenly pops up next to our table. "Can I answer any questions for you folks?" he says, pointing at the greasy laminate menus. He stares at Mom with a weird grin on his face.

"Can you turn on the Red Sox game?" Roddie says, gesturing to the TV, which is showing recaps of some kind of fishing tournament.

"I think we need a minute with the menus, please," Dad mumbles.

After Just-Call-Me-Reese shuffles off, Mom clears her throat again. "Well, we're glad that you shared that with us,

Roddie," she says. "We'll have to work on finding some ways to make school more fun for you."

"Yes," says Dad. "Maybe you could even ask about starting a baseball team."

"Whatever," says Roddie, whose attention is now turned to the game.

"What about you, Ethan?" Mom asks. "Tell us about the friend you were with today."

"Her name is Coralee," I say. "She's new too, kind of. She got expelled from boarding school because she used dish soap to turn the dance studio into a Slip'N Slide. So she came back to Palm Knot."

"Your friend was expelled from boarding school?" Dad asks, shooting Mom a look of alarm.

"Only because a girl broke her ankle," I explain. "By accident. It's actually a funny story."

"A Slip'N Slide in the dance studio? I don't know why that rings a bell," Mom muses. "I must be having déjà vu."

"Are you sure this friend is a good influence?" Dad asks.

"Please listen to your brother, Roddie," Mom commands. "And take off your baseball cap."

Roddie's eyes stay glued to the screen. "The game's on."

"Your brother listened to you," Dad says. "Now you need to listen to him."

"I *am* listening. Ethan's got a friend, and you don't like it because she got expelled. I say let him have a friend. Isn't that why you dragged us all the way to this hellhole? So he could pretend to be a normal kid?"

"Roddie!" Mom yelps. "You apologize to Ethan this instant."

Roddie crosses his arms over his chest.

Dad slams his hand down on the table, something I've only seen him do a handful of times. The customers around us go quiet, and I sink a little lower into my seat.

"Roderick Truitt!" he exclaims. "You apologize to your brother or leave this table."

"It's okay, Dad," I mutter. But no one listens.

"And take off your baseball cap!" Mom snaps.

Roddie sneers. "Fine. I'll walk home."

I stare at the walls so I don't have to see my parents' faces when Roddie gets up and stalks out. There are pictures of smiling people barbecuing on the beach, volleyball teams posing in the sand, and painted signs that say things like *It's 5 O'Clock Somewhere* and *Beach Is a State of Mind.*

Mom and Dad have a quiet argument over whether to follow him, which ends with Dad reminding Mom that Roddie is old enough to take care of himself.

For some reason it makes me a little sad, that they let him go so easily when they haven't wanted to let me out of their sight for weeks.

"Ethan?" Mom says gently. "Don't think about what Roddie said, okay, honey? He's still angry that we made him leave Boston. He's mad at us, not you."

"We think it's great that you have a new friend," Dad says.

"How was the rest of your day?" Mom asks, patting down her hair. She is trying to make things feel normal again. Another of Dr. Gorman's cardinal rules. Normalcy is key to healing. As if anything in my life will ever be normal again.

I tell them about the diorama projects and the red wolves. Dad says one weekend we'll take our own field trip to see them if I want. Maybe my new friend Coralee could come too.

"That would be cool, Dad," I say. "Thanks."

By the time we order and Just-Call-Me-Reese brings out our fish and shrimp sandwiches, nobody is very hungry.

On the way home, we pass Roddie walking on the side of the road. Dad rolls down the window and tells him to get in, but he glares into the car and shakes his head.

"No *thanks*," he spits.

Dad punches the gas and mutters something about teaching him a lesson.

Off-Limits

∽

GRANDPA IKE'S TRUCK IS gone when we get back to the house, even though he said he was staying home for dinner.

He's gone a lot for an old man who just wants to be left alone. I wonder where he goes. It's not like he has a lot of choices in Palm Knot.

Maybe he just leaves to get away from us. Maybe he just drives.

I go into the kitchen, still hazy with leftover smoke, to get a snack before creaking up the stairs to start on my English homework. But when I reach the landing, my eye catches on Grandpa Ike's door.

It's been firmly shut ever since we arrived, but now it stands just a crack open.

I hesitate for a moment. I know I shouldn't, but I can't help myself. I want to know what's in there.

I raise my hand to the knob and start to push.

"Hey!"

My hand wrenches back to my side, and I turn to see Grandpa Ike towering over me. He must have gotten home while I was making my snack.

His eyes are bloodshot, his cheeks red with fury.

He reaches past me and slams the door shut, making my heart jerk in my chest.

"Did you open it?" he says, cornering me against the wall. "Did you touch anything?"

I shake my head. "N-no. No, it was open already."

He mutters something under his breath.

How can this be the same man who just this afternoon was teaching me to drive?

"You tell your mother she is not welcome in my room. Same goes for you, you hear me?"

I nod furiously.

"This room is off-limits. Off. Limits."

Then he shoulders past me and shuts the door before I can even open my mouth to say "I'm sorry."

Company

⌘

THE NEXT MORNING, I don't mention anything to Mom or Dad about what happened with Grandpa Ike, whose truck is already gone again from the driveway. I feel sticky with shame thinking about him catching me pushing his door open.

But I also can't stop wondering what's in that room.

I take my bike to school, so that Coralee won't have to ride around me in slow circles when we go to Mack's. Suzanne doesn't speak to me or look at me all day, not even in social studies class when we're assigned to be in the same small group to make a poster about the Mayans. At lunch, Coralee and I sit together with a few other kids on the opposite side of the cafeteria from Suzanne's table.

After school, we head straight for Mack's, just like yesterday, but when we get there, a sign hangs on the door. *Gone to*

Pleasant Plains to pick up feed. Back tomorrow.

"Looks like we're not going to get to use the library today," Coralee grumbles.

"Should we go to the Fish House?" I ask. "Reese might give us free hush puppies. I think he has a crush on my mom or something."

"Gross," Coralee replies, wrinkling her nose. "His eyebrows are, like, one mega-eyebrow."

"Definitely," I agree.

"Anyway, we could go. But I saw your best friend Daniel walking in there with Jonno when we passed by."

I pull a face. "Let's not do that, then."

I'm not afraid of Daniel and Jonno, but I would rather not have to worry about them taping a *Kick Me* sign to my back in the Fish House like they did during English today. ("That's all they could come up with?" said Coralee. "Pathetic. They're like cartoon bullies. They're not even worth the title.")

"Do you want to come to my house?" I ask after a minute. "It's a couple miles, but I don't think my parents would mind."

"Sure," Coralee says without a pause. "Does your mom make saltwater taffy?"

"Um. No?"

"Just asking. I have low blood sugar, so I always like to have some taffy on me. Let's stop at the Sand Pit and get some first."

After a quick taffy run, we start toward home. Coralee pumps her short legs twice for every pump of mine. Once we hit the gravel road, she skids to a stop.

"Hey!" she calls. "What's that house?"

She's pointing to the abandoned Blackwood house. It looms crookedly out of the tangled, cricket-filled forest like an ancient shipwreck. Green fuzzy moss has taken over the roof. The gutters are rusted over, and long tangles of Spanish moss cascade down from them, obscuring the front porch from view. Sharp slivers of glass, like daggers, are all that remain of the second-story windows.

"I'm not sure," I say, stopping and planting a foot in the gravel. "It's just some old house that used to belong to a family called the Blackwoods. No one lives there now."

Coralee frowns. "There's something weird about it," she says. "Something spooky."

"There's a *lot* that's spooky about it." I don't tell her that it's actually giving me the creeps just standing here looking at it. "Should we go? I'm thirsty."

Mr. Bondurant, who is sitting on the porch of his trailer across the road, stares curiously at us. I avoid his gaze, but Coralee waves and shouts hello. To my surprise, he waves back at her.

"Do you know him?" I ask.

"Nope," she says. "Just being friendly. Aren't people friendly in Boston?"

"They keep to themselves, mostly."

Coralee follows me the rest of the way home, and it's not until we come to a stop in front of my house, gravel spraying behind our back wheels, that I start to feel self-conscious. The gray paint on the wooden facade is chipped and faded, grime covers the attic windows, and Mom hasn't gotten around to ripping up all the weeds in the garden yet.

But Coralee is looking up and grinning. "Cool house!" she exclaims. "I like the porch swing."

"Thanks," I reply, flustered but happy that Coralee is impressed.

The garage is open, and she follows me in to park our bikes beside the Fixer-Upper.

When we enter through the garage door, which leads straight into the kitchen, Mom is standing at the counter in stretchy pants, with one foot planted on her inner thigh so that she's balancing on the other foot with her hands in the air above her head. She's reading an open magazine on the counter.

"Um, Mom?" I call.

"Oh, hi, Ethan!" She turns around and sees Coralee standing behind me, watching her with interest. She drops her foot down and laughs.

"You didn't tell me you had company," she chides me. "You must be Coralee."

"Yes, ma'am. Coralee Jessup. Thank you for having me to your home."

She holds out her hand and smiles toothily up at Mom.

"Jessup," Mom says. "That sounds familiar. Was I at school with your mother?"

Coralee shrugs. "It's a small town."

"You're right," Mom says. "Way too small for a yoga studio, and I've got exterminators working upstairs, so you'll have to excuse me. I don't normally practice in the kitchen. Does your mom do yoga, Coralee?"

Sometimes when Mom is caught off guard, she rambles. I roll my eyes, ready to pull Coralee into the living room, but she doesn't seem to notice that anything embarrassing is happening.

"I can't speak for my mother," she says. "But my guess is she wouldn't know a *vinyasa* if it bit her in the butt."

Mom laughs again, and some of the lines around her mouth soften, so for an instant she looks much younger. I guess it's probably been a while since she's heard a joke. "That's really funny," she says unnecessarily.

"Okay, well, we're going to go work on our homework on the back porch," I say.

"That's fine," Mom says, nodding. "Should I bring out some sweet tea?"

"None for me, ma'am," Coralee says, patting her pockets. "I have some taffy that needs eating. Do you ever make salt-water taffy for Ethan?"

"I can't say that I ever have," Mom replies, shooting me a bemused look.

"I can share my recipe with you if you want," Coralee says. "It was the blue ribbon winner at the county fair a few years back."

"I would love that," Mom says. "I didn't know we still had a county fair. When is it?"

Coralee pauses thoughtfully. "They brought it back. I think it's in the fall. Plenty of time for you to learn."

Mom laughs again. "We'll have to have you back, then," she says.

"That would be lovely."

We don't get much work done that afternoon. Instead, Coralee shoots questions at me, which I bat away with my own. From the way she fires them one after another, I get the feeling that she's been waiting to interrogate me ever since she met me.

"Do you have any brothers and sisters?"

"Just Roddie, but we don't get along very well. What about you?"

"My brother, Calvin. He's way older than me. He lives in California now. I'm supposed to go visit him this summer, when school lets out. He's going to be a doctor. He got inspired after he saved my life when a copperhead bit me two summers ago. So why don't you and your brother get along?"

"It would be cool if you got to go to California."

"What do you usually do in the summer?"

I usually go on camping trips with Kacey.

"The usual stuff," I say. "Are you gonna visit Atlanta, too? I bet you miss it."

"Not really. I didn't make a lot of friends there. What about your friends back in Boston? What were they like? Do they miss you?"

I lean down and start rummaging through all the papers in my backpack, hoping Coralee hasn't seen my jaw tighten. "We really should start on this homework."

A New Normal

❧

BEFORE I KNOW IT, Coralee and I are spending most afternoons together after school.

Mack sure doesn't seem to mind having us over. Every day that we've come in for the past two weeks, she lets us pick from the jar of saltwater taffy ("It's not as good as mine," says Coralee, "but it'll do") and shoos us into the library like a mother hen. Sometimes she even brings soda, which Mom doesn't let me have at home.

Zora and Zelda usually slink into the library after us and jump up next to where Coralee sits on the couch, purring while she rubs their bellies.

"They know I like animals," she says. "Cats can sense that kind of thing."

Mom still makes me call her every day when I get to

Mack's so she knows I haven't decided to hitchhike back to Massachusetts. She usually sends Grandpa Ike to pick me up.

For the first few nights after he caught me outside his room, we drove in silence. I was starting to wonder if we were ever going to talk about anything again, or if he was going to start treating me like Roddie does instead.

Then one night, he was waiting for me in the passenger seat of the truck. "You drive," he said through the open window.

I noticed that his eyes were kind of puffy and bloodshot, just like the night he yelled at me. But he didn't seem angry. Just weary.

I opened the door and slid into the driver's seat.

"Nice and easy," he said as I released the clutch too early and the truck jerked forward. We stalled, but on my second attempt, we rolled smoothly toward the inlet bridge.

"Thatta boy," said Grandpa Ike.

Ever since then, things have been normal again. Grandpa Ike lets me drive home almost every night now, and even after just two weeks, I've improved so much that I hardly ever stall out anymore. Sometimes we talk and sometimes we don't, but he seems to have forgiven me for trespassing in his room.

It feels nice. Being forgiven.

A couple of days Coralee and I have gone to my house instead of Mack's, but we never go to Coralee's. She doesn't offer, so I don't ask. That's okay, because she seems happy enough to hang out in my living room or on the porch. She likes to tease Grandpa Ike about his truck. "Is that thing still running? Bet my bike is faster."

Whenever Coralee comes over, Mom shows her what's changed in the house, and Coralee oohs and aahs over the new additions. "Mrs. T, did you get this wallpaper from Buckingham Palace?" or "I could fall asleep on this couch and never wake up!" and "Your color scheme in the study is truly inspired, ma'am." It makes Mom happy since she lives with all boys, and we don't notice things like that. Except Grandpa Ike, who just complains.

Sometimes I think Coralee doesn't actually care about that stuff, that she just says those things to make Mom happy, the same way she asks Dad to explain his job to her and listens attentively while he talks her ear off about coding languages. But either way, I'm grateful.

Only Roddie seems immune to Coralee's charms. He just scoffs at her when she asks him if he knows whether the eggs in his omelette are free-range and rolls his eyes when she asks what song he's been blasting in his room. Coralee doesn't seem to mind, though. "Teenagers," she mutters. "Always so moody. Did I ever tell you about the time my big brother got so mad he hopped a train all the way to Mobile . . ."

I still don't know much else about Coralee's family besides the fact that she has a brother.

Which is funny because she knows almost everything about mine.

Almost.

When she asks me why we moved here, I give her the same line Mom gives to everyone. "My grandpa Ike needed help around the house," I say.

"Your grandpa Ike seems fine to me. Did you know that he does the *Daily Journal* crossword every morning? And he doesn't have any trouble getting around."

I lift my shoulders in a defensive shrug. "It's lonely being an old man. Maybe he needs somebody, even if he doesn't know it."

"That's definitely true, Ethan," Coralee says. "Everybody needs somebody."

What I Know about Coralee

1. Coralee is twelve years and two months old. She's young for seventh grade because she skipped kindergarten.

2. Coralee has lived in Palm Knot her whole life, except when she went to the school in Atlanta.

3. Coralee has a brother named Calvin, who is studying to be a doctor in California and who never comes home.

4. When she was little, Coralee was bitten by a copperhead snake and had to have Calvin suck the poison out of her ankle before he took her to the hospital.

5. Another time, Coralee's life was saved by a rolling pin. I'm not exactly sure how.

6. Coralee likes to play violin and make blue-ribbon-winning saltwater taffy.

7. Coralee runs faster than anyone in our class, and she talks even faster than she runs.

8. Coralee rides her bike everywhere.

9. Coralee has gotten a perfect score on

every spelling test she's ever taken.

10. Coralee insists the meat industry is inhumane. Which is not specifically about Coralee but is something she tells me a lot because she loves animals.

Field Trip

〰

EVEN THOUGH I LISTEN to Coralee's stories all the time, sometimes I feel like I still don't know very much about her. I've never met her family or been to her house or heard her play the violin. I don't know who she was friends with before she left to go to school in Atlanta or why Suzanne was so upset when she showed up again.

One day at lunch, I catch Suzanne glaring at her from across the cafeteria. Coralee doesn't see. She's telling a story about accidentally setting her Halloween costume on fire, and miming how her hands flailed in the air trying to put out the flames. Behind her back, Suzanne and Maisie start doing the same thing, collapsing into laughter at their own impressions.

Seeing my gaze over her shoulder, Coralee turns around and spots them.

She lowers her arms and goes back to picking at her lunch.

"Why does Suzanne dislike you so much?" I ask.

Coralee seems to get along fine with everyone besides Suzanne's gang. We sit with lots of the other kids at lunch, and she can find something to talk about with anyone, even Herman.

She thinks about the question for a minute. "Suzanne wants everyone to be afraid of her. That way she has more power. That's what being popular is all about. But I'm not afraid of her. Maybe she worries that if people see that, they won't be afraid of her either, and she won't be popular anymore."

"So did something happen before you left—"

But Coralee has already turned to Herman, sitting next to her. "You know, Herman, those chips are full of preservatives," she says. "Have you ever thought about trying apple chips? Or carrots and hummus?"

Herman's eyes widen.

"Hey," I say. "I thought maybe we could go to your house after school today. You could play your violin for me."

"We co-ould," says Coralee, the corners of her mouth drawing down into a pensive frown. "But I had another idea in mind."

"What?" I say, pushing away the remainder of my chicken nuggets and okra.

"A little field trip. There's somewhere I want to go."

"What kind of field trip?"

She grins. "You'll find out."

The Blackwood House

THAT AFTERNOON I BIKE behind Coralee all the way to the gravel road that leads up to my house. We stop at the mouth of the drive, where the trees on either side bow together to form a thatched roof of leaves over the road.

"I thought we were going somewhere," I say.

"We are," Coralee responds. She stops in front of the Blackwood house and points toward it. "We're going *there*."

My skin begins to creep. Whenever I pass this place, with its blank face and broken windows, I look straight ahead, toward the Milsaps' colorful house. I look there now and see a little boy making mud pies next to the pen where they keep their goats.

If I can't even *look* at the Blackwood house, how am I supposed to just walk in?

On the other hand, this is kind of an adventure. If Kacey

were here, she would tell me to stop being such a wuss.

Come on, Ethan, she'd say. *I dare you.*

So I say, "Okay."

Then I add, "But why?"

"I just want to check something."

"Check something?"

But Coralee has already dropped her bike in the weeds, so I do the same and follow her through the yard toward the front steps. There used to be an iron gate, but it's lying beside the hedge. A set of rusty white chairs is strewn about the yard like skeletons. Years of branches and leaves and acorns from the oak trees above us have drifted into haphazard piles, smothering the brown, calf-high grass. Something rustles off the path in front of us, and Coralee shrieks.

"Snake!" She sounds nothing like herself, and I realize this is the first time I've ever seen her scared of anything. I guess it's because she's been bitten by one before.

"Is it poisonous?" I ask, craning my neck to see its scaly tail slither into the grass.

"No," she says, already shaking off her shock. "Just a black snake. Not a copperhead. Did I tell you about the time I got bit by the copperhead?"

"Yeah," I say, suddenly eager to make it to the porch steps. Until I realize that it is probably just as likely that snakes live inside the house as out here.

Coralee goes first up the stairs. We have to be careful

because the wood has rotted so much that holes the size of tennis balls pepper the steps.

When she tries the knob of the front door, it won't budge. She moves to the door knocker and drops it. It bangs against the wood and echoes like a gunshot.

The sound makes me flinch, and I look to see if anyone is around to witness our trespassing. Mr. Bondurant is nowhere to be seen, and the Milsap kid is elbow deep in his mud pit.

"I don't think anyone's been home for a while," I say.

Coralee slinks over to the windows and tries to lift them, but they stick in their frames.

I'm secretly hoping that she'll give up now, that we'll turn around and go home.

But then I hear Kacey's voice in my head again. *Boo, you wimp!* Like she's standing there next to me.

Suddenly I feel like I need to be moving, like I can't stand on this porch for another second, so I aim a hard kick just below the doorknob. For a second, Coralee looks at me like I'm a stranger she's never seen before. Then the door squeaks open, and an incredulous smile spreads across her face.

I manage a sly grin. "I saw it on TV."

Coralee nods, impressed. She doesn't see that my arms and legs are shaking.

This time, I go first. The floorboards moan as we step inside. Darkness descends, and the air grows thick and mossy. Something brushes past my arm, and I jump to the side. Coralee glides around me into the hall as I pull cobwebs from my T-shirt, then raise it up over my nose. "It stinks in here."

I keep my voice light and steady, but my heart drums as my eyes adjust to the darkness. Something is off. I don't know why, but I can't shake the feeling that there's someone else here. That Coralee and I aren't quite alone.

My gaze flits around the entry hall, as though I'm expecting to pick out a third, shadowy figure lurking in a corner. I can make out a curving staircase in front of us and closed doors to our left and right. I suck in my breath when I catch sight of a looming silhouette next to Coralee.

But it's just an old coatrack with a ratty raincoat hung on it.

There's no one else here.

"I knew it," Coralee whispers. "I knew I remembered this place."

"What?"

"The first time I came over to your house and saw this place, I had a feeling I had been here before, and now I know I have," she says, her voice quick with excitement.

I shake my head in disbelief. This has to be some practical joke Coralee has cooked up.

"That's why you wanted to come here?"

Coralee turns to me. "Look," she commands. "This is the entrance. That's obvious, okay. But that door to the left leads to the kitchen, and then—yeah, then there's a dining room. That corridor goes to the living room, and the door to the right is a study with a big coat closet."

I stare at her. This is no joke. I can tell she believes what she's saying.

She grabs my wrist and drags me through the door on our left. "I'll prove it to you," she says. "See? Kitchen."

A counter covered in plastic sheeting and a thick layer of dust juts from the wall to our left. I can make out a sink and an ancient oven to our right, and a space where a refrigerator used to be.

"Lucky guess?" I venture.

But then she takes me to the next room, which boasts a long dining table and a chandelier that has become a nest for some kind of animal.

"And through here is the living room. There used to be a piano. And a fireplace. And everything was yellow."

She is right about the living room and the fireplace. But if there was a piano here, it's long gone, and any hint of color was sucked out of the walls years ago.

I hear a groan that sounds like a footstep on the floor-boards above us. "Did you hear that?" I whisper.

I look up. Watery light catches on the cobwebs that cling like draped sheets to the ceiling. Everything is quiet now.

Coralee shakes her head. "Probably just a rat. Come on."

We walk through the living room and into a corridor with

a few smaller rooms. Coralee points out each one. "Drawing room, bathroom, study," she lists. She opens the door to the study, walks through it, and then swings open the one that leads back to the main entrance. "Oh, and coat closet," she adds, pointing to the right wall of the study.

A chill trickles through me like someone has spilled ice water down my neck.

"How do you know all this?" I ask. The thought crosses my mind that she could have come in and scouted the place out one day on her way home from my house. But the door and the windows were all locked, and Coralee couldn't have kicked the door open on her own.

"I'm not sure," she replies, and I'm surprised to hear a shiver in her voice. "I don't remember *being* here. I just remember *here*. Like I lived here in a past life or something."

"Well, now you've seen it," I say. "Let's go."

She follows me back into the main entry hall, where I almost run into the coatrack.

"Can we go upstairs first?"

My eyes catch on something and I freeze. The ratty raincoat I saw earlier. It's not ratty at all. I reach my hand out. It's not damp and dusty, like a coat that's been rotting away in this house for years. It's crisp and dry and smells of perfume. Like someone might have just taken it off.

"Coralee," I whisper. I can barely hear my voice over the thrumming of my heart. "I don't think we're alone here."

Coralee stands next to me, so that our shoulders are touching, and examines the raincoat. She reaches for the pockets and begins to pat them down.

"What are you doing?" I rasp, my throat suddenly dry. "We need to go. Now."

"Maybe there's something in the pockets that will tell us who—"

But before Coralee can finish, I hear a thud from upstairs and spin around. My heart does a running backflip in my chest, and a rush of adrenaline surges through me.

Then Coralee turns too, and I see her jump like a scalded cat, her spine arching in midair. She raises a shaking hand and points to the second floor landing, where we can both clearly see the shadowy outline of a woman standing motionless at the top of the stairs. She's so still, I think she must be a dummy. Until she takes a step forward.

Coralee's scream rings out. I grab her shoulders and turn her toward the door, and we tumble out of the house and down the stairs. Her foot falls through one of the holes in the wood, and she gasps.

"Help me!" she cries. I pin my shoulder under hers and lift her out and down the last two stairs.

Together, we sprint to our bikes and pick them up out of the weeds.

"This way!" I yell to Coralee, who starts to bike toward the main road, away from my house.

She shakes her head. "No way am I passing this place again today," she says. "I'll see you tomorrow."

I don't want Coralee to go. I want to know how she knew everything about this house. I want to know who she thinks the woman is. But if I make her come home with me now, I'll have to bike back out here with her later, which means *I'll* have to pass the house by myself to get home again.

So I start pedaling and yell, "See you tomorrow!" over my shoulder.

And then I ride like the devil himself is chasing me.

The Voice
on the Phone

I CAN'T SLEEP THAT night, and it has nothing to do
with the angry music Roddie is blasting. My head reels, and
every time I close my eyes, I see the silhouette of the woman
standing at the top of the stairs. Surely no one would choose
to live there if they had another place to go. She must be a
squatter.

Unless.

I remember the feeling I had when we first walked into the
house, like someone else was there beside us.

"No," I whisper aloud. "There's no such thing as ghosts."

And even if there were, that wouldn't explain the raincoat.
Right?

Finally, I throw my covers off and pick up the phone sitting in the cradle on my dresser. It's late, but I'm sure Coralee

will still be awake. She told me she practices violin every night for two hours after she finishes all her homework. I have to talk to her. I rummage in my backpack for the sheet of paper where she wrote down her number weeks ago. When I find it, I pick up the phone, but there's no dial tone.

I listen for a moment and hear a man's voice. Not my dad's, or Roddie's, or Grandpa Ike's. But the voice on the phone is familiar.

"—have just been so hard. On all of us, but her mother is taking it the worst."

A pang of hurt shoots through me, skewering me like I'm a human kebab. I know that voice. It's a voice I never thought I'd hear again. One I never wanted to.

It's Mr. Reid. Kacey's father.

"I'm sorry, Rick. When we got your message this morning, we thought maybe—"

"No, but thanks for calling back. I feel very—"

I press the red "end" button on the phone and let it fall onto the floor. Then I drag myself back to bed and curl into a ball. My mouth goes sour, and the room starts to spin.

I lie still, the covers above my head, letting my breath in and out in careful measures. Just like I did the nights after the incident. I know if I lie here long enough, the room will stop spinning.

The shadow woman is pushed from my mind completely.

A real ghost takes her place.

I stuff my pillow over my head, trying to block out the sound of Mr. Reid's voice.

And the words that have haunted me since Boston.

You killed her, Ethan Truitt.

What I Remember from after the Incident

1. My hands, sticky with dark blood.

2. Yelling for help until Mrs. Juarez, Briana's mother, ran out of the house and found us.

3. Being frozen at Kacey's side. Mr. Juarez shouting for me to move out of the way.

4. Someone screaming her name.

5. Mrs. Juarez pulling me away from Kacey and holding me.

6. Loud, flashing lights.

7. Spinning darkness.

8. Waking up to mechanical ticks and beeps, bright plastic lights, and a sore throat.

9. Telling Mom and Mrs. Reid about the dare and the tree branch and the rock; Mom smoothing the hair from my forehead, whispering, "It's okay, you're okay," because she didn't understand what I was telling her.

10. Asking about Kacey. "Where is Kacey, is Kacey okay, when can I see Kacey?"

11. Whispers outside my room.

12. Driving home with Mom and Dad in the rain.

13. Staring at Kacey's empty house, her dark window, willing her to come home.

14. More darkness. Darkness that just wouldn't lift until . . .

15. A light flashing on in Kacey's window.

Eavesdropping

❧

SO MUCH OF THE days after the incident still blurs into a blank in my mind. I've seen TV shows where someone loses their memory and spends the whole hour trying to put together the pieces. But I'm grateful I don't remember more than I do.

The dare. The tree branch. The rock.

The light in Kacey's window.

The square of white paper.

You killed her, Ethan Truitt.

After running over the list of things I remember in my head a couple hundred more times, I finally fall asleep for a few hours, waking up to an ashy sky.

I can't go back to sleep once I'm awake, and I'll have to get up for school soon anyway, so I go downstairs and pour myself a glass of milk.

I tiptoe past Grandpa Ike's room and Mom's study. But as I'm passing Mom and Dad's room, I hear my name. I pause outside their door. Eavesdropping is why I couldn't sleep last night and what will probably keep me awake again tonight.

On the other hand, why are they talking about me?

I press my ear up to the door.

"—just stirred up a lot of emotions that I would have liked to forget about for a while."

"But we don't need to tell Ethan that Rick called, do we?" says Mom.

"No, of course not," says Dad. "But it just started me thinking about everything again. Ethan was so close with Kacey. I worry that his new friend—"

"Coralee."

"Right, Coralee. What if she's just his substitute for Kacey? What if he's using her as an excuse not to move on, not to process his emotions?"

I wonder if Dad has been talking to Dr. Gorman. It sure sounds like it.

There's a pause, and I hear one of them open the wardrobe.

"You think he should start going to therapy again?" Mom asks.

"I think we should be cautious about how much time he spends with Coralee. I don't want him to get too attached to her. What do we know about her, anyway? Besides the fact that she got expelled from boarding school, that is? What if she's taking advantage of him? He's so vulnerable right now."

"She does tell some *interesting* stories," Mom admits. She sounds uncomfortable. "But she's a lovely girl. Very different from Kacey, but lovely."

I hear footsteps moving toward me and run on light feet back to my room. I dive through my door just as I hear theirs creak open.

I listen as they move downstairs and into the kitchen. My heart is pulsing in my ears, and it's not just because I was almost caught eavesdropping.

Is Dad right? Is being friends with Coralee just my way of replacing Kacey? Is Coralee somehow "taking advantage" of me? What did Mom mean by "interesting stories?" Did she mean stories like stories, or stories like *lies*?

I think of Coralee leading me through the Blackwood house, pointing out where everything would be. Was it some kind of trick after all?

I wish I could talk to Kacey. She would know what to do.

But then, if I could talk to Kacey, I wouldn't be here.

I pull the covers up over my head again, and I don't move until Mom comes to shake me awake.

Space

WHEN I WALK INTO homeroom, I don't make eye contact with anyone, especially not Coralee. Ms. Silva announces the winner of the red wolf diorama contest, who, depressingly, is Suzanne. Her diorama of the pup den will be sent to the wolf preserve to be displayed for visitors. After everyone applauds, Suzanne's little doll ears go annoyingly pink with pleasure, homeroom is dismissed, and I hurry out into the hall.

I don't make it far before I feel someone tugging on my sleeve.

"Hey," Coralee says. "Are you okay?"

"I'm fine," I reply. "I just need to—"

"Because we have to talk about yesterday," she chitters. "I have to tell you—"

"I need to—" I interrupt, pointing toward the bathroom. I

make a beeline for the door before she can object, and I decide to stay in there until everyone else has already gone to first period. I stand by the hand dryer and pretend to be finishing homework that's due today. When I hear the bell ring, I peek out the door. Coralee is gone. I walk to health, where we're watching another movie (today it's cardiovascular disease), and slip into an empty desk in the front of the room at the opposite corner from where Coralee and I usually sit.

"You're late, Truitt," Coach Sluggs barks.

"Sorry, Coach."

Suzanne and Maisie sit in the two desks to my left. They're laughing about something, but their giggling stops when I sit down. Suzanne shoots me a suspicious glance, then writes something on the corner of her paper and shoves it toward Maisie, who nods wisely.

I can't see Coralee, but I can feel her eyes on me: a silent, questioning rebuke.

I dodge her for the rest of the day, trying to remember everything I've ever heard Roddie say about how to break up with a girl. He went through a lot of them before he got together with Grace.

Not that Coralee and I are breaking up. We weren't dating or anything like that. I just need some space. I sit next to Herman in science and English and stay with Ms. Silva to do extra credit during lunch. I don't want to have to sit next to Coralee and wonder if Dad was right, if being friends with her is just my way of forgetting about Kacey. I don't want to listen to another one of her stories and wonder if she's telling the truth.

After school, I hide out in the gym until I'm sure Coralee will give up and go to Mack's without me. And when I go home, I cycle the long way around Main Street so I won't pass Mack's Hardware Store at all.

The Ethan
I Was Before

WHEN I GET HOME after school, Grandpa Ike's truck is in the driveway, and Mom and Dad are working in the yard, pulling up weeds and replacing them with new plants.

"Where's Coralee?" Dad asks, taking a sip from his water bottle and spilling some down his shirt.

"She had something to do after school, I think."

Mom and Dad exchange a silent look. Since the incident, they have perfected the art of the silent look. I think sometimes they have whole conversations that way. Dad pushes his glasses up the ridge of his nose and lifts his chin approvingly.

"You look tired, Ethan," Mom says. She takes off her gardening glove and touches the back of her smooth hand to my forehead. "You don't feel hot. Are you sick?"

I shake my head. She runs her fingers through my hair.

"Why don't you go lie down for a while anyway? You have dark circles under your eyes."

Her voice trembles with a chord of worry, one I haven't heard since before Coralee started coming around.

"Thanks, Mom." I can't muster the energy to force any enthusiasm into my voice. "I think I will."

I almost wheel my bike over Roddie when I take it into the garage. I see his legs sticking out from under the Fixer-Upper just in time. But he must hear me, because he scoots out from under the truck, brushing his hands together. Then he stomps off into the kitchen without a glance in my direction.

"'Lo, Ethan," Grandpa Ike calls from the other side of the car's hood, which is popped open.

"Hi. What's going on?"

"Your brother asked if he could try to fix up the Fixer-Upper," he says. "I'm showing him some basics. If you want—"

"That's okay," I say before he can finish. "I'm going to lie down."

I pass Roddie coming out of the kitchen with two bottles of water, stumble up the stairs, and collapse into the window seat.

My stomach churns like a lava pit. I feel guilty for ignoring Coralee today, but guiltier for abandoning Kacey. I know Dr. Gorman would say that I haven't *really* abandoned her, but I have stopped thinking about her all the time, which is almost the same thing.

But that's not Coralee's fault. Sure, she tells some pretty wacky stories, but she also makes me laugh. She makes me feel almost like the Ethan I was before the incident. Like everything I do isn't going to be wrong.

The Ethan I was before liked diving and baseball and video games and skateboarding. He was always up for a practical joke, always ready for a dare.

But that Ethan disappeared after the incident. That Ethan is gone forever.

Isn't he?

Why Coralee and Kacey Are Completely Different

1. Kacey played soccer, but Coralee just likes to run. Kacey skateboarded, but Coralee rides her bike.

2. Coralee always volunteers to talk in class, but Kacey never did unless the teacher called on her. Coralee talks a lot in general, but Kacey liked to listen.

3. Kacey's favorite color was green, and Coralee's is pink. Kacey hated pink.

4. Coralee's favorite food is saltwater taffy. Kacey liked beef jerky, which Coralee would never eat.

5. Kacey's family was always around, at school and at her soccer games, and Coralee never even talks about her family.

6. Coralee is a violin prodigy, but Kacey couldn't carry a tune to save her life.

7. Kacey's favorite movie was The Secret Garden, even though I always thought it was too girly for her. Coralee says she doesn't really watch movies.

8. I knew everything about Kacey. Coralee is still a mystery.

Amelia Blackwood

❧

I MUST HAVE DRIFTED off, because the next thing I know there's a knock on my door.

"Come in," I call, groggily blinking the room back into focus.

Grandpa Ike pushes the door open. "Your mother said to come check on you."

"You're taking orders from Mom now?"

He grimaces. "Well, she was going to come herself, but I thought you might like to take a drive with me to the store instead. I'm out of ham. So I told her I'd handle it."

"Oh," I say. "Yeah, I guess."

I need *something* to take my mind off things.

Grandpa Ike drives us down the gravel road and stops. Right outside the Blackwood house.

I sneak a glance at it while we switch places so I can drive. The front door is closed, so someone must have shut it after we left. There's no movement in any of the windows.

"What's the deal with that place?" I ask once Grandpa Ike is settled. I try to keep my voice casual.

He glances at the house. "No one's lived there in a long time," he says.

Wrong, I think as I press down on the gas a bit too hard.

"Easy, kid."

"Sorry. Why did they leave?"

"They didn't."

I look over at Grandpa Ike, who strokes at his beard. His face is hard to read under his old hat.

"What do you mean?"

"Well, Arnold Blackwood died a long time ago, back in the eighties, and Amelia lived there by herself for another twenty years. She had a nurse or someone taking care of her, but eventually she left. Not long after, Amelia took a tumble down the stairs. No one found her for days."

"You mean she died in that house?" I ask, picturing the woman silhouetted at the top of the staircase. "On the *stairs*?"

Grandpa Ike shoots me a sideways glance. "Never mind all that," he says. "Anyway, she never had any kids, so her nieces and nephews own the place, but they live in Michigan or Minnesota or some other icy wasteland. So they've let it go to pot."

I'm thinking so hard about Amelia Blackwood that I miss the turn onto Main Street and have to pull into someone's driveway and turn around.

I'm still thinking about her that night as I wait for sleep to come.

There's no such thing as ghosts, I tell myself.

People don't come back from the dead.

But I can't stop the small voice in the back of my head from asking.

What if?

A Lesson

❧

CORALEE IS NOT IN homeroom the next morning.

She's not in gym, either.

Or in science.

I feel a flicker of worry when I remember that Ms. Silva is planning to give us a spelling test in English. Coralee loves spelling tests because she always finishes first and hands in her paper before Ms. Silva says the words for the second time.

Why isn't she here?

At lunch, I sit in our normal spot by myself. I think someone will probably come and sit with me. School is lonely without Coralee. I talk to some of the other kids, like Herman, but Coralee's the only one who feels like a real friend.

Back in Boston, I wasn't popular, exactly, but I definitely wasn't unpopular. Kacey was pretty and athletic, and everyone liked her. People always sat with us at lunch and assemblies and pep rallies. Once, I told Kacey she was the reason people hung out with us. She rolled her eyes and punched me in the shoulder. "Like all the other girls don't have a crush on you? *Oh, Ethan!*" she said, swooning. "He's so dreamy! Those dark curls! Those blue eyes!" Then she fake fainted.

No one comes to sit with me.

In Palm Knot, I am an outsider.

When I'm halfway through my tasteless hamburger, someone finally slides into the seat across from me.

Suzanne.

"Where's your little friend today?" she asks.

Her hair is in two blond braids that rest on her shoulders. Kacey used to wear her hair like that to play soccer.

"I don't know," I say. "She's not here."

"Duh," Suzanne sighs. She spoons out some yogurt and smacks on it.

Why is she sitting with me?

"Are you two having a lovers' quarrel?"

"What?" I sputter. "No, we're not—we're just friends."

Suzanne smirks. I can see Maisie craning her neck around like an owl, trying to see what Suzanne is up to. I glare at her.

"Well," Suzanne says, "I hope you've learned your lesson."

"My lesson?"

"Tsk, tsk, tsk," she clucks, shaking her head. "You chose to be friends with Coralee, and now look at you, sitting all by yourself. If you had just listened to me, you could have saved yourself a lot of trouble."

By trouble, I guess she means all the times I've heard Daniel and Jonno laughing and making fun of me in class, or when Jonno "accidentally" knocked my lunch off the table, or the time Daniel elbowed me in the face during a basketball game in gym class and gave me a bloody nose.

Suzanne bats her eyelashes at me as she digs into her yogurt cup for a last spoonful. "Anyway," she says, "that's all I wanted to say. I have to get back to my friends now."

I'm overcome with a desire to take her spoonful of yogurt and flip it into her face. I think back to my third day of school, when Coralee demanded Daniel give my money back while Suzanne watched without a word. Hot splotches of shame splash across my face. How did I not see it before now—how lucky I've been to have a friend like Coralee?

"Hey, Suzanne?" I call, just as she's turning away.

She looks back at me.

"You're right," I say. "I did learn my lesson. One real friend is worth more than a hundred fake ones. Maybe you'll figure that out one day too."

The Wall
of Coralee's Past

AFTER SCHOOL, I COLLECT extra copies of all our home-work assignments. Then I go to the main office and ask Mrs. Oakley for Coralee's address.

"I'm her friend," I say. "She wasn't at school, and I need to take her make-up work to her." I wave the worksheets convincingly.

"Well, aren't you a sweet thang," Mrs. Oakley coos. Her yellow hair is piled up on her head like an abandoned beehive, and I can't stop staring at it as she prints out Coralee's address and gives me directions to get there.

"Oh, and can I call my mom? To let her know where I am?"

Mrs. Oakley's hand flies to her chest. "That is just *the* most considerate thing I have ever heard. Your mama sure did raise you right. Go on ahead, honey."

She tosses me two mini Snickers bars while I'm on the phone. I pocket them to give to Coralee later.

Riding my bike to her house takes fifteen minutes. Instead of turning left after the strawberry farms, I head straight past the marshes and keep going for two miles or so. I don't have to make any more turns. Coralee's house is on the highway.

I lay my bike down in the shell-splattered gravel next to a mailbox that looks like it might be rusted shut. The house in front of me is built in the shape of a perfect hexagon. Two concrete pillars run from the small porch to the dark shingled roof. A pair of rocking chairs adorns the porch, which is not in the same state of disrepair as the Blackwood house, but it's pretty close.

I can see remnants of an old barn in Coralee's backyard, which stretches out into what once might have been a crop field but looks more like a swamp now. Even the house sits low to the ground, like it's been slowly sinking into the muddy earth over many years.

In fact, it looks like it might slip into the ground at any moment.

I feel a twinge of guilt pinch my stomach. Is this why Coralee never invites me over? Because she doesn't want me to see her house?

I could slink back to my bike, hop on, cycle away, and never tell Coralee I came. But no. I owe Coralee more than that. I owe her an apology.

Cautiously, I inch my way up the stairs and to the porch, where a screen door hangs off its hinges, welcoming me to knock on the wooden door behind it.

I knock three times and wait for a long minute.

Just when I start to think no one's home, a woman comes to the door. She is whip thin like Coralee, and her skin is the same smooth dusky brown, like I imagine the polished wood of Coralee's violin must be.

I attempt a smile and say, "I'm a friend of Coralee's."

She opens the door wider so I can see she's dressed in navy scrubs. "You here to see Coralee?"

"Yes," I say. "Ethan, from school. I brought her work for today."

The woman eyes me for another minute and then steps aside, ushering me in. "I'm Adina," she says. "Are your shoes clean?"

"I think so." But Adina's mouth curves down at the corners, so I take them off anyway and place them by the door.

"Coralee!" she calls. "You have a guest!"

I look around the small house: dining nook to my left, living room to my right, kitchen straight ahead, separated from the dining table by the back of a staircase. In the living room, where the walls are covered in peeling floral paper, a television flickers, playing a game show with canned laughter.

Even though everything is old, the floors shine and the windows gleam. The house is spotless.

"Coralee doesn't have many friends over," Adina says. "That's why I didn't let you in right away."

"Oh. Well, I'm her friend."

"So you said." Adina raises an eyebrow. "I'm just gonna go get her. I don't think she heard me call. Probably playing that violin."

She gestures to the couch. "Have a seat."

I walk over to the sofa as Adina disappears upstairs. I have a strange sensation of eyes upon me, but I still jump when I hear a voice croak, "Hello."

My eyes land on an armchair, where an old woman curls up under a quilt, her form so frail she almost disappears into the chair completely.

"Oh!" I cry. "Hi."

"I'm Coralee's granny," she huffs. My eyes fall on the oxygen tank next to her chair. "I'm sorry my daughter didn't introduce me."

"That's okay," I say. "I'm Ethan. I'm a friend of Coralee's."

Coralee's granny puts a finger behind her ear, and I repeat myself louder. Unlike Coralee's mother, her granny accepts my answer happily once she hears it.

"That's nice," she says. Her voice comes out in a coarse chirp, like a grasshopper song. "Can I get you some lemonade? Cookies?"

"No, thank you," I half shout. Granny doesn't look like she could even make it to the kitchen, let alone fix me an afternoon snack.

She nods and gives me a toothless smile. She has a crop of iron-gray hair, and lines cut so deep into her face that her skin looks like tree bark. Her brown eyes glaze over, and she turns her head back toward the TV.

My gaze wanders to the wall behind her, in the dining room, where dozens of pictures and mementos have been tacked up. I walk over to examine them. A picture of a family barbecue on the beach. A photograph of the barn out back when it still gleamed with red paint. A man in a white coat holding a diploma. Coralee's old yearbook pictures. A fishing hook. Half a dozen newspaper clippings. A few programs from school plays and rehearsals, and one from a funeral of someone called Calvin Jessup, who must be the man Coralee's brother is named after. Handwritten recipes. A homemade shelf boasting a wooden rolling pin and what looks like a stack of poker chips.

I'm so busy soaking up the wall of Coralee's past that I don't notice Coralee behind me until she speaks.

"You're here," she says.

I jump-spin around. "Give me a heart attack, why don't you!"

She scoffs and flicks a few braids behind her shoulder. "It's *my* house."

Her eyes glint like new pennies, and I think I detect some

of the same suspicion in them that I saw in her mother's.

"This is a cool wall," I say as a peace offering.

"Yeah, well, we're redecorating the rest of the house soon," she says defensively. "We just haven't had time to do it yet."

"I think it's a great house."

Her eyes soften a bit. "My grandfather built it himself," she says. "And Granny won't live anywhere else. Anyway, why are you here?"

"I wanted to bring you your homework," I say. "And to apologize."

Some of the fight goes out of her shoulders.

"Oh."

"Is that the rolling pin you told me about?" I ask. "The one that saved your life?"

"Coralee?" calls Granny. "Is that you?"

Coralee goes to the old woman and puts a hand on her shoulder. "It's me, Granny."

"All right, dear," Granny says, patting Coralee's hand.

Coralee returns to my side and runs her fingers over the rolling pin. "That's it," she says.

"How did it save you?"

I may not know everything about Coralee, but I have a feeling that the fastest way to make her forget she's mad at me is to get her telling a story.

"We were visiting relatives in Ohio for Christmas," she says. "And I fell through thin ice. My aunt saw me from the

134

kitchen and ran out to save me. She was making sugar cookies, so she had the rolling pin in her hand. She used it to pull me out of the water. If she hadn't had the pin, she couldn't have fished me out."

"Cool," I say with a grin. I reach out and touch the rough surface of the pin. I hear Mom's words in my head. *She does tell some* colorful *stories.* Maybe so, but this one must be true. Why else would they keep a rolling pin on the wall?

And maybe that means they're *all* true.

I hear Adina's footsteps thudding down the stairs. Coralee takes my arm in one of hers, grabbing her backpack with the other, and tugs me along so that I have no choice but to follow her out onto the porch and back into the sticky afternoon air.

She throws herself into one of the rocking chairs, and I take the other.

"I, um, I missed you at school today," I say.

"Adina had to work a double shift at the hospital," she explains, pulling her knees up into the chair and rocking herself back and forth. The floorboards creak with her weight. "Granny wasn't having a good day, so I had to stay home and watch her."

"She's sick?" I ask.

Secretly, I'm relieved that *I'm* not the reason Coralee wasn't at school today.

"Emphysema," Coralee confirms. "And dementia."

"Oh." I'm not exactly sure what those words mean, but

135

they don't sound good. "That's horrible."

"Adina takes care of her most of the time, but it's hard. Her bills are really expensive and Adina has to do a lot of double shifts to cover them."

"You call your mom by her first name?" I ask.

Coralee shrugs.

"That's cool. If I called my mom by *her* name, she would probably ground me."

Coralee looks at me like she's waiting for something, so I clear my throat.

"I wanted to say sorry for the way I acted the other day. I don't know—"

"It's okay," Coralee interrupts. "I'm just glad you're here. I thought you didn't want to be my friend anymore."

We sit listening to the *cre-EE-ak, cre-EE-ak* of the floorboards under Coralee's rocker.

"I need to tell you something," I blurt out.

It has just dawned on me that I am not only here to apologize for not trusting Coralee. I am here because I *do* trust Coralee.

This house with its peeling wallpaper and sagging porch— this is the secret Coralee has been hiding. She deserves to know mine.

The creaking stops, and Coralee turns to me.

"I need to tell you something too," she says. "Let's go."

Coralee Cove

∾

CORALEE AND I BIKE almost all the way back to school. After we cross the bridge over the inlet, just before we get to Mack's, she pulls off the road, into a gnarled grove of wind-warped trees. She drops her bike in the sandy soil.

"We walk from here," she says.

I lay my bike next to hers and follow her down a narrow footpath that winds its way between the inlet and the grove. Yellow lichens speckle the trees that grow at funny angles from the ground. The ever-present cricket chorus is rowdy here, like they have to chirp louder to be heard over the waves lapping against the shore.

"Watch out for snakes," Coralee calls over her shoulder.

The trek is short, just a couple of minutes. The path ends, and Coralee cuts through the brush, weaving between the stunted trees. Then the soil turns to rocks, the underbrush disappears, and we are standing a few feet above a slice of beach that looks out on the inlet.

"Wow," I say. "This place is awesome."

"Yeah," she says, climbing onto the rocks. "I found it a couple of years ago. I've never brought anyone here before."

I can't decide if I should be hurt that Coralee hasn't shown me her hideout sooner or honored that she is showing me now.

I decide on honored.

She hops down onto the beach. When I follow her, I see that the rocks are built up around a large storm drain. Its mouth opens tall enough that Coralee could probably walk in without having to duck down and wide enough that I could spread my arms without my fingertips reaching the concrete. The tunnel rests at the edge of the sand, but otherwise the little beach is pristine.

"Don't alligators live in those?" I point to the drain mouth, remembering something I read in Mr. Charles's class about gators traveling from pond to pond through the drains.

"That's what this is for," Coralee replies. She points to a chicken-wire grid, which has been duct taped over the entire entrance.

"Did you do that?"

She nods proudly. "Mack gave it to me. I couldn't have any alligators coming to spoil my spot," she crows, puffing out her chest and grinning. "No alligators allowed at Coralee Cove!"

"Coralee Cove?" I ask. "You named it after yourself?"

"Sure did," she says. "Who knows if anyone or anything else in this world will ever be named after me? But this bit of beach is mine."

She plops down, planting her feet in the sand and squinting up at the late-afternoon sunlight. I sit down beside her. There is suddenly nothing I would like to do more than just sit here, feeling the sunlight soak into my skin and watching the inlet waves lick at the shore.

But Coralee is looking at me expectantly. "You still want to tell me something?"

I nod, dig out the mini Snickers, and hand them to her. "It might take a while."

"That's okay," she says, taking the chocolate. "I've told you lots of my stories. But I don't know any of yours. I don't know Ethan's story."

Ethan's Story

〰

THE FIRST THING YOU have to understand about me and Kacey is that we have been best friends since before I can remember. Literally.

Our families lived on the same street since before we were born, four days apart at the same hospital. When our moms brought us home, they put us down for naps in the same crib while they had coffee or made lunch together. Our parents grew apart, but not me and Kacey. Most years we had all the same classes and teachers at school, but even the years we didn't, we still spent all our time together. Roddie even treated Kacey like his own little sister, racing her at sprints and stealing food off her plate when she came over for dinner.

Over the years, lots of kids at school and even some of our teachers would say how weird it was for a boy and girl to stay best friends. But it wasn't weird to us.

The second thing you should know is that, even though she *was* popular, Kacey didn't act like most of the popular girls we went to school with. Instead of wearing trendy labels or expensive boots, she usually wore gym shorts or sweatpants and tennis shoes. She kept her hair in a ponytail or braids because she didn't like having it in her face (and because most days she didn't bother to brush it in the morning). Instead of posters of boy bands on the wall in her room, she hung posters of the US women's national soccer team.

But Kacey was so pretty that it didn't matter that she kept her hair back and only wore sweats. And she was so funny and easy to talk to that people who should have been intimidated by her weren't. She had this laugh like ribbons blowing in the wind. It made everyone around her want to laugh too.

She also played starting forward on the girls' soccer team.

She probably could have been the star of the boys' team too, if they had let her. Because it wasn't just that Kacey could *keep up* with boys. She was better than almost anyone at almost everything she tried. Like, when I bought a skateboard, she bought one too, and within a week she was doing kick turns and board slides. When I told her I was going to try out for the baseball team, she agreed to be my practice pitcher. She got so good that Brandon McDavies, the boys' pitcher, told us we weren't allowed to practice on the school field anymore. Even though he said the field was reserved, we both knew it was because Kacey had embarrassed him by being better than he was.

Seventh grade started out just like every other year. We walked home from school together, helped each other through our homework, and sometimes played baseball or video games when we were done.

But it got boring, passing day after day doing the same stuff in the same quiet neighborhood. Some days you felt like you were too big for it, like you were a ten-pound lobster trapped in a grocery-store fish tank, like you might explode if you didn't get out or do something new.

So we dared each other.

Dare you to cannonball off the high dive.

Dare you to say "quack" after every sentence at school.

Dare you to skateboard down the windshield of Ms. Kim's minivan.

Dare you to order thirty pizzas to Brandon McDavies's house.

Sometimes we completed the dares, sometimes we didn't. Either way, we always laughed about it afterward.

When Kacey joined her club soccer team in October, she had less time to hang out. She went to team dinners after practice on Thursdays and competed in tournaments that lasted all weekend long. She even had to miss school sometimes to travel for games.

You probably think that we were finally drifting away from each other. But we weren't. Okay, sure, I didn't get to see her as much, but when Kacey and I were together, it was like we had never been apart.

After Thanksgiving, Kacey started bringing one of her soccer friends around the neighborhood to hang out with us. Her name was Briana Juarez, and she played keeper. She stood a few inches taller than Kacey and had crinkly brown eyes and freckly cheeks. I liked Briana okay, but she mostly talked to Kacey about things that I didn't know or care about, like Lydia's fake-out in their last game or the US women's team's chances in the next World Cup.

But what bugged me more was that I had never seen Kacey look at anyone the way she looked at Briana. It was almost like she *admired* her or something. Which was odd because Kacey didn't *admire* anyone. She didn't admire me. And it's not like I admired her, either. You don't admire someone who you've seen puking on the carpet in the movie theater lobby because she was dared to eat two whole buckets of popcorn during *Lethal Force III.* You don't admire your best friend because you don't need to. You're equals.

When Kacey asked me to go with her to Briana's birthday party the weekend after winter break, I said yes. It didn't really matter to me what we were doing, as long as we got to hang out together. She had been invited to some prestigious soccer camp in Europe for the entire summer, so there were already two months ahead that I wouldn't get to see her at all. It would be the first summer I could remember that she wasn't going to come camping with us.

A huge snowstorm struck a couple of days before the party, which was great because it caused the power to go out, and Kacey's practice got canceled, so she came over to our house to roast marshmallows and play cards by the fireplace with me and Roddie.

By the day of Briana's party, the power was back on. But another flurry the night before meant there was a fluffy coating of fresh snow atop the packed icy layer beneath. It was the perfect kind of snow, because you could sled in it, build with it, and make snowballs out of it.

Which is why it was particularly annoying that Briana's party was inside.

When we got to her house, Mrs. Juarez ushered us down to the basement, where a dozen or so other kids played pool or watched a movie. I didn't know any of them, and as it turned out, neither did Kacey. They all came from Briana's school.

I wondered if that was why Kacey had chosen today to wear eye makeup for the first time ever. Because maybe she was nervous about meeting all these new people. That's why I decided not to kid her about it, even though it looked so weird to me.

Briana gave me a quick hug and talked with Kacey for a

while about their upcoming game. But then some kid wearing a cloud of cologne arrived, and Briana let out a squeal and ran to hug him. After an hour of watching them flirt, Kacey and I finally laid down our pool cues. We had already beaten some guys we didn't know three times in a row.

Which was just like Kacey, to be able to beat anyone at pool even though her eyes had been glued to Briana the whole time.

"Let's get out of here," I whispered.

"My dad isn't coming to get us for another hour," she replied.

"Yeah, I know we can't leave," I said. "But we can go outside. Do something fun. I'm bored down here, and that guy's cologne is making me want to puke all over this carpet. Oh, wait, that's your thing."

Kacey laughed and followed me upstairs. We walked through the kitchen, where Mrs. Juarez was pulling a cake out of the oven.

"Looking for the bathroom?" she asked.

"No," I said. "We were wondering if we could hang out in the backyard for a while."

Mrs. Juarez cocked her head and wiped her hands on her apron. "I suppose that's okay for a few minutes," she said. "As long as you wear your coats and boots. I'll make you some hot chocolate to warm you up when you come back in."

After we had wrapped ourselves up in our parkas and

snow boots and wool scarves, we wandered around in Briana's yard, dodging each other's lazy snowballs. I could tell that Kacey's heart wasn't in it. Otherwise her snowballs would've stung like punches when they hit me, which they always did.

Another thing about Kacey is she was almost never upset, not even when she lost an important soccer game or when she fractured her ankle when we were ten. "It's no biggie," she would say. Or, "At least I'll get to miss school for a few days."

But now she stared up at the slate sky, which was threatening another storm, and sniffled like she was holding back tears. I figured it had something to do with Briana ignoring her.

"Hey!" I called, tossing a snowball at her. "What's wrong?"

"Nothing," she said, catching my snowball before it could hit her shoulder. She dropped it and kicked it into a spray of powder. "It's nothing."

I didn't know how I was supposed to make Kacey feel better. I'd never had to do it before. So I did the only thing I could think of.

"If it's nothing, then you won't mind if I dare you to climb to the top of that tree."

I pointed to the far end of the yard, where a huge tree rose out of the ground, its snowy limbs like a collection of giant bones.

"That is, *unless* you're too scared."

For a second, she didn't respond, and I thought I had made her feel worse. Then she attempted a grin. "Scared? I don't *do* scared. How about I climb to the top of that tree and peg you with a snowball?"

"Dare you to try."

"Dare accepted."

Kacey took off, with me chasing behind her. The air was thick with sugary snow that sprinkled down from the tree as Kacey made her way up. I stuck my tongue out to catch some of it in my mouth. Then I cheered her on from below by yelling insults at her.

"You call that climbing? My grandma could climb faster than that!"

"Both your grandmas are dead," Kacey called down.

"Which should tell you how slow you're going!"

Two-thirds of the way up, a big gap between branches made her pause. She couldn't quite reach the higher one. So she edged farther out to where the one above her bowed down toward the one she was standing on, which had begun to buckle under her weight.

"What are you doing?" I called.

"I can grab it," she said, pointing to the higher branch, "if I can just get a little farther out."

She was right. She could reach it if she shuffled out a few more feet. But a few more feet and the branch she was standing on narrowed to the size of my arm.

"I don't know, Kacey. The branch you're on doesn't look that stable," I said.

"Who's scared now?" she called down. "Even if I fall, I'll just land in a foot of snow."

So I closed my mouth and said nothing else.

And that's the last thing Kacey ever heard me say.

Nothing.

I watched her make her way farther out onto the branch. Her feet dragged sideways, first the right sliding out a few inches, then the left shifting to meet it. The branch above her was within her grasp. She reached her arms up to grab it, the tips of her fingers brushed against it, and then *crack!*

That's when the branch broke.

It felt like she took forever to fall.

But really it was over in less than a second.

That's how long it took for a life to end.

She fell in a shower of white and landed with a sickening *thwack* on the snow-covered ground. Then she was still.

I screamed her name.

But I knew she couldn't hear me. I ran to her and knelt beside her. A thick halo of blood seeped into the snow around her head. My hand trembled against her snow-cold cheek.

I started shouting for someone to come help us.

That was the last time I ever saw Kacey, lying there, arms and legs sprawled out, spilling red blood into the snow.

And then Mrs. Juarez was there, pulling me away from

148

Kacey, and then the red lights and the hospital and the afterness.

The light in Kacey's window.

The square of white paper.

You killed her, Ethan Truitt.

The Mysterious One

CORALEE DOESN'T SAY ANYTHING when I've finished. Not at first. Hot tears are splashing down my face, and I swallow a sob, which makes me hiccup. The sun still shines bright and white-hot, but it can't seem to warm me. The sand feels like snow on the bottoms of my feet.

Coralee doesn't stare at me or shush me like I'm a baby. She looks out at the water and scrunches her toes up and down in the sand until I've wiped my tears away.

"Did she break her neck?" she asks gently.

I cringe as I remember the paramedics easing Kacey's body up from the snow. Her head lifting to reveal the rock, gray with jagged edges, smudged with dark blood.

"Her head hit a rock," I whisper.

Coralee doesn't flinch. "So you think it's your fault?"

"My psychologist back in Boston calls it survivor's guilt," I say. "She says it's common in people with post-traumatic stress disorder."

"That may be true," Coralee says. "But I don't see any expensive doctors hovering behind you now. So why don't you tell me what *you* think."

"What I think?"

"Do you think it was your fault?"

I can feel frustration begin to simmer inside me. Coralee doesn't understand. No one does.

"I don't *think* it was my fault," I say. "I *know* it was my fault. If I hadn't been there, if I hadn't dared her, she wouldn't have been in that tree. She wouldn't have fallen. And she wouldn't be—"

But I can't finish. If I finish, my anger and sorrow will swallow me whole.

To my surprise, Coralee doesn't argue with me. "Okay," she says. "So it's your fault."

I nod. "She wouldn't have fallen if I hadn't been there."

"No question," she replies. "But let's say it was you in that tree instead of her. Let's say she dared you, and you fell."

I don't tell her that I wouldn't have fallen, because I'm taller than Kacey and I would have been able to grab hold of the branch she was trying to reach. I don't tell her how often I've thought about the exact same thing.

"What's your point?" I ask.

"Would you blame her? If it was you?"

Coralee is staring at me now. I grab a handful of sand and let it run slowly through my fingers.

"No," I say finally.

"And if she was here, do you think she would be mad at you?"

I breathe out a long sigh. "No."

"So maybe it is your fault," Coralee says. "But that doesn't mean you have to blame yourself."

I've never thought about it like this before, and I can't think of anything to say. After a while, I feel Coralee's slight arm drape around my shoulder, and I'm reminded again of the day in the cafeteria when she led me to her table.

"I haven't told anyone," I say. "Nobody here."

"I won't either," she replies solemnly. "I promise. Is that the real reason your family moved here? So you could start over?"

"Yes."

The sun has begun to drop. I haven't called Mom since I told her I would be a little late coming home from school. She's probably worried sick.

"We should go," I say.

"Yeah. It's almost dinnertime."

"Do you want to come over to my house? For dinner? Grandpa Ike and I can drive you home so you don't have to bike in the dark."

And, I think, *Mom can't be too mad at me in front of Coralee.*

I stand, brush the sand off my hands, and hold them out to help her up. She doesn't take them at first, and I'm afraid she's going to shake her head and make an excuse about needing more taffy to keep her blood sugar up or having to study for the make-up spelling test we both know she'll ace. Maybe now that she knows what I've done, she won't want to be my friend.

But then she puts her palms in mine and lets me lift her easily to her feet. "Dinner sounds great," she says. "As long as there's no meat."

"My mom's making lasagna," I say. "It's vegetarian. My favorite."

"Careful, Ethan," Coralee cautions, wagging a finger at me. "If you tell me too much more about yourself, there will be no mystery left."

I muster a small smile. This whole time I've been thinking that Coralee is the mysterious one, when it's been me all along.

"So you can really skateboard?" she asks. "Can you teach me?"

"Sure," I say, surprised. I think of my skateboard, which has been sitting in a box since we arrived, along with my baseball glove, my video games, and all the other stuff from Boston I can't bear to look at anymore.

I lead the way back to the path that will take us to our bikes and the road. Halfway there, I remember something.

"Didn't you want to tell me something too?" I say.

"Oh, yeah. It's about that night at the house. That woman."

The way she lowers her voice almost to a whisper, like she's afraid of being overheard, makes me feel uneasy. I hear a loud snap somewhere in the trees behind us and I startle, then stumble over a tree root.

"What was that?" I say, spinning around.

Coralee keeps her head down and pushes me forward. "Keep walking," she says quietly. "I'll tell you everything when we get to your house."

Followed

❧

JUST AS I SUSPECT, Mom is flittering around the front porch like a moth as we pull into the driveway, where Roddie and Grandpa Ike are working under the hood of the Fixer-Upper.

"Where have you been?" she says to me, a tremble in her voice. "You told me you were just going to drop off Coralee's homework. I called, and Adina said you weren't there."

"He was with me, Mrs. T," Coralee answers. "I had to be absent from school today, and I made Ethan catch me up on what I missed. It was my fault he forgot to call you."

"Oh." Mom looks from me to Coralee. I can tell she's struggling to swallow down the lecture she had prepared for me. "Well, just don't let it happen again. Okay, Ethan?"

I apologize for worrying her and ask if Coralee can stay for dinner.

Mom has miraculously managed to make the lasagna without burning it, and we all help ourselves to seconds (except for Grandpa Ike). Maybe it's because Coralee is here, but everyone gets along better than usual. Even Roddie takes off his Boston College cap without being asked.

"Why don't you tell everyone your news?" Mom says once we're all digging into our second portions.

Roddie stares at her blankly.

"What your gym teacher said?"

"Oh," says Roddie, looking down at his plate. "He wants me to help him start a baseball team for next year."

"Isn't that wonderful?" Mom asks, beaming.

"Sure is," Coralee affirms.

"It's not for sure yet," Roddie says, grinding pepper over his lasagna. "They might not have funding."

"How much funding does it take to stick a couple kids out on a dirt field, for God's sake?" Grandpa Ike says.

"It still won't be anything like my old team. It's not like any Boston schools are going to send scouts down here."

Dad wipes his mouth with his napkin and clears his throat. "Actually, Roddie, your mom and I thought we might plan a weekend for me and you to go visit some colleges in the area. There's some good schools in Georgia. In-state tuition here is, well, it's a lot more affordable than—"

Roddie's fork clatters to his plate. "No."

"We need to start thinking realistically about—"

"I'm not going to some podunk Georgia school!" Roddie shouts. "Why should I have to be punished just because you decided to move us away? I'm going to Boston College with Grace!"

I glance at Coralee, who is frozen, her fork halfway from her plate to her mouth.

"Um, Mom?" I mumble. "Can Coralee and I be excused?"

Mom nods distractedly, and we slink away from the table. I jerk my head toward the back porch, and Coralee follows.

It's a relief when I close the glass door behind us, blocking out most of the yelling.

Coralee curls up on a wicker couch while I flip on the porch light and then take the matching chair. The insects and frogs screech loud enough that I have to move one of Grandpa Ike's junk boxes and pull the chair closer to the couch so Coralee and I can hear each other.

"Roddie really doesn't like it here, huh?" says Coralee.

I shake my head. "It's not his fault he's so unhappy," I say. "Not really. I screwed his life up pretty bad. That's why he won't speak to me anymore."

"Maybe you should talk to him."

"No," I say, picking uncomfortably at the chair arm. "Not a good idea."

Coralee doesn't understand. And how can she?

She wasn't there in the street when Roddie caught me

157

trying to run again. She doesn't know what happened between us that day.

"So what did you want to tell me?" I ask, eager to change the subject.

Coralee curls herself more tightly around her legs and scans the dark horizon like she's on the lookout for something.

"What's going on?"

She won't meet my eyes. Instead, she looks up at the porch light, where a half dozen insects are throwing themselves toward the bulb.

"Okay," she says. "Here goes. Ever since that day in the Blackwood house, strange things have been happening. I think—I think I'm being followed."

"By who?"

"You remember that woman we saw? Standing at the top of the staircase?"

The hairs on the back of my neck prickle.

"How could I forget?"

"Well, I saw her again."

Goose bumps creep up and down my arms.

"Where?" My voice cracks. Like I'm not sure I want to know.

Coralee gulps.

"Where, Coralee?"

When she answers me, her voice is a mere whisper. "Right outside my bedroom window."

The Red Velvet Box

～

Now I understand why Coralee rushed us away from Coralee Cove when we heard the tree branch snap, and why her eyes keep flickering toward the sweep of darkness beyond the porch.

Who knows what could be out there, hiding in the shadows?

Coralee tells me everything, and then I make her tell me again.

"So you think the woman followed you from the Blackwood house?" I ask.

She nods.

"You woke up in the night?"

"No, I wasn't asleep yet, and I went to the bathroom—"

"And when you came back—"

"I was closing my blinds, and I saw her standing there. Right below my window."

"You're sure it was the same woman?"

"I'm sure. She was the right height. She stood the same way. Really proper, kind of old-fashioned."

"It couldn't have been your mom? Or Granny?"

"Granny hasn't been able to go farther than the front porch for the past two years. And Adina is too tired at night to creep around underneath my window."

"So then what did you do?" I continue.

"What would *you* do? I hightailed it back into bed and pulled the covers over my head."

"And the next night?"

"Same thing, except—"

"Except what?"

"Well, this time I waited up to see her, and when I did, she raised her hand really slowly toward the window."

"Like she was waving at you?"

"Like she was reaching for something."

My mind whirs. How could the woman from the house have followed Coralee? She was on her bike. There's no way anyone could have trailed her on foot, and there were no bikes or cars parked outside the house.

Unless . . .

The palms of my hands have gone sticky with sweat.

"Coralee? I think I have a theory."

"Me too," she says.

Then we both blurt out what we're thinking at the exact same time.

"What if she's a ghost?" I say.

"It's because of what I took," says Coralee.

"Wait, *what?*" we say together.

"You took something?"

"You think she's a *ghost*? Why would you think that?"

I can feel my cheeks warming. "I just thought—something that Grandpa Ike said about the woman who used to live there. She died on the stairs and— Why are you looking at me like that?"

Coralee is gazing at me with an expression I've seen on Mom's face a thousand times, her eyebrows knit with worry, her eyes wide with concern.

"I get why you thought that," Coralee says slowly. "I probably would have thought the same thing if I had heard that story. But I found, well, I found tennis-shoe prints outside my window. Ghosts don't wear tennis shoes, right?"

"Of course not," I mumble. "I didn't mean I actually *believed* she was a ghost. It was just a stupid theory."

She puts a hand on my arm. "I can understand why you would want to believe that ghosts are—"

"Like I said, I don't believe in ghosts," I snap, moving my arm to scratch a fake mosquito bite, trying to ignore the feeling in my stomach, like a balloon being punctured.

161

People don't come back from the dead.

"So you were saying that you took something?" I say, needing to change the subject.

Coralee hesitates before reaching down into her backpack. She pulls out a red velvet box. "I didn't mean to take it," she says. "Honest. But I was looking in the pockets of that raincoat for something that might tell us who it belonged to, and right when I found this is when we saw that woman. And then we were running, and I didn't even realize I still had it in my hand."

It's not until now that I notice Coralee doesn't look like herself. She's got dark circles under her eyes, and even though the skin on her lips looks raw, she's still chewing on it.

"Did you look and see what's in it?" I ask.

Without a word, she slides the red box across the glass table between us, and I pick it up.

It's a bit wider than my palm, and heavier than I expected it to be.

I press my fingers against the plush fabric and pull. The lid springs open.

I gasp.

Even in the hazy porch lighting, the contents of the box gleam and twinkle like Christmas lights.

What's in the Box

1. A pair of shiny diamond earrings.

2. A string of milky pearls as long as my arm.

3. A golden ring with blue stones, which Coralee calls "sapphires."

4. A heart-shaped locket, its face made of rubies, that hangs from a silver chain like a ripe strawberry on a dewy stem.

5. A delicate silver watch, crusted with tiny diamonds around the face.

6. A gold pendant shaped like a peacock, its feathers rippling with emeralds and crystals and more sapphires than I can count.

Treasure

~

ONCE I'VE LAID OUT all the treasures on the table and examined each one, I look up at Coralee again.

"Do you think these are real?" I ask.

"They're heavy," says Coralee. "And shiny. And some of them look really old. If they aren't real, they're really good imitations."

I pick up the strand of pearls again and run them through my hands. They're smooth and cool. "So you think this woman saw you take the box and tracked you down somehow?"

"Yes."

"And she's been there two nights in a row?"

Coralee nods.

"Why didn't you just leave them out on your porch for her

or something? Then maybe she'd go away."

Coralee clucks her teeth. "What would happen if Adina found them first? Or if that lady came up onto the porch to get them and Adina heard her and called the police?"

"Why *didn't* you call the police?" I ask. "Why don't we call them right now?"

Coralee stiffens and she shakes her head. "Go to the police? Think about it, Ethan. What was that lady doing with this kind of jewelry in an old, abandoned house? She probably stole it and was hiding out there. If this stuff actually belonged to her, she would have gone to the police by now. But if we go to the police with some story about a mysterious woman hiding out with a box full of jewels, they'll think we're lying. Whoever she is, I'm sure she's found a new hideout by now. They might think I stole all this stuff. Ethan, they could put me in jail!"

"Okay, okay," I say, holding my palms up. "No police. You're right. But we have to do something. We have to tell somebody. This jewelry could be worth a lot of money. If someone knows you have it and wants it back, you might not be safe."

"I know," Coralee whispers, bringing her knees to her chin and wrapping her arms around them.

Just then, Mom calls my name, and we sweep the jewelry back into the box as fast as we can. Coralee slips it into her bag as Mom opens the porch door. "It's getting late, kids. I think Coralee might want Grandpa Ike to take her on home."

But one look at Coralee's face tells me that home is the last place she wants to go.

Ghosts

❧

ONCE GRANDPA IKE AND I get home from dropping Coralee off, I spend most of the night tossing and turning, worrying about Coralee and trying to convince myself that I never actually believed the woman we saw was a ghost.

Believing in ghosts is dangerous. It gives you hope when there is none.

I can't let myself forget. Kacey is gone.

You can't be with her. You can never be with her again.

Help

~

THE NEXT MORNING, I get up early for school and pedal the wrong way, toward Coralee's house. I don't want her to have to bike to school alone.

When I pass by the Blackwood house, I pause and look it over.

No movement. Except for the door being closed, there's no sign anyone's been there since we left. Coralee was right. The woman we saw is probably long gone by now.

I don't stop again until I get to Coralee's house.

I breathe a sigh of relief when she emerges, but as she draws closer and brushes a few braids back from her face, I see her eyes are puffy.

"Did you get any sleep?" I ask.

"Not really," she says.

"Me either."

Coralee climbs on her bike, and we set off at a much slower pace than usual.

"Did she come back?" I ask.

"I don't know," she says. "I shut the blinds as soon as I got in."

We get to school late since Coralee was too tired to bike very fast, and she spends half of science class dozing before Mr. Charles wakes her up and threatens to give her lunchtime detention.

"You should fall asleep more often at school," Suzanne says to her at the end of the period. "It makes class so much nicer for everyone else."

Coralee is too weary to even roll her eyes.

At lunch, we grab a table no one sits at because the uneven legs make it wobble. This way, we definitely won't be interrupted.

"So," I say. "What are we going to do? We have to tell someone."

"I know," Coralee says, unwrapping her sandwich and taking a small bite. "That's why after school today we're going straight to Mack's."

When we get to Mack's, she sees how upset Coralee is, hangs a *Back in Fifteen* sign on the door, and ushers us into the library. She listens to Coralee tell about going to the

Blackwood house. How she felt like she'd been there before, how the woman appeared just as her hand closed around the box, and how when she got home and opened it, she couldn't believe her eyes.

Mack doesn't say anything, but her mouth tips into a frown that deepens as Coralee tells her about the woman standing outside her window. Finally, when Coralee is through, Mack leans forward and says, "That's some story."

"You believe me, though, don't you, Mack?" Coralee asks, a tremble crossing her lower lip.

"Course I do," says Mack. "Now about this jewelry. Did you bring it with you?"

Coralee nods and pulls the velvet box from her backpack.

"You took that to *school?*" I ask.

"I couldn't leave it at home," says Coralee. "That woman might have broken in and stolen it back."

Mack takes the box and opens it. She studies its contents, her expression impossible to read.

"Do you think they're real?" I ask.

"Yes," says Mack. "No doubt about that."

She examines the jewelry for another minute, then shuts the box tight. She closes her eyes too. "Let me think," she mutters to no one in particular. "Let me think."

"Should we go to the police?" I ask.

Mack's eyes flutter open. "No," she says. "No need for police. You leave this with me. And you leave your mysterious

170

woman to me too. I'll take care of it."

"But—how?" I ask.

"There's nothing to worry about," Mack says. "No one's going to bother y'all again, and I'll make sure these jewels find their way back to where they belong. You trust me?"

"You know I trust you, Mack," says Coralee.

"And you?" Mack says, turning her gaze to me. "Can you trust me to protect Coralee?"

I nod. "I trust you. I just wish—"

"Then no more questions. And no more trespassing in abandoned houses. You promise me? Nothing good ever came from snooping around an abandoned house."

"Promise," Coralee and I say together.

"Well, then. I gotta open the shop back up now before I lose all my customers. And I'm doing inventory, so I'm afraid y'all have to play somewhere else today."

Without another word or a backward glance, Mack lifts herself from her chair and strides out the door.

One Heck of a Story

≈

CORALEE AND I SHOW ourselves out while Mack points a lady to the fertilizer aisle. We sit at the edge of the curb, the same place I sat on my first day in Palm Knot, and squint into the hot sun.

"That was weird," I say. "What do you think Mack's plan is?"

Coralee scuffs her shoe back and forth against the pavement. "I don't know," she says. "But Mack always does what she says she's going to. If she says she'll take care of it, then she will."

"Yeah, but how? Do you think she knows who—"

"I'm too tired to think about it," says Coralee, turning toward me. Her head is drooping from her neck like a wilting flower, like she's too weary to hold it up. "I'm just relieved Mack's helping us."

172

"Yeah," I say. "Me too. You wanna come over to my house? Mom's making tofu teriyaki for dinner."

She shakes her head. "I have a bed at home with my name on it."

"All right," I say, standing up and wiping a sheen of sweat from my forehead. Coralee lifts her hand toward me. I grab it and pull her up.

We bike together over the bridge and past the empty fruit stands until my turn. "See you tomorrow," I call.

"Hey, Ethan?"

I slow down and look back. Coralee's face splits into the first smile I've seen all day.

"Yeah?"

"This is going to make one heck of a story someday."

"Yeah. Someday."

Then I pedal off, wondering all the way home what Mack has planned and why she won't tell us what it is.

Roddie's Moment

❧

As soon as Coralee walks through Ms. Silva's door the next morning, I can tell that the mysterious woman failed to make an appearance during the night. The circles under Coralee's eyes aren't quite as dark, and her tiny braids swing confidently from the high ponytail she's tied them into.

She gives me a thumbs-up on the way to her desk, which I return with a grin.

The woman doesn't come back that night either. Or over the weekend, which Mom makes me spend hauling out the rest of Grandpa Ike's old boxes, and which Coralee has to spend at home with Granny while Adina works back-to-back shifts.

Whatever Mack's plan was, it must have worked.

With every day that passes, I find myself thinking about

the woman and the jewels less and less. But maybe that's because when we get back to school on Monday, our teachers keep us really busy with practice tests and extra homework to try to get us ready for our end-of-year standardized tests next week.

Or maybe it's because Coralee and I barely have a chance to talk the whole week. Having a conversation in class is out, since all the teachers are being extra strict. Mr. Charles threatens to call Coralee's mom when he catches her passing a note to me during our math quiz ("Go ahead and try," she grumbles), and even Ms. Silva snaps at us for whispering while we're supposed to be writing practice compare-and-contrast essays.

We can't really talk during lunch, either, because Herman sits with us every day, and we don't hang out after school because Adina is still working afternoon shifts, which means that Coralee has to take care of Granny. "Sorry, Ethan," she says every day. "I would invite you over, but Granny's having another bad day. I don't think it's a good idea to have company."

"Yeah, no problem," I reply casually, trying to hide my disappointment. Because the afternoons feel a lot longer without Coralee to fill them, with nowhere to go but home. When Coralee's here, no one fights as much as they usually do. But when I get home after school on Wednesday, Mom and Grandpa Ike are shouting at each other in the living room.

"Your mother gave that chair to me for our tenth anniversary!" Grandpa Ike shouts, throwing his faded baseball cap across the living room floor, where it whacks against the glass door. "And I've sat in it every night since. You had no right to throw it out!"

"You'd think you could manage to take better care of the things you apparently love so much. The stuffing was coming out. It was falling apart—"

"Don't think I don't know you've been trying to get in my room, too."

"Because the exterminators needed to get in!" Mom cries. "You're too busy out doing God knows what every day to take care of basic—"

"You're a guest in *my* house, damn it. But you set foot in that room one more time and you won't be anymore."

"What is going on out here?" Dad shouts, marching out of his office. "How am I supposed to get any work done with all this screaming?"

Grandpa Ike glares at Dad for a moment before storming upstairs and slamming his door just like Roddie.

He doesn't come back down for dinner, so I make a ham-and-mustard sandwich and bring it up to his room.

Mostly, I just want him to know I'm sorry that Mom is changing all his stuff, even though I don't think he actually means all that about kicking her out of the house.

But a small part of me is hoping he'll let me in, so I can see what's in his room.

Then I could have solved at least *one* mystery around here.

When I knock on Grandpa Ike's door, he opens it after a minute, but only gives an inch or two.

He looks surprised to see me, but he takes the sandwich. "Heard your mother and me fighting, huh?" he says without opening the door any wider.

"Yeah. I wish I knew why you didn't get along. Maybe I could do something to help."

"Your mother's problems with me have nothing to do with you. Nothing for you to feel upset about."

An awkward silence falls over us.

I guess he's not going to invite me in after all.

"Haven't been driving for a while," Grandpa Ike says finally. "How about we go for a spin soon?"

"Yeah," I say. "That would be great."

Grandpa Ike and Mom aren't the only ones fighting these days.

Later that night in my room I hear Mom and Dad arguing. I can't make out what they're saying, just the dull hiss of their conversation like hot water running through the pipes. They've been fighting like this almost every night.

Usually it starts a few minutes after the phone rings.

I wonder if it's Mr. Reid who keeps calling, but I'm usually too afraid to pick up the phone and listen. I pick it up once, just for a second. Just long enough to hear a man's voice crying before I punch the "end" button and dive back into bed.

Why is Kacey's father crying on the phone? Why is it making my parents fight?

The only person who seems to be feeling better about things is Roddie, who is spending less and less time in his room these days. The school board approved the Palm Knot High baseball team for next year, so he's been staying late at school to organize tryouts and to get the field cleaned up. He spends his evenings out in the driveway working on Grandpa Ike's Fixer-Upper until it gets dark. Grandpa Ike helps too, when he's actually here.

On Thursday, while Dad's helping me with my science homework and Mom's cooking dinner, we hear a *clunk, clunk, clunk*, followed by a loud whooping. We all pile out onto the porch in time to see a black puff of smoke blooming from the exhaust pipe of the Fixer-Upper, now whirring with life. Roddie's sitting in the driver's seat, his left arm out the window, his hand raised in a triumphant fist pump. Grandpa Ike looks on with a satisfied expression.

"I can't believe it!" Mom calls. "I can't believe you actually did it!"

Dad runs down from the porch and peers under the hood, which is being propped up by an umbrella. "She's a beaut," he says, a big sappy grin on his face.

I wish I could run down too, trace my fingers over the red stripe of the truck that Roddie has washed and polished meticulously, and high-five my brother.

Mom must know what I'm thinking, because she gives me a gentle push. "Go on," she says. "Why don't you go congratulate Roddie? Maybe he'll take you for a ride."

But I shake my head. "No," I say. "I don't want to spoil this for him."

This is Roddie's moment. I know he doesn't want me to be a part of it, so I turn and walk back inside, trying to ignore the twist in my gut. I guess a part of me was hoping now that Roddie doesn't seem completely miserable, he might stop hating me quite so much. That he might start looking *at* me again instead of *through* me.

Later that night, I do catch him glancing at me across the dinner table. His face reminds me of the way he looks at the players of the losing team when he shakes their hands after a game.

I don't want Roddie to feel sorry for me, but it's kind of nice to know I'm not completely invisible to him after all.

Pool Party!

❧

WHEN CORALEE GETS TO school on Friday morning, she looks tired again.

"Is everything okay?" I whisper as Ms. Silva goes over the testing schedule for next week. "You haven't seen—"

Coralee shakes her head. "I'm fine," she says. "It's just all this testing stuff."

"Coralee and Ethan. Eyes up here and mouths closed, please."

We turn our attention toward the timetable on the board, but it's hard for me to concentrate. I can't help but feel like there's something Coralee's not telling me. Since when does a test make her anxious?

Ms. Silva dismisses us to first period, and everyone gathers their things.

"Wanna go to Mack's after school today?" Coralee asks. "Adina finally has an afternoon off."

"I have to leave early for a dentist's appointment. What about tomorrow?"

Coralee nods. "Definitely," she says, and her smile makes me feel slightly better.

Daniel and Suzanne push past us as they're walking toward the gym.

"Did you hear about the hurricane they think might hit us next week?" Suzanne asks loudly.

"Yeah," says Daniel. "It would be so awesome if they canceled school. Awesome for most people, that is. If I lived in a shack like Coralee's, I'd be pretty worried."

Suzanne looks over her shoulder and giggles. "That thing could blow over with a slight breeze."

Coralee's mouth tightens into a scowl, and her hands clench into fists. She squares her shoulders and takes a step forward, but I grab her by the arm. Coach Sluggs is standing at the end of the hall, his whistle in his mouth, watching us.

"I'd be hoping for school to get canceled too," I say just loud enough for Daniel and Suzanne to hear me, "if I knew I was going to fail all our end-of-year tests and get held back for a second time."

Daniel spins around, his lips drawn up in a snarl, but Suzanne pulls on his arm. "Coach Sluggs is right there," she hisses. "You'll get suspended. Get him back later."

Daniel hesitates, glaring at me, then allows Suzanne to lead him into the gym.

When I look over at her, Coralee isn't upset. She's beaming.

"That was a good one," she says. "Thanks for sticking up for me."

I shrug. "It was nothing."

Before we can follow Suzanne and Daniel into the gym, Herman shuffles up and hands us both thin envelopes. "You probably won't want to come," he mumbles. "But my mom is making me give invitations to everyone."

Coralee rips hers open, revealing a square piece of paper with a picture of three kids jumping into a pool. It says *POOL PARTY!* in big letters at the top. Then, below the picture: *Please join us this Sunday 2–4 p.m. at the Pink Palm Motel to celebrate Herman's 13th birthday.*

"It's okay if you don't come," Herman says quickly, see-sawing from one foot to the other.

But he's looking at us, his wide eyes like soggy green Froot Loops in pools of milk. They hold a silent plea. If Coralee and I won't agree to come to his pool party, who will?

"Of course we'll be there," Coralee says.

"We wouldn't miss it," I add.

Herman's body sags with relief. "Really? That's great! That's— Yeah!"

The bell rings, and Coach Sluggs calls from the end of the

hall. "Let's go, let's go, people!"

Herman's face breaks into a grin, and he looks back and forth from me to Coralee. "I have to go give Suzanne and Daniel theirs now," he says. Then he pats me on the back with one of his massive hands, knocking me off balance. "See you Sunday!"

"Poor kid," Coralee says. "I think we've given him a false sense of confidence."

Once we get into the gym, we watch as Herman taps Suzanne on the shoulder. She turns away from her conversation with Daniel, who's still scowling, and looks at Herman like he's some bum on the street about to steal her purse. He hands them their invitations, swipes his hand nervously through his greasy hair, and disappears into the locker room.

Suzanne opens the envelope and wrinkles her nose. Daniel says something that makes her shriek with laughter, and they drop their invitations in the trash can as they turn the corner.

Grandpa Ike's Errand

WHEN I GET HOME after my dentist appointment, Grandpa Ike is in his new chair, waiting for me. He gets up when I walk in.

"I have an errand to run," he says, raising his eyebrows. "Want to come?"

"An errand?" I ask. Then I remember his promise the other night to take me driving. "Oh! You mean—"

He puts his finger over his lips and tips his head toward Mom and Dad, who are sitting at the kitchen counter. They still don't know he's been teaching me to drive.

Grandpa Ike mumbles something to Dad about going into town, and we head out together. He drives until we get to the Blackwood house. Then he stops and climbs out so we can switch places.

The house is just the same as always, rotting and silent and still. Almost still enough to make me wonder whether there was ever any woman there to begin with, or if it was just our imaginations.

Almost. But not quite.

Grandpa Ike tips the brim of his baseball cap across the drive to Mr. Bondurant, who sends a salute back.

"It's weird how he's always on his porch like that," I say, shifting gears.

"Some people have nothing better to do with their time," Grandpa Ike mutters.

But what does Grandpa Ike do with *his* time? According to Mom, he's barely ever home during the day, when Roddie and I are at school. The question sits on my tongue, ready to spring out.

"Where do you want to go?" I say instead.

"I need to stop by the hardware store," Grandpa Ike replies, pointing toward town.

"For what?"

"Just an errand, like I said. How's that friend of yours, Coralee? Why hasn't she been around much lately?"

"She has to take care of her grandmother sometimes."

"Good kid."

When we get to Mack's, Grandpa Ike tells me to wait in the truck.

"I won't be a minute," he says.

"That's okay," I reply. "I don't mind coming in."

I haven't seen Mack since the day she took the jewelry from Coralee and promised that no one would be bothering her again. Maybe there's a chance she'll tell me how she got rid of the woman and what she did with the stolen jewelry.

"No," says Grandpa Ike. "The truck doesn't lock anymore, so it's better if you stay here."

And before I can protest, Grandpa Ike has slammed the door behind him. I watch as he walks into Mack's and stands at the counter for a minute, talking with her. Then he returns to the truck, empty-handed.

"Mack didn't have what you need?" I ask.

He shrugs. "Mack always gets me what I need."

It's funny, I think, how Grandpa Ike sounds a lot like Coralee when he talks about Mack. People in this town seem to trust her a lot.

As I steer us out of the parking lot, Grandpa Ike punches on the radio, which is basically just static, so I guess he doesn't want me to ask any more questions.

Mack's Desk

∿

ON SATURDAY, WE MEET at Coralee Cove and spend the entire morning going back and forth between the secret beach and Mack's store, floating in the warm salt water and lying in the sun, which is out in full force. By noon, the air sticks to me like a second, scorching skin, and I make Coralee follow me to the Fish House for air-conditioning and milk shakes. It feels great to be out of the house, away from all the fighting.

After our shakes, we promise Mack to spend the afternoon potting and watering her new summer plants, and in exchange she gives us two beach chairs to take with us to the cove. Once we're done potting, we wash off our hands and trudge back to the library, thoroughly exhausted. Even in here, the May air is as thick and sticky as warm honey, so we fan ourselves with Mack's paperbacks.

"My arms are so sore," Coralee complains. She isn't even five feet tall, but she somehow manages to drape herself over the entire couch.

"My whole *body* is sore," I say.

"I'm too tired to even unwrap a taffy," she moans.

"Well *someone* has been eating a lot of taffy," I say, pointing to the trash can beside Mack's desk, which is overflowing with waxy wrappers.

"Weird," Coralee says with a small frown. "Mack doesn't usually eat it. She just keeps it for kids."

I shrug as I slump into one of Mack's overstuffed armchairs. Mack greeted us in her usual way this morning, asking us how we were and throwing us each a taffy.

She didn't ask Coralee if she'd had any more trouble, or offer up any information.

It didn't seem to bother Coralee, though, so I didn't ask any questions. I guessed I'd just have to trust Mack, like Coralee and Grandpa Ike do.

"We should start on our essays," Coralee says finally, reaching down to pull her binder out of her backpack.

I groan. "Do we have to?"

We're supposed to write a three-page essay on our favorite character in the time-travel book for Ms. Silva's class. Neither Coralee or I have started yet.

I force myself to get up and rummage through my

backpack until I find my copy of the book and my binder.

"Do you have an extra pencil?" I ask. "I have a mechanical one, but it's out of lead."

"Nope," says Coralee, sitting up and plonking her binder across her lap. "Check Mack's desk."

"Are you sure?"

"She won't mind."

Coralee heaves a long sigh as I walk over to the desk. Outside, Mack laughs with one of her customers. Above us, something scrapes against the floorboards.

I open the top middle drawer. Nothing there but stamps and envelopes and address labels. The drawer on the left is full of files.

I open the drawer on the right just as we hear a loud *thump* from above us.

Coralee's spine straightens. We both lift our chins to look up at the ceiling.

"Is someone upstairs?" I ask.

"Mack's apartment is on the second floor," Coralee says. "It's probably just her. There's a back way up."

"No," I say. "Mack's in the store. Listen."

Sure enough, we can hear her instructing a customer on how to get rid of mold.

"That's *really* weird," Coralee replies. "Mack lives alone."

I glance down to shut the desk drawer.

"Maybe it's just Zora and Zelda," says Coralee.

But I don't respond.

In the desk drawer, there are piles of pens and pencils.

And behind them, at the very back of the drawer, something has been tucked away.

"Um, Coralee?" I say, looking up.

"Yeah?"

"I don't think it's Zora and Zelda up there."

"Why?"

I can hear myself gulp as I reach into the drawer.

"Because of this," I say, holding up the red velvet box.

The Face in
the Window

~

"THAT DOESN'T MEAN ANYTHING," Coralee says, standing up and squinting at the box. "It's probably empty."

But it's not. I can feel by how much it weighs in my palm. I open its lid and show her the glittering jewels inside. Her shoulders slump.

"Maybe she's just keeping it safe until she can find the owners," says Coralee.

"Maybe," I reply. "But who's upstairs?"

"Let's ask," Coralee says, marching toward the door. I put the box back in the desk drawer and follow her through the store, to where Mack is scribbling something on a sheet of paper filled with numbers.

"Mack?" Coralee asks.

"Mmm?" Mack doesn't look up from her list. The radio is

on next to her, and the weatherman is talking about the hurricane that could be headed toward us.

"Is someone staying with you?"

Now she raises her head and gives Coralee a sharp look like I've never seen before. Like Coralee's crossed a line. Just as quickly as I see it, it flickers away, and her features return to normal. Mack wipes her hands on her overalls and pours herself a glass of iced tea from a pitcher on the counter.

"Why would you ask that?" she says calmly.

"We heard something upstairs," I say. "It sounded like someone was up there."

Mack looks from Coralee to me and back again. "It's just me here," she says. "You know that, Coralee. Y'all probably just heard some mice. They get in the walls sometimes. I'll have the exterminator come next week."

"But—" Coralee starts.

"What about all the taffy wrappers? Who's been—" I say.

Mack cuts us off. "It's almost dinnertime. And I have plenty to be getting on with here. Maybe it's time y'all head out for the day."

A look of almighty surprise crosses Coralee's face.

"Can we come back tomorrow?" she says, her eyes narrowing in suspicion.

"I got business in Savannah tomorrow," Mack replies. "Best you find somewhere else to play."

Coralee purses her lips and places her fists on her hips.

"Fine," she says. "Come on, Ethan. Let's get our stuff and go."

She stalks back between the shelves to the library, where she's already throwing her binder into her backpack by the time I follow her in.

I open my mouth to speak, but she shakes her head. "Not here."

I sling my backpack over my shoulder and stop halfway to the door.

Then I turn, stride back to Mack's desk, and stuff the velvet box into my bag.

Coralee's eyes widen, but now I'm the one shaking my head. "Let's go," I say.

Coralee suppresses an indignant sniffle as we pass Mack on our way out. I think I hear her call good-bye to us, but it's hard to tell if it was really her or just the wind chimes over the door.

Once we're out on the sidewalk, Coralee jerks her head toward the inlet bridge. "Come on," she says. "Let's go to the cove. We can talk there."

As we walk past the shop, I glance up, shading my eyes from the sun and squinting toward the second-story windows. And that's when I see it.

Even though I'm sweating all over, my blood freezes.

"Coralee," I whisper.

"What?"

She doesn't see it. She doesn't see the woman's face in the window above Mack's store.

"What?" she repeats again. And then she cries, "Oh!"

My gaze locks with the eyes staring through the window for just a moment. Just long enough for me to be sure of what I see. Then a curtain falls, and she is gone.

X Marks the Spot

❧

"I KNEW IT," I say, pacing the narrow beach. "I knew there was something weird going on. That's why she didn't want us to ask any questions. Why she wouldn't tell us what she had planned."

Coralee sits slumped in one of our new beach chairs, holding the red box in her hands, prying it open and snapping it shut every so often without speaking.

"You saw the woman in the window, right?" I say.

Coralee nods.

"It has to be the same one who we saw at the Blackwood house," I continue. "Why else would Mack lie about her being up there? Maybe that's why she didn't want to go to the police. Maybe it's because Mack knows her. Maybe they're both in on it."

"I can't believe it," Coralee murmurs finally, shaking her head. "I can't believe Mack would lie to me."

I fall into the chair beside her. "I'm sorry," I say. "I know you trusted her."

She holds up the box. "What are we going to do with this now?" she asks.

"I don't know," I say slowly. "I just didn't want to leave it there. Now that we know we can't trust Mack."

Coralee furrows her brow and twists her lip back and forth, like she's deep in thought. She keeps opening the box and snapping it shut.

"I don't think either of us should take it home," she says. "Sooner or later, Mack's going to realize it's gone missing and come looking for it. We need to put it somewhere safe, where no one would ever look for it. Just until we figure out what to do."

"Where do you hide a box full of treasure?"

Coralee snaps the box closed, jolting to her feet. "That's it, Ethan!" she says. "Treasure! We should bury it!"

"Like pirates?" I ask. "Like 'X marks the spot'?"

"Exactly like that. We can bury it right here at Coralee Cove."

I frown. "Isn't that risky? Leaving it out in the open?"

"But it won't be," says Coralee. "No one but us ever comes here anyway. If we bury it deep enough, up past where the tide comes in, it'll be really safe."

"How will we find it again?"

Coralee walks to the far corner of the beach, where the rocks meet the sand, and draws an X with her foot. "We'll bury it here, then put a rock over it. One we can remember."

She looks over her shoulder to where I'm still sitting in the beach chair. She must be able to read the uncertainty on my face, because she pops one hip out and crosses her arms. "You got a better idea?" she asks.

"No," I admit.

"Then let's get digging."

After we dig for almost an hour, we've carved a hole in the mostly dry sand that must be at least three feet deep. We cast aside the sticks and sharp rocks we've been using to help us dig, and bend over the hole to examine our work.

"That should be deep enough," I say. I glance into the trees again to make sure no one's watching, like I've been doing every couple of minutes. Then I reach for the velvet box.

"Wait," Coralee says, wiping a drop of sweat from her cheek. "One more thing."

She pulls her pink lunch box from her backpack, empties it out, and carefully places the velvet box inside, then lowers them both into the hole.

"There," she says. "Now it'll stay dry."

"Good thinking."

It takes only a couple of minutes to fill the hole back up again. Once we're done patting the sand down, Coralee looks for a rock to mark the spot with while I count the paces from the hiding spot to the beach, like I guess people who bury treasure are supposed to.

"Look!" she says. "This one's shaped kind of like a horse."

I stare at the rock, screwing up my face and squinting, but I don't see it. "Nope," I say. "Not a horse. What about that one with all the barnacles on it? That's easier to recognize."

Coralee agrees, and we haul the rock over, dropping it on top of our hiding spot.

We fall into the sand and sit for a minute, catching our breath.

When I look over at Coralee, I glimpse a spark of excitement in her eye, and suddenly her whole face lights up in its glow. "This is kind of fun, huh? Like a real adventure."

"Yeah," I say, feeling a sudden squeeze of guilt.

It's exactly the kind of real adventure that Kacey and I always wanted to have together.

The kind we'll never have.

You can't be with her. You can never be with her again.

Bullies

❧

WHEN I GET TO the Pink Palm on Sunday for Herman's party, Coralee hasn't arrived yet, so I go to the Sand Pit to buy a handful of taffies for her. When I get back, she's waiting for me at the gate to the pool, wearing a sun-faded pink swimsuit.

"I guess Herman didn't need to worry about the turnout," she says. I see what she means when she swings open the gate to the pool.

Colorful clumps of balloons hang from the backs of some of the pool chairs, all of which are taken, and the water is full of kids playing Marco Polo or paddling on foam noodles. A banner hangs above the pool that reads *Happy Birthday, Herman!* and a huge ice cream cake is slowly melting on a glass table.

It looks like almost the whole seventh grade has turned out for Herman's party, except for Suzanne's crew. It's the hottest day of the year so far, and I bet the number of guests who have shown up has something to do with the temperature.

A woman who can only be a couple of inches taller than Coralee greets us at the gate. I can tell by her crinkly green eyes that she is Herman's mother.

"Welcome!" she cries. "Welcome to the party!"

She hands us both party hats, the kind that are shaped like a cone and have straps that bite into the skin under your chin. I look around to confirm that no one else is wearing theirs before dropping mine to my side. "Grab some snacks," she says, gesturing to the table behind her, where she has set out a cooler full of soda and bowls of chips and dip.

"Thanks, Mrs. uh—"

"Thanks, Mrs. Florence," Coralee says, coming to my rescue. "This looks great."

Herman's mom rushes to greet someone behind us who has just come in, and Coralee and I wave to Herman. He gets up from his chair, which has been wrapped in streamers, trips, and stumbles toward us.

"You made it!" he says, beaming.

He's wearing bright orange swim trunks and a soggy party hat on his head. "We have lots of snacks, and there's cake later, and—"

Herman freezes. He's staring over my shoulder. "I can't believe it," he murmurs. "They actually came."

I turn to see Suzanne, Daniel, Maisie, and Jonno walk past us.

Coralee makes a noise like an angry cat as they stop in front of Herman's chair.

"Guess we'll have to share this one," Suzanne says to Maisie, her eyes flickering over the streamers before she sets her bag down, tearing some of them in two. "The boys can just lie on their towels."

Herman's face falls.

"Don't worry, Herman," says Coralee. "We'll take care of it."

"No," he pleads. "Please, don't. I'm just glad they came. I don't need to sit down."

"They're bullies, Herman," I say. "You shouldn't care so much what they think."

"Yeah," says Herman, looking down at his bare feet, which he keeps lifting up and down off the hot pavement to keep them from burning. "I know that."

Suddenly, I have an idea.

"Actually," I say, "it just so happens that Coralee and I got you a present that might come in handy right about now. Right, Coralee?"

Coralee blinks at me.

"We just have to go get it," I say. "We'll be back in a minute."

"Right," Coralee says blankly. "Back in a minute."

"What exactly is this gift we got Herman?" she asks once we're out of earshot.

"The beach chairs!" I say. "The ones Mack gave us. We'll give one to Herman. Then those jerks won't have ruined his party."

Coralee smiles. "Excellent."

The Tunnel

꩜

My heartbeat picks up when I see Mack watering plants on the sidewalk in front of her store. As we approach, Coralee lifts her nose up in the air and crosses to the other side of the street.

"Hi, Coralee. Ethan," Mack calls.

"Ma'am," Coralee retorts. I put up one hand in a feeble wave.

Coralee doesn't even look at Mack, but I do, and I see hurt written on her face. Her mouth hangs open, like she wants to say something else, but she lets us keep walking.

I guess that means she hasn't realized the jewelry is missing yet. Which is good, because Coralee and I still haven't figured out what to do with it next.

"Coralee," I say as we turn down the path toward the cove.

"We need to come up with a plan. What are we going to do when Mack realizes the jewelry is gone? What if she—"

But Coralee stops dead in her tracks as the cove comes into sight.

Everywhere I look, holes have been dug in the sand. There are food wrappers strewn about, too. Steaks chewed to the bone, foil knots emptied of baked potatoes. Like someone got hungry after so much digging and stopped for dinner.

I jump down onto the beach and head straight toward the barnacled rock. I see with relief that it's still there, still in the exact same position we placed it.

"Someone's been here," I murmur. "Looking for the jewelry."

Coralee hops down after me, wearing a dazed expression. "Someone must have been watching us."

"But how?" I say. "I kept an eye out the whole time we were digging. There was no one there. And besides, if someone was watching us, why didn't they see where we hid the box?"

"Ethan. Look."

Coralee points to the storm drain, where the chicken wire she taped to the tunnel has been peeled back in one corner, leaving a quarter of the mouth exposed. A hole just wide enough for someone to crawl through.

Someone could have easily been in there yesterday, spying on us, without us seeing a thing. But their view of our hiding spot would have been blocked because of the angle and Coralee's duct tape job.

The hairs on my neck prickle when I realize someone could be in there right now.

My heart quivers in my throat, but I put my eyes up to the chicken wire and cup my hands around my face to shield out the sunlight. I still can't make out anything in the darkness.

"Hello?" I yell. "Is someone there?"

At first, I hear nothing. Then there's a scuffle and a scratching sound.

"Coralee, someone's in there!" I cry.

I fall back from the wire as Coralee's foot makes contact with it. "Go away!" she screams, kicking. "Whoever you are. Leave. Us. Alone!"

From my place in the sand, I hear the muffled echo of someone splashing away from us through the tunnel.

Big Trouble

~

CORALEE STANDS GUARD WHILE I dig as fast as I can. I heave a sigh of relief when I see the neon pink of the lunch box. I pull it out by its strap and fumble with the zipper.

The red velvet box is still there, and so is all the jewelry.

But there's no way we can bury it again. Not now that someone knows it's here.

I sling the lunch box over one shoulder and grab one of the beach chairs in my other hand as we leave, just barely remembering the reason we came down to the cove in the first place.

Herman's eyes light up when we return and hand him his "present."

I follow Coralee to the edge of the pool, where we find a space by ourselves to sit. I keep a firm grip on the lunch box, not caring how funny I must look clutching a bundle of neon pink.

"Coralee," I murmur, looking around to make sure that no one is close enough to overhear us. "This isn't fun anymore. This is serious."

"I know," she replies.

"There was someone watching us in there. Someone who might be dangerous. We could be in big trouble."

Coralee still wears a blurry expression, and I wonder if her blood sugar is low. I offer her one of the taffies I got at the Sand Pit, which are probably melted by now, but she shakes her head. Then she lowers herself into the pool without a word and turns around to face me, resting her forearms on the wet concrete.

"These jewels could be worth a lot of money," I say. "We don't know what someone might do to get them back. We have to tell someone. The police, or your mom. Or maybe Grandpa Ike."

Coralee takes a big gulp of air and submerges herself underwater. She stays under for at least a minute. Long enough that I would be worrying if her fingers weren't still grasping the pool ledge. Finally she shoots up with a gasping breath.

She looks at me, little beads of water streaming down her face. With her braids limp and wet, she looks even younger than usual. "You're right," she says finally. "But we have to be careful about it. We could get into big trouble that way too. Let me think about it tonight, okay?"

"Yeah," I say reluctantly. "Yeah, okay."

The Evening News

CORALEE AND I LEAVE the party as soon as we can politely excuse ourselves. I try to take the lunch box home with me, but she holds on to it with an iron grip. "I'm the one who took the jewelry from that house," she says. "I got us into this mess, so it's my job to get us out."

Finally, I let her take it, once she promises she'll call me if she senses anything out of the ordinary.

On my way home from the party, I cycle extra fast past the Blackwood house and keep my eyes on the gravel beneath my tires.

When I get home, Roddie's out in the driveway, snapping pictures of his newly restored truck with his phone from every angle. I think I see him glance up at me just as I wheel my bike into the garage.

I hear voices shouting before I even get through the door.

"—have to tell him."

"It won't do any good. We don't know anything yet, so—"

Mom pauses when she hears the door click shut behind me. "Ethan?" she calls. "Is that you?"

"Yeah." I take off my shoes and walk through the kitchen into the living room, where I see Dad sitting on the sofa and Mom standing beside the coffee table. Grandpa Ike sits in his new chair, staring at the Weather Channel, which is forecasting hurricane models. He doesn't look at me when I come in. Neither does Dad, whose cheeks are flushed and whose hair sticks up in the back like he's been running his hands through it. His fingers are tapping at a furious pace on the couch arm.

Mom looks flustered too, but she quickly slaps on a smile. "How was your party?"

"It was okay. What are you guys talking about?"

I'm not sure I really want to know, but the words are out before I can stop them.

Dad shoots a dark glance at Mom.

"It's nothing you need to worry about, sweetie," she says. "It's just something about Roddie. That's all. Nothing to do with you."

I look at Dad and then at Grandpa Ike to see if I can read the truth in their expressions, but their faces are frozen with discomfort, like ice sculptures on a hot day.

"Why don't you go take a shower," Mom suggests. "And then dinner will be ready."

I do as she says, trying to push the raised voices from my mind as the lukewarm water washes over me. Maybe they really were talking about Roddie. Maybe they've been fighting about whether they can afford to send him to Boston College if he doesn't get a scholarship.

Except: why would they be yelling about Roddie when he could probably hear them from out in the driveway?

My stomach twists like a wet dishcloth being wrung out. I'm worried about Coralee. Maybe I should have fought harder to make her let me take the jewelry.

I comfort myself with the thought that even if Mack did lie to us, I still trust one thing she said. She won't let anything happen to Coralee.

We eat our grilled-cheese-and-tomato sandwiches in front of the TV that night. Mom insists that we watch the evening news so we can see the updated hurricane coverage. Of course, we have to sit through all the boring local stories, too. These include:

1. A used car salesman being investigated for fraud.
2. A red wolf that escaped from the local preserve (which, okay, is not that boring a story).
3. And the results of a city council vote on whether to expand a local highway (not enough traffic to justify an expansion at this time).

210

Then the pretty newscaster ("This is Maria Olivas reporting for Channel Eight") shows satellite pictures of the storm, which is still in the Caribbean, and asks an older man about the odds it will hit locally ("Jason, your thoughts?").

Jason's thoughts are that chances are high the storm will hit us later in the week, but it's uncertain if it will turn into a major hurricane. "At this time, no one is talking about an evacuation, but coastal residents should prepare for flooding and widespread power outages. Although it's early in the season for a large storm system, it's still too soon to rule out the chance that this could be a major event."

"Cool," Roddie murmurs.

"I should get to the grocery store early tomorrow," Mom mutters to herself. "Before they sell out of everything. And we need to make sure we've got supplies to prepare the house for a storm."

"Maybe we should take a trip inland," Dad says nervously.

"The only storm you need to worry about is the one you're huffing up over there," Grandpa Ike says. "It'll blow over like they almost all do. Or it won't, and we'll ride it out. This house has been through worse."

"Did you know hurricane winds can blow faster than a cheetah can run?" Roddie asks, surprising everyone by joining the conversation. We all turn and stare at him.

"What?" he asks. "It's true. I learned it in school."

When the news ends, Mom claps her hands together.

"Time for bed," she says to me, even though it's still really early. "You have your math test tomorrow, so you need to get a good night's sleep."

I think about calling Coralee from my room, just to make sure she's okay, but I'm afraid I'll hear Kacey's dad on the other end of the line again, so I read Ms. Silva's time-travel book until I fall asleep.

Testing Day

❧

I GET TO SCHOOL early on Monday morning. The teachers
are cooking us a special pretesting breakfast in the cafeteria.
I know because Mr. Beasley must have announced it twenty
times last week. Coralee told me it's the best breakfast I'll get
all year.

And at lunch, we get to have pizza delivered.

Mr. Beasley doesn't want *anyone* absent on testing day.

It's only seven thirty when I arrive, but by the time I
put my bike in the rack and make my way into the cafeteria, it seems like the whole school is already there. Ms. Silva
is passing around a tray with homemade biscuits and jam,
while Mr. Charles serves bacon. Mr. Beasley and Coach
Sluggs are flipping pancakes at a griddle that's been set up
in the corner. The sixth grade teachers, who are wearing

T-shirts with peppy slogans, are handing their students plates and cups of orange juice.

I search the sea of kids for Coralee, but there's no sign of her. So I take a seat next to Herman, who immediately begins thanking me again for his birthday present.

"Don't worry about it, Herman, seriously," I say. "Have you seen Coralee this morning?"

He shakes his head woefully, as if he's afraid that his answer might make me mad.

"Okay. Did you have a good birthday?"

Herman starts in about the cannonball contest and the new Xbox games he got from his mom and dad. I try to nod my head like I'm listening. But I can't. I'm too worried about Coralee.

What if something happened? What if the jewelry thief followed her from the pool yesterday and kidnapped her before she made it home? Or while she was on her way to school this morning? Coralee wouldn't miss the best breakfast of the year because she had a tickle in her throat or a sprained ankle. And Adina wouldn't keep her home on testing day. No one's mom keeps them home on testing day.

As I pick at my biscuit and eggs, I curse myself for not calling to make sure she got home okay last night. For not insisting that we tell someone yesterday about everything that's happened. For not taking that box home myself.

Next to me, Herman is making his best attempt at conversation.

"Are you nervous about the test?" he asks. "I am. I'm terrible at math. Not like tomorrow will be any better. I'm even worse at English."

"I'll be right back, Herman."

When I approach her, Ms. Silva is wiping her forehead off with the bottom of her apron, which she must have forgotten is covered in flour.

"Ms. Silva?"

"Good morning, Ethan," she sings. I mean she *actually* sings it. "Are you ready for your test?"

"Yeah. Kind of. I wanted to ask a favor?"

She cocks her head. "Go on."

"Coralee isn't here, and I'm worried that something might have—that she might not be okay. Can I go to the office and call her?"

Ms. Silva frowns. "What makes you think that?"

Just then, the morning bell trills, and Mr. Beasley starts bellowing out orders to get to our homerooms.

"I can't explain right now," I say. "But I need to get in touch with her."

Ms. Silva puts her finger to her mouth and taps it thoughtfully against her lips. "You need to get to class," she says. "You can't be late for the test. But Mr. Beasley is calling the families of any students who aren't here yet, so we'll find out what's going on. Okay?"

"Thanks, Ms. Silva," I say, trying to let her soothing voice calm me down. "Um, one more thing?"

215

"What is it? We need to hurry." She's already started toward the door.

"It's just—your forehead? You have some flour."

Ms. Silva laughs and wipes her forehead again, this time with the underside of her apron. "Thank you, Ethan."

No Answer

❧

I JUST HAVE TIME to slide through Ms. Silva's door before the test proctor closes it.

"You must be Ethan Truitt. Tha-aat's everyone!" he calls. "Except—is there a Jessup here? Coralee Jessup?"

I take my seat and look at him blankly. I can't bring myself to say the words "She's not here." He adjusts his glasses and makes a mark on his roster.

We're halfway through bubbling our names when Ms. Silva comes in. I stare at her, willing her to give me some signal as to whether she's heard any news of Coralee. But she doesn't. She just writes the start and end times of each test section on the whiteboard.

My knee jiggles up and down, and I realize I've written my old Boston address on my test instead of Grandpa Ike's. I erase it and start over.

Where is Coralee? Why won't Ms. Silva look at me?

I jump, startled, from my seat, when the test proctor lays a hand on my shoulder. "You're going to disturb the other students," he says, frowning at my knee, which is still jiggling up and down.

"And your hand," he says, sighing like he thinks I'm making trouble on purpose.

I've been tapping the fingers of my left hand against the desk while I've been bubbling in my social security number.

Great. On top of everything, I am turning into my dad.

Ms. Silva tells us to open our test books and begin.

Just as we're finishing the first section, the door opens, and Mr. Beasley struts in. He takes his suit jacket off when he comes into the classroom, and I see a thick glaze of sweat on his forehead and two dark patches blooming under his arms. Jacket in one hand, clipboard in the other, he surveys the classroom and writes something down.

Ms. Silva weaves on tiptoe among the desks and meets him at the front of the room. He whispers something in her ear, and she shoots me an almost unnoticeable glance before turning her back to the class.

It doesn't matter that she only looked at me for half a second. I had time to read the unease written in her eyes.

Mr. Beasley leaves, shutting the door quietly behind him. I stare down at my test. The numbers don't make any sense.

It's like looking at random scribbles made by a three-year-old.

I put my pencil down.

Halfway through, we get a break. While all the other students file quickly out of the classroom, eager for their three minutes of free time, I sit at my desk as if I've been glued there. Once my classmates are gone, Ms. Silva kneels beside me.

"Ethan? It looks like you haven't answered very many test questions."

I bite back a retort. I like Ms. Silva a lot, but her priorities are way out of order here. "Did you hear anything about Coralee?" I ask. My voice cracks, but I don't even care.

She bites her lip and adjusts her headband. "There was no answer at her house," she says gently. "But I really wouldn't worry, Ethan. I'm sure everything is fine. Do your best on your test, and we'll try again later."

Explanations for Why Coralee Is Not at School (and Why No One Is Answering Her Phone)

1. The jewelry thief kidnapped her while she was riding her bike home yesterday. She's still got Coralee and has told her mom not to talk to anyone or Coralee will be killed.

2. She was kidnapped on the way to school today. In which case her mom probably doesn't even know she's missing yet.

3. Her mom didn't cook dinner all the way through, and now all the Jessups are too busy puking to come to the phone.

4. Someone reported the missing jewelry, and the police somehow found out that Coralee has it. They've taken her to the station and are threatening her with jail time unless she gives up her partner in crime.

5. She forgot to eat her saltwater taffy last night, and her mom had to take her to the hospital to treat her low blood sugar.

6. The boarding school in Atlanta called and offered Coralee her spot back, but only if

she would agree to start today.

7. Coralee is too scared to come out of her house. And her mom forgot to pay the phone bill, so it's disconnected.

Skipping School

❦

I HAVE TO GET to Coralee.

Is the only thought in my head.

When the test is over, I jostle with the other kids toward the cafeteria. I have a plan. I grab a slice of pizza from the lunch line and sit down at a random table.

I don't touch the pizza, though. Instead, I wait just a couple of minutes, until all the kids are in the cafeteria. Then I drop my plate, pizza uneaten, into the trash can and walk toward the doors. I'm lucky. All the teachers are busy turning in their testing materials, so it's just a volunteer monitor who's guarding the exit.

"Bathroom," I mumble, pointing toward the restroom.

She arches her gray eyebrows. "Is that allowed?"

"It's an emergency."

I even bounce back and forth a little for good measure. She moves aside, and I head toward the bathroom, the opposite direction from the front doors and my bike and freedom and Coralee. But as soon as she turns back toward the cafeteria, I make my move, sprinting the other way.

As I burst through the double glass doors, I think I hear someone yell my name, but I keep going.

I can't lose another friend.

I can't lose Coralee.

I'm pedaling out of the parking lot before the heavy door even shuts behind me. I don't look back to see if anyone is coming after me.

My bike seems to propel me forward with supernatural speed, like it understands that this is an emergency. I fly down Main Street, past the Fish House and the Pink Palm and Mack's—where I think about stopping first, to confront Mack, but decide it's better to go straight to Coralee's house.

Finally, I skid to a halt in Coralee's driveway. I trip in my haste to get off, and end up falling on my side into the gravel, pinned down by my bike. I push it off me, ignoring my stinging knee and throbbing arm.

There's a black van with tinted windows parked in the driveway. A police van? I fling myself up the stairs and onto the porch. My hand hits the door with more force than I mean it to, and I can't stop pounding.

Adina opens the door. She's not wearing her scrubs. Today

she's in sweatpants and a tank top. Her face is puffy, and her eyebrows crease when she sees me.

"Ethan? What are you doing here? Shouldn't you be in school?"

I haven't yet caught my breath from the biking and the running and the pounding.

"I was worried," I pant. "Coralee isn't at school. Do you know she isn't at school?"

Adina casts a furtive glance behind her and steps out onto the porch, closing the door. In the daylight, she looks even worse than she did standing in the house. Her shoulders slump, and her eyes are rimmed in red.

"Of course I know."

"Oh. Is she okay?" Adina stares at me like I'm in worse shape than she is. I swipe some of the sweat from my face and hastily try to tuck my shirt in. I look down at my knee and realize it's dripping blood onto my sneaker.

"Coralee had to stay home to deal with a family matter, Ethan."

"Can I see her?"

"I'm sure when she's ready to talk about it, she'll call you." Adina says. "In the meantime, you need to wash that cut out and put some Neosporin on it. You got some at home, right?"

"Yeah, probably. But—Coralee isn't—she's okay?" I ask, my frustration mounting.

"She's fine," Adina replies. "I'm going to call the school

and your parents and let them know you're okay. I suggest you go straight home, and don't let me catch you skipping class again."

She says it firmly, but in a way that makes me think she's not trying to scold me. I suddenly feel stupid, ditching school and riding all the way here and pounding on the door. Obviously Coralee doesn't want my help, doesn't even want me to know what's going on.

"Okay," I agree defeatedly.

Adina waits to go back inside until I am on my bike again, pedaling away.

The Battle

∽

I KNOW IT'S GOING to be bad when I see Mom and Dad standing on the porch, arms crossed, waiting. They stare me down as I trudge up the stairs toward them. Dad shakes his head back and forth. Mom says, "*In,*" and opens the door for me.

Grandpa Ike sits in his chair reading the newspaper, and Roddie is slumped on one of the couches, typing away at his laptop. I wonder why he isn't at school either.

They both look up when we walk into the room. Roddie straightens, and I think I see him let out a sigh of relief. Or maybe it's disappointment.

"*Sit,*" Mom says, pointing to the couch across from Roddie. I wonder if she's only going to talk in one-word sentences. She brings me a blob of wet paper towels to place on my still-bleeding knee.

Mom and Dad both start at once.

"Don't know what you—"

"—worried about your behavior—"

"—could you leave school?"

They glare at each other hotly. "You go first," Mom snaps.

Dad clears his throat and starts pacing up and down the carpet between Roddie and me. "Ethan, you ditched school."

"Yes," I admit.

"To see Coralee."

"Yes, because I thought—"

"You *ditched* school," Dad says again. "And that is unacceptable. You're grounded for a month, and that includes seeing Coralee."

"Coralee isn't the issue here," Mom interjects. "Ethan has to take responsibility for his actions."

"Yes, but—" Dad starts.

"How could you do this to us, Ethan?" Mom cries suddenly. "We get a call from school saying you took off on your bike. We pulled Roddie out of class. Your father was already on the phone with the sheriff's department when Adina Jessup called."

I wasn't thinking about my parents when I took off from school. Of course they would think—

"We thought it had started again. That we would find you at some godforsaken bus stop somewhere between here and—and—or not even find you at all until it was too late—"

227

"Oh, come on."

Mom and Dad, both openmouthed, pivot slowly to look at Grandpa Ike.

"Did you want to add something, Ike?" Dad says, his voice razor-sharp.

"The boy was obviously worried about his friend. He wasn't trying to run away. He did what he did out of loyalty, and now we should all just leave him alone."

Mom's cheeks go from white to red in the blink of an eye. *"Excuse me?"* she says, quietly at first. Then she says it again, her voice high and almost giddy, and her body jerks sharply, like she's a possessed puppet. *"You* are giving *me* parenting lessons? You are trying to tell me how to raise my child? That's rich, *Dad."*

It's the first time I've ever heard her call him that, and somehow it comes out sounding like an insult.

"I appreciate your advice, I really do," she says sarcastically. "But I've got the parenting thing under control. Maybe if you had had some words of fatherly advice thirty years ago, I would be a little more willing to take them now."

Grandpa Ike's face twists into a snarl. Dad raises a hand and lowers it between him and Mom as if to stop them from physically attacking each other. Then everyone starts shouting at once.

"—have no idea what's best for my son—"

"—keeping secrets from your own boy—"

"—never should have let him get attached to this girl—"

No one seems to be paying the slightest bit of attention to me anymore. My eyes swing back and forth between my parents and my grandfather and finally settle on my shoes. In my head I collect all the words I can make out, so that later I can try to piece them together. *What's best. Secrets. Attached.* I glance toward Roddie, but he's gone. Somehow he slipped out of the room without anyone even knowing. I wonder if I could do the same.

Mom's voice bellows out above the others. "The only reason we agreed to come here is because we thought it would be best to give Ethan a new start," she yells, finally saying aloud what I've known all along. "But if he can't get that here, then we might as well go back to Boston."

"Fine," Grandpa Ike spits. "Fine! The only reason you *agreed* to come here? How about the only reason I *let* you come here. No one asked you to be here. No one is making you stay. I certainly don't want you here. Any of you."

The words *any of you* sting like salt water on my scraped knee. I knew Grandpa Ike didn't get along with Mom, but I actually thought he liked taking me for driving lessons.

Mom is about to argue back. Grandpa Ike is getting up from his chair. Dad is pacing and running his fingers over the stubble on his chin. And that's when I hear Roddie.

"Mom?"

He stands in the doorway to the kitchen, holding his hand

over the receiver of the phone.

"What do you want, Roddie?" Mom says. Her eyes dart around the room, skipping over Grandpa Ike and Dad and landing on me before spotting the phone in Roddie's hand.

"It's just—" Roddie glances at me, and again, I get the weird feeling that he's pitying me. "It's Mr. Reid. He's on the phone for you. He says it's important."

And then, before I can stop them, his words ring out in my head, silencing everything else.

You killed her, Ethan Truitt.

Defiance

༄

EVERYONE IS FROZEN IN place, except for Mom, who whisks the phone away from Roddie and stomps out onto the front porch.

"Why is Kacey's dad on the phone?" I ask finally.

Dad looks from Roddie to Grandpa Ike to me as if waiting for someone else to answer. "Mr. Reid is having a hard time, Ethan. It makes him feel better to talk to us."

Grandpa Ike, still only half out of his chair, mutters something under his breath that sounds like "disgrace." Then he pulls on his baseball cap and lurches out of the room and through the kitchen. We all listen as the engine of his truck coughs to life and his tires fly through the gravel.

"Why would talking to *you* make Mr. Reid feel better?" I ask. "Last time I checked, he never wanted to see any of us again."

"Go to your room, Ethan. Your mom and I will be up later to talk about this more."

A few weeks ago, I would have accepted Dad's orders unquestioningly. I would have been too tired to put up a fight. But I'm not tired now.

I am angry.

"There's something you're not telling me." I force myself to shift my gaze from my bloody shoes to Dad's face. I look him squarely in the eye. I'm not going anywhere until he answers my questions. His mouth is open in surprise.

"What is it that you're not telling me? Why does Mr. Reid keep calling?"

"I want you to go to your room," Dad says again, "and think about how your actions have affected this family. I've already told you why Mr. Reid keeps calling."

"Dad," says Roddie. "Don't you think it's—"

"Room! Now!" Dad yells. Dad almost never yells. I glare at him. That's when I notice his hands are shaking.

It's this, and not his raised voice, that finally makes me stride across the room, pound up the stairs, and slam my door behind me, twisting the lock. If they're not going to tell me the truth, I don't want them talking to me at all.

I pick up the phone and click it on, thinking I might as well find out for myself what's really happening. But all I get is a dial tone. Mom has already hung up.

Words

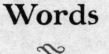

MOM AND DAD KNOCK several times that afternoon. They alternate between anger ("Open this door right now, young man!") and regret ("I'm sorry things got so heated, but we still have to discuss this.")

I don't open the door for them. I don't respond. I lie on my bed and stare at the ceiling and turn everyone's words over, trying to use them to answer the questions whirling around in my head.

It makes me think of last year, when we had a fair at school, and Kacey made me get in one of those booths with wind machines that make dollar bills fly around your head. No matter how I reached and clutched for them, the bills kept slipping through my hands.

Kacey did impressions of me for weeks after.

When the insect chorus gears up on the marsh, and I know evening is approaching, I hear a tentative knock on my door, but no voice. I ignore it.

Later, when the sky is dark, I finally come out of my room. I have to go to the bathroom *sometime*. There's a plate of food sitting on the floor in the hall. I pick it up and look it over. Ham sandwich and salt-and-vinegar chips.

I hear Grandpa Ike's words again.

I certainly don't want you here. Any *of you.*

Even though I haven't eaten since breakfast, I toss the food back to the floor and step over it. It's going to take more than a ham sandwich to make me forget those words.

Breaking the Silence

～

MOM KNOCKS SOFTLY ON my door the next morning.

"Ethan? It's time to get up for school, honey."

Her voice is shredded with worry, and I almost feel guilty for giving her the silent treatment.

After I get dressed and brush my teeth, I go downstairs to find something to eat. My stomach growls like a rabid animal when I open the refrigerator.

"Can I fix you something?" Dad says behind me. Which is pretty funny, since Dad couldn't break an egg to save his life.

Ignoring him, I pull out some leftover pasta bake and spoon it onto a plate, which I thrust into the microwave.

Dad watches me scarf my food and gulp down two glasses of milk while I'm standing at the counter. When I'm done, he says, "Your mom and I agreed that it's best if we drive you to school today."

So I don't have my bike. So I can't get to Coralee's.

I wasn't planning to go again anyway. I thought she might call me yesterday to explain what was going on, or at least thank me for risking being grounded for life just to check on her. But she obviously didn't feel the need to talk to me. Which makes her just one more name on the list of people who I can't trust anymore.

"I'm not going with *you*," I say.

Dad looks at the ground and shuffles his feet. Like he's ashamed of himself. "I'll get Ike to take you."

"No," I say sharply. "Not him, either."

"I'll take him," Roddie says, appearing in the doorway.

I nearly choke on my last bite of pasta.

Why would Roddie volunteer to take me to school?

Dad lifts an eyebrow. He looks at me questioningly, and I nod slowly.

A few minutes later, I brush a few stray sunflower seeds off the seat and climb into Roddie's truck.

He starts the engine and turns around in the driveway. "Listen, Ethan," he says as he presses hard on the accelerator and shoots us forward. "I know things have been, you know, hard for us since Boston. But if you need to talk . . ."

The rest of his sentence trails off. An unspoken offer. I let the silence hang for a minute before shaking my head. Roddie

236

may have had a shift of heart, but that can't make me forget what he said to me in Boston. It doesn't erase the fact that he's ignored me for months.

"So anyway," he says, "I looked online this morning and it seems like Anastasia is on track to hit us."

"Anastasia?"

"The hurricane," says Roddie.

"Oh." I've barely even thought about the brewing storm. "Will it be bad?"

"Nah. Grandpa Ike says we'll be fine. But we might get a day or two off from school. A hurricane day. Like we used to get snow days back in Boston. That's cool, right?"

"Yeah. Sure."

It's weird to hear Roddie talk to me about Boston. It's weird to hear Roddie talk to me at all.

"I've been meaning to tell you hi from Grace. She always asks me how you are."

I wonder what he tells her.

"Tell her hi back," I say.

"Yeah. Yeah, I will."

Roddie clears his throat and finally punches on the ancient truck radio. He spends the rest of the drive trying to find a station that comes in clear enough to listen to, but all he gets is a lot of noise.

It's still better than silence.

People I Can't Trust

1. Mom
2. Dad
3. Coralee
4. Adina
5. Ms. Silva
6. Mack
7. Grandpa Ike
8. ~~Roddie~~ (?)

Lies

❧

I'M NOT SURPRISED WHEN there's no sign of Coralee in the cafeteria that morning. I knew somehow she wouldn't be here today. When Ms. Silva sees me, she glides over and kneels down next to me. "It's nice to see you this morning, Ethan," she says. "After the test we'll talk with Mr. Beasley about what happened yesterday. Okay?"

She keeps a close eye on me during the test session, circling around my desk more often than anyone else's and glancing at my answer sheet. I think I do surprisingly well on the test, considering I'm so distracted that I have to read every word three times to work out its meaning. I get answers bubbled in for almost all the questions anyway.

When we get dismissed for lunch, Herman tags along with me in the hall. "Are you feeling better?" he asks.

"Huh?"

"They said you got sick yesterday and had to go home," Herman explains. "Are you better today?"

"I wasn't sick."

"Oh."

I want to sit by myself in the cafeteria, but Herman follows me from the pizza buffet to the lunch table. I notice the same monitor I tricked yesterday guarding the door again today. She keeps her beady eyes trained on me.

"How do you think you did on the test?" Herman asks. "That passage about—"

"I don't think we're allowed to talk about it," I say shortly.

Herman slumps forward in his seat with a shrug. "Yeah," he says, taking a huge bite out of his first slice of pizza. "I guess not."

The test proctors announce that once we're done eating, we can go to the gym for games. I guess they want us to blow off some steam. But I stay put while everyone else piles out of the cafeteria doors. Herman stays too.

We're sitting in silence when someone flops down in the chair next to me.

Suzanne.

"Hi, Suzanne," Herman says hopefully.

She ignores him.

"Girlfriend absent again today?" she asks me, flipping her yellow hair over her shoulders. As she does, I see her glance around the cafeteria, like she's making sure no one will see her sitting with us.

"She's not my girlfriend," I say wearily. "Just go away, Suzanne."

"Oh, so you're not together anymore. I guess that means you found out, huh?"

She stares at me, studying me for a reaction.

"Found out what?"

"That's why I came to talk to you. I thought you'd figure it out eventually, but in case you didn't, I just wanted to make sure you knew not to believe anything she told you about me. It's all lies."

"What are you talking about?"

"Oh," she says with a smirk. "I guess that means you haven't figured it out. I mean she lies about everything. Like, all the time. I heard she told you that she was at some boarding school for music. Yeah, right. She went to live with her daddy in Atlanta because her aunt didn't want her anymore. But obviously her daddy didn't want her either, because he sent her back."

Suzanne sits in smug silence, waiting for me to respond. But I don't. I can't.

"What else has she told you?" she continues. "That she almost died of malaria? That she's descended from royalty? That she has a brother who's going to be a doctor?"

"No," I reply uncertainly, ignoring the thing Suzanne

says about Coralee's brother. But I think about what I over-heard Mom saying, about Coralee telling stories. I think about the times I asked Coralee to play me a song on the violin and she refused. I think about her blue-ribbon-winning saltwater taffy and her pet alligator and her copperhead bite and her near miss on the ice in Ohio.

"Really? Because that's what she told me, back when we were friends. Before I figured it out."

I scramble to keep up with what Suzanne is saying. "You're wrong," I say. "Coralee doesn't even live with her aunt."

It's weak, but it's the best defense I can come up with.

Suzanne stares at me sympathetically. "Oh, Ethan, honey, who did she tell you that was? Beyoncé? That woman Adina *is* her aunt. Herman can tell you."

Herman drops his gaze from Suzanne back to his plate.

"Herman?" she chides. "Tell him. It's for his own good. Is Coralee a liar, or not?"

Herman looks at me, his eyes full of regret. "She exagger-ates sometimes, I guess," he mutters.

"Stop it, Suzanne," I command. "Leave Herman out of it. Even if what you're saying is true, who cares? I don't."

"I know," Suzanne says. "That's because you're a nice person. But Coralee is not a nice person, Ethan. She tells lies about you, too, just like she's probably told you lies about me."

"She never tells me anything about you," I say. "And she wouldn't tell lies about me, either."

"Oh yeah? Then how come she told me that you moved here because you killed some girl in Boston?"

My heart slams into my chest like a fist pounding on a locked door.

"Wh-what?" I stutter. "When did she say that?"

"When you were at the dentist last week."

Suzanne drums one of her neatly manicured hands on the table. "Of course, I didn't believe her, Ethan. She doesn't want you to have other friends. She just said it so no one else would like you."

"You're lying," I say feebly.

"I've never heard Coralee say that," Herman squeaks.

"No one is talking to you, Herman," snaps Suzanne.

Did Coralee really say those things? *Why* would she say them? But how else could Suzanne know anything about Kacey?

The bell rings.

"Look," Suzanne says, narrowing her eyes. "All I'm saying is that I'll keep that to myself, as long as you keep whatever she's told you about me to yourself, too. 'Kay?"

I stare down at the table. Suzanne's chair scrapes against the floor as she gets up.

"At least now you've finally learned that good friends are hard to come by. Next time, maybe you'll choose better." She giggles. "But at least you have Herman."

Once Suzanne has skipped off, Herman pats my back with

an awkward hand. "I'm sorry, Ethan," he says. "I didn't know Coralee was saying those things, or I would have told you."

"That's okay, Herman," I croak back. "You're—you're a better friend than Suzanne will ever be."

The monitor I tricked yesterday stalks up to our table.

"Get to the gym, young man," she scolds. "No more shenanigans. Not on my watch."

I glare at her but do as she says. Where else do I have to go, anyway?

Truth

❧

I BARELY REACT IN Mr. Charles's class when I get called to the office over the intercom. Ms. Silva told me to expect a meeting with Mr. Beasley. I take my time getting there, dragging my hand along the lockers.

The air-conditioning is broken in the main office, and the first thing I see is Mrs. Oakley, sitting at the front desk, using a packet of paper to fan herself. When she sees me come in, she drops the paper and gives me a faltering smile.

The second thing I see is a group of three people standing in a conspiratorial clump. Mr. Beasley, Ms. Silva, and, to my surprise, Grandpa Ike. Mr. Beasley catches my eye and clears his throat. Ms. Silva is wringing her hands.

"What are you doing here?" I ask Grandpa Ike, not bothering to conceal my disdain.

"I'm taking you home, Ethan."

I look at Ms. Silva in confusion. "I thought we were having a meeting? Because I'm in trouble?"

"Well, your grandfather is here now, Ethan," Ms. Silva says. "And he thinks that it would be best if you went home with him. We can have our meeting another time."

Mr. Beasley nods eagerly, crossing his hands over his jutting belly. "Don't think about it, sport," he says. "We'll sort it out when you get back."

"When I get back?" I ask. "Where am I going?"

"Ah—well," Mr. Beasley starts.

"There's a storm coming," says Grandpa Ike. "So there might not be any school tomorrow."

"Exactly," Mr. Beasley says, nodding. "So stay safe, and we'll see you soon." He claps Grandpa Ike on the back, throws me one last pained glance, and disappears into his office.

"C'mon, Ethan," Grandpa Ike says, taking my shoulders under his firm grip and steering me from the office.

I shiver involuntarily as we walk into the air-conditioned hall.

"Why are you taking me out of school if the storm's not coming until tomorrow?"

"Your mom and dad just want you home," Grandpa Ike says, wiping his creased brow.

Unlike you, I think.

"Are they going to tell me what's going on?" I ask.

"Because if not, then I don't see any reason for me to miss more school."

It's not like I want to be here, either. The only place I *want* to be is with Kacey.

The only person left I can trust, and I can't ever be with her again.

"They're going to tell you," Grandpa Ike replies. "They're going to tell you the truth."

"Oh," I say, taken aback. "Well. Good."

But suddenly every muscle in my body is tense, like it's preparing for a fall.

We sit in silence as we move through town at a crawl. We have to wait for a long line of cars turning into the Sand Pit.

"Everyone is stocking up for the storm," Grandpa Ike says.

I look out over the bay, where men in orange reflective vests are stacking big bags of sand atop the rocks that separate land from sea. The sky is already a deep shade of gray, with hives of angry purple clouds hovering in the distance.

"Ethan, about what I said last night. I didn't mean it, about wanting you to leave. Sometimes I let my anger get the best of me."

Grandpa Ike doesn't usually string together so many words, which makes me think that he's spent a while planning this pathetic apology.

I don't reply.

A taut silence stretches between us as we drive over the inlet bridge, past the strawberry fields and the empty farm stands.

"Listen, Ethan," Grandpa Ike says when we reach the driveway. He turns the ignition off and tucks the key underneath the visor. "Before we go in there—you remember what I said, back when you first got here, about kids being stronger than their parents give them credit for?"

"Yeah," I say, my hand hesitating on the door handle. "I guess."

"You remember that, whatever happens. You are stronger than you know. You hear me?"

My hand trembles against the metal of the handle as Grandpa Ike's words crash down on me, like the first rain of the coming storm.

That's when I know that something is truly, desperately wrong.

Mr. Reid

∿

WHEN WE ENTER THE living room, Mom and Dad are sitting on the couch that faces the kitchen. Mom's skin has gone white, except for her nose, which is red. Her hands are folded gently in her lap like a pair of doves. Dad taps his pointer finger around his knee in a feeble way, and Roddie slouches on the little cushioned bench, which is too small for him, in front of the darkened fireplace.

"Sit down, son," Dad says, gesturing to the opposite couch.

Dad never calls me "son."

Grandpa Ike pats my shoulder and takes his usual seat.

Then silence prowls between us, an unspoken threat.

"Ethan," Mom says finally, "we need to talk."

It's the same thing she said to me after I ran away for the

second time. The time I almost made it.

Ethan, we need to talk. You can't keep running away.

The first time I ran away, the night I stole the bill from Kacey's doorstep and found the address for the nursing home, I only made it to South Station before the police caught me, so it wasn't as big a deal. But the second time—

"You know we've been talking to Kacey's dad."

The second time, I almost made it to Kacey before Mr. Reid stopped me.

Kacey's dad, blocking my way to Kacey's room. Kacey's mom, exhausted, crying next to him. My voice: Where is Kacey, is Kacey okay, when can I see Kacey?

I braced myself for what he was going to say.

"Kacey's dead. You killed her, Ethan Truitt."

But that's not what he said at all.

What he said was worse.

"Ethan?" Mom repeats gently. "Are you listening?"

"Yeah," I say. "Kacey's dad. He's been calling here."

"Right. Your father and I, well, we thought it was best not to talk with you until we knew anything for certain. We didn't want to upset you again."

I struggle to keep Mom's words and Grandpa Ike's living room in focus.

The stench of sickness and sorrow hitting me as I run through the doors of the nursing home where Kacey's parents have taken her without telling me. Kacey's dad advances toward me, like he's about to hit me. His back is as straight as a baseball bat; his eyes burn with fury. I take a step back in my sneakers, soggy from running through the rain to get here.

His voice cuts into me like a bolt of jagged lightning. "What are you doing here?"

"I came to see Kacey. To see how she's doing."

"Even if she could see you, what makes you think she would want to? You're the reason she's here in the first place."

"Please, if I could just—"

"You don't deserve to be here. Not any more than my daughter deserves to be lying in a nursing home, being kept alive by machines."

"Kacey's going to be okay. I can make things okay."

Kacey's dad points his finger at me and pushes it into my chest.

He looms over me.

"You? You *can* make things okay? Because of you, she's never going to wake up. You did this to her. Now get out. *GET OUT!*"

Kacey, Kacey, Kacey

❧

I SQUEEZE MY EYES shut, and Mr. Reid disappears. Mom and Dad are staring at me. Dad opens his mouth to speak, but I wish he wouldn't. I really wish he wouldn't.

I already know what he's going to say.

"Mr. Reid has been calling to let us know, er, how Kacey is doing," Dad says. "They've been hoping that Kacey will show some signs of progress."

Signs of progress.

He means signs that Kacey is still in there somewhere, trapped in her own body.

"Kacey's family has been thinking a lot about what's best for her," says Mom.

I wish I could slow time down, to stop Mom's words from spilling out.

But she keeps going. "Mr. Reid has felt for a while now that it would be kinder to Kacey to let her let go. He called a little while ago to let us know that— Oh, Ethan."

Her voice breaks.

"Mrs. Reid has finally agreed with him," Dad says. "They'll be taking Kacey off life support in a few days. Once the family has had time to say good-bye. Which means—"

I don't hear Dad's voice anymore. I don't see the living room. I don't see Mr. Reid gnashing his teeth at me. I see Kacey falling through midair. I see early-morning Kacey sleeping next to me on the bus, afternoon Kacey on her skateboard, blond hair tangling with the wind, summer Kacey on a rope swing, screaming with joy as she lets go and splashes into the river, my Kacey smiling as she comes up with her best dare yet.

Kacey, Kacey, Kacey. Fearless, beautiful, daring Kacey.

Kacey lying in a nursing home bed, unable to move or think or laugh or breathe.

Still falling.

But not for much longer.

The words that have haunted me since we left Boston are finally about to be true.

You killed her, Ethan Truitt.

Pain

❧

MOM KNOCKS ON MY door, which I haven't bothered to lock. She holds a glass of water and a little white pill in her hand. I recognize the sleeping pill. I used to take them at night sometimes after the incident. They turned the pain from a thousand pricking needles to a dull, fuzzy stomachache.

"I don't want it," I moan into my pillow.

This is *my* pain.

I need to feel it.

"Okay. I'll leave the water here for you. What else can I get you? Something to eat?"

"I'm tired," I lie. "I want to sleep."

Mom doesn't take the hint. She pads across the room and perches herself on the edge of my bed. "I know we've been over this," she says. "But I need you to remember that this is not your fault."

"Mmm."

"Do you want me to get Dr. Gorman on the phone?"

"No."

"Kacey won't be in pain soon, Ethan. She'll be somewhere else. Somewhere better."

Mom reaches to smooth my hair down over my forehead. I roll to my other side. I can't tell her what I'm thinking. That part of me is jealous of Kacey, because she won't be in pain soon, but the pain of missing her will stay with me forever. That she might be going somewhere better, but the world she's leaving me in will always be a little bit worse without her.

"I'm sorry, honey, but I have to help get the house ready before Anastasia. It's supposed to hit tomorrow afternoon. I'll be back to check on you later. Shout for me if you need anything."

I stare out at the marsh. The rippling water and the tangled reeds and the tumble of moss in the trees. It's all so wild and free. And alive.

You Killed Her,
Ethan Truitt

I MUST HAVE SOMEHOW managed to fall asleep, because when my eyes fly open again, the marsh is bleak and gray, like a dark veil has fallen over it. The clock on my table says it's only 6:32 p.m. Not late enough to be this dark. It must be the storm clouds.

Or maybe knowing Kacey will soon be gone from the world has sucked out all the light.

Mom knocks on the door three times before it cracks open.

"Ethan?" she calls softly. "Coralee is here to see you, honey."

I sit straight up in bed. "What?"

"You don't have to come down if you don't want to," she says. Her nose is still red, her hair a mess. "I told her you weren't feeling well."

"No," I say, putting my feet to the floor and testing how it feels to stand. Unsteady. "I'm coming."

How dare Coralee come here? How dare she come here *now*? After she ignored me? After she told Suzanne that Kacey was dead? That I had killed her?

Mom's eyes widen as I brush past her. Coralee is sitting on the sofa in the living room, watching the news with Grandpa Ike and Roddie. She turns around when she hears me coming down the stairs.

"Ethan!"

I jerk my head toward the front door. "Porch," I growl.

I open the door and let it slam shut in the wind behind me, so that Coralee has to open it again. Then I throw myself down on the porch swing.

"Ethan?" she says, perching next to me. I shift over, away from her. "Is something wrong? I'm sorry I didn't call or come by. It's just—"

Hearing her voice sends hot flames of anger licking up my neck and cheeks. "I don't want to hear it, Coralee," I interrupt. "I don't want to hear any more lies."

I look straight ahead at Grandpa Ike's truck. But I can hear the confusion trickle into her voice. "L-lies? What do you mean?"

I bark with hollow laughter. "I know you didn't go to boarding school. I know Adina's not your mother. I know everything you say is a lie."

I fight to keep my voice calm because I don't want Mom to come out here. I need to be angry.

I am so angry.

"Listen, Ethan, I don't know who you've been talking to, but did you ever think that maybe *they're* the ones lying? Did you ever think about trusting me?" There's an edge of anger to Coralee's voice too.

"Trusting you?" I bellow. "*Trusting* you?" I'm on my feet before I realize it, looking into Coralee's eyes, which have gone wide with shock. "I did trust you! I stuck up for you! I believed all those ridiculous stories you told me. Until Suzanne told me what you said about Kacey. You told her—you told her that Kacey was dead. And now she's going to die! You said it, and now it's happening!"

But even as I accuse Coralee, I know my words aren't true.

Kacey isn't going to die because of what Coralee said. Coralee isn't even the first person to say that Kacey was already dead.

Everything goes blurry once again. Coralee's face is gone, the porch is gone, the driveway and the truck are gone. Hot tears pool in my eyes and splash down my face, and I hear my own voice howling into the wind.

The door opens, and someone steers me inside. Coralee is shouting something, but all I hear is "sorry" before the door closes again behind me.

A strong grip on my shoulders, pulling me upstairs.

Pulling at me like it did that day in Boston, the very last time I tried to run.

A strong grip on my shoulders, pulling me back, making me

258

lose my balance and fall onto the pavement.

"Where do you think you're going?"

I'm going toward my room, stumbling down the hall, being guided by sturdy hands.

"Let me go! I have to get to Kacey! I can fix her!"

"Ethan, listen to me. You're not going anywhere. You can't fix Kacey. She was dead from the moment her head hit that rock."

"You don't understand. I can make her better!"

Rough hands hoist me up off the pavement and pin me against a parked car.

Gentle hands lay me down on something soft. My bed. The sheets are still warm.

"You act like if you can see her, you can make her okay. You walk around all day talking about her like she's going to ring our doorbell any second."

"Miracles happen! Even Dr. Gorman admitted that miracles sometimes happen. Mrs. Reid thinks she could still wake up. That's why they moved her to the nursing home."

"They moved her to the nursing home because it was the only place in the state that would take her. Because everyone knows she's already dead. Her mom's in denial, just like you."

"No one knows Kacey like me. No one can help her like me.

259

That's why you have to let me go. LET ME GO!"

A hand pounds the metal of the car, close to my head.

"Damn it, Ethan. Mr. Reid doesn't want you there! And even if he did, she wouldn't really be there. You can't be with her. You can never be with her again. People don't come back from the dead. Mom and Dad are talking about moving us away from Boston if you can't get a grip. Is that what you want? Why can't you just accept that she's gone, and move on?"

"Because if she's dead, if she's really dead, I killed her, didn't I?"

I tell myself to stay very still, like I've told myself before. If I stay still, eventually everything will stop spinning.

Or maybe it's Roddie who says it. Roddie, who's hovering over me, asking if I'm okay.

"Is that what you need to hear?" Roddie asks. I can hear a car door slam in the street and Mom and Dad yelling at him to let me go, but he leans in closer.

"You need someone to tell you what a bad thing you did so it can finally be real to you?" Roddie whispers. "Fine. I'll say it. You killed her, Ethan Truitt. You killed Kacey. Now get on with your life."

The Storm

~

WHEN I WAKE UP again, Roddie has gone. It's pitch-black outside, and the winds howl like a pack of prowling wolves across the marshes. Someone has turned my bedside table lamp on. Memories keep coming back to me in sharp fragments.

Remembering each one is like cutting myself on a shard of glass.

"*Coralee had to stay home to deal with a family matter, Ethan. . . .*"

"*Coralee is not a nice person, Ethan. She tells lies about you, too. . . .*"

"*They'll be taking her off life support in a few days. . . .*"

"*You told her that she was dead. And now she's going to die!*"

All those nights I waited, watching Kacey's window, sure she would come home.

Kacey could do anything.

Kacey's heart thirsted for life.

Nobody understood that about Kacey the way that I understood it.

Kacey could do anything, and Kacey would never leave me.

Which meant that she would come back to me, no matter what.

Even when Mr. Reid told me she was never going to wake up and threw me out of the nursing home, I didn't believe it. That's why I tried to run again the third time.

If I could just get to her, make her realize I was still there, waiting for her to come back to me . . .

But then, when Roddie caught me trying to run the last time, something snapped.

Even as Dad pulled him away from me, I knew what he said was right.

Kacey wasn't coming back.

Mr. Reid was right too. I was the reason she was gone in the first place.

I sit up. The clock reads 6:17 a.m. I look outside again, and only then do I realize that the reason it looks pitch-black is that the storm shutters have been closed over the window.

My mouth feels like dried mud, and I ease my way out of bed and down the hall to the bathroom to brush my teeth. I notice as I brush that the bathtub is full of water.

Even though it's early, I hear the TV on downstairs. When I lean over the banister, I see everyone awake and huddled around the blue screen. Even Roddie. Which is odd, since I don't remember the last time I saw him up before eleven on a day he didn't have to go to school.

Mom catches sight of me. "Ethan!" she calls, standing up and dropping the remote. "You're up."

"Is Anastasia here?" I ask.

"Not yet," Dad says. "Not the worst part. It's still a few hours out."

"Come downstairs," Mom says. "I'll make you some breakfast."

I hesitate. I don't want breakfast, and I'm not sure I want company. But the alternative is sitting in my dark room, listening to the wolf-wind and thinking about Kacey lying in her nursing home bed, waiting to die. So I trudge downstairs and flop next to Dad on the couch. He rubs a hand over my shoulders. Roddie sits on the floor in front of the TV with a blanket around him. He gives me a faltering smile.

"Morning, bro," he says.

He hasn't called me "bro" since before the incident.

Grandpa Ike nods at me from his chair, and I drop my eyes to the floor.

"What can I get you?" Mom asks. She's wafting around the room like a bedraggled butterfly, picking up paper plates and plumping pillows, as if all my problems might just be fixed by some good housekeeping. "Eggs? Toast? Bacon?"

She must be really worried if she's offering to cook me bacon. "Nothing now," I say.

"I'll just get you some water, then."

I can feel everyone's eyes on me, but I don't want to talk. So I stare at the screen, where a lady in a yellow raincoat huddles in front of a beach, trying not to get blown away by the wind.

"At this point, we have power outages reported in over ten counties in Florida, and two so far in Georgia," she yells. "If you still have power and you're in the storm's path, get your flashlights, candles, and water ready."

The TV flashes to a radar screen, showing the storm's predicted path.

"Looks like it could go either way," Grandpa Ike mutters, studying the two possible storm patterns, one of which spirals back out to sea; the other keeps tumbling inland. "If it hits us square-on, it could be a big one."

The show returns to the news desk. "We have a local casualty being reported," says the male anchor, whose hair is too slick and tie too pink. "Unfortunately, the missing wolf from the Georgia Red Wolf Preserve has been found dead. Local restaurant owner Reese Magellan found the body late last evening, collapsed behind his Dumpster."

"That's right, Lou," says Maria Olivas. "Representatives

from the preserve say they believe the cause of death was likely accidental rat poisoning, though they have not been able to get to the body to confirm. The wolf is thought to have already given birth to her pups, but authorities are not hopeful for their chances of survival without a mother and in this storm."

Mom clucks her teeth sadly.

I think numbly about what Coralee said the first day I met her, about all animals needing someone to look out for them.

"Now we're back to Andi to give us some tips about staying safe indoors. We are reminding all our viewers again that within the next few hours, Anastasia will be bearing down on the southern Georgia coast, and at that point no one should be outdoors under any circumstances."

The coverage goes on like this for an hour or so. When my legs get stiff, I stand up.

"Everything okay?" Dad asks.

"Fine," I lie. It's a stupid question. How could everything be okay? "Just going to go change."

I'm still wearing the outfit I wore to school yesterday. No one has bothered to force me to put clean clothes on.

The stairs take all my energy, so when I get to my room, I'm out of breath. I flick on the overhead light and lean down to get fresh clothes from my dresser. Just as I reach it, the phone trills to life.

Before I have time to think about it, I grab it and punch it on.

"Hello?"

"Ethan?" Coralee's voice pipes feebly through the phone line.

"What do you want?" I ask.

I feel bad about what I said to Coralee. It's not her fault Kacey's going to die. It's mine.

But it doesn't change the fact that she lied, that she broke her promise not to tell anyone about Kacey. That she told *Suzanne*, of all people.

"I know you're mad at me," she says. "But I need you to meet me at the cove."

"Are you kidding? There's a hurricane outside, in case you haven't noticed."

"I know, and I know you're really upset right now, but we have to get there. It's important. It's the tunnel. I think I know who—"

I hear a click. "Hello? Ethan?" It's Mom. "Are you on the phone?"

"Just hanging up."

And then I end the call before Coralee can say another word.

Where Coralee Is

❧

THE LIGHTS FLICKER A couple of times the next hour, but the power stays on. Rain drills down so hard that there's a constant low roar. Wind sweeps around the house, and every floorboard seems to moan with the effort of staying put.

It feels right, somehow, the storm rattling the house. Like the wind is feeling everything I'm feeling.

At eight, Mom forces me to eat some toast, which I choke down by taking big sips of water after every bite.

At eight thirty, I say I'm tired and go back to my room. I flip to the end of the time-travel book. Of course, the hero saves the day. He goes back in time and sacrifices himself to save his friend's life.

The ending, which I liked when I first read it, just makes me angry now. I throw the book against the wall.

At nine o'clock, the phone rings. I don't answer it. I don't want to talk to Coralee again.

Less than a minute later, there's another knock on my door.

Dad comes in with the phone in his hand. His mouth is set in a frown.

"Hang on," he says into the receiver. "I'll ask."

Placing his hand over the mouthpiece, he says, "Adina Jessup is on the phone. She can't find Coralee. She wants to know if Coralee is here, but I told her no. She didn't say anything to you about coming over, did she?"

I stare at him, speechless, before slowly shaking my head.

Dad repeats this message into the phone. "Of course, we'll let you know if we see her."

When he's hung up, he leans his shoulder against the doorframe. "Can you think of anywhere she could be?" he asks. "This is important, Ethan. If she's out in this storm, she could be in real trouble."

I open my mouth to answer, but Mom calls Dad's name from downstairs. He looks over his shoulder and back at me. "If you think of anything," he says, "come tell me immediately."

Then he shuts the door.

Which leaves me by myself to wonder why I didn't tell him that I know where Coralee is.

At least, I think I know. What did she say earlier this

morning? "I need you to meet me at the cove. . . . I think I know who—"

Who what?

Who the thief is?

Who we heard in the tunnel?

I rub my hands over my face, racking my brain, listening to the howl of the wind.

And for some reason, Suzanne's face flashes into my mind. Suzanne in Mr. Charles's class.

Then the holes dug in the sand and the empty food containers from the Fish House.

Then the reporter on TV.

And suddenly, I know why Coralee has gone to the cove.

Now I just have to figure out how to save her.

The Plan

～

MY FIRST THOUGHT IS Roddie. Roddie seems to be trying to make things up to me, and he's way more likely to let me
leave the safety of the house to go out into the hurricane than
my parents, or even Grandpa Ike.

But when I get to Roddie's room, I hear a stifled sob. I also
hear a girl's voice, and she's crying too. It's not my mother, so
it has to be Grace, talking to him on the computer. I lean my
ear to the door.

"I love you," Roddie says. "This is so hard."

"I know," Grace's voice hiccups. "But it's for the best."

They're breaking up. No way is Roddie going to help me
right now.

I run through my options in my head. If I tell one of
the adults, they won't let me go. They might decide it's too

dangerous for any of us to go, and Coralee will be stranded. Or Dad will go by himself, or Grandpa Ike. And what if they don't come back? It will be my fault. Again.

I could call Coralee's house and tell Adina, but it would end the same way. Adina would go alone into the raging storm.

No. I can't put any of them in danger to fix *my* mistake. I won't let anyone else die because of my mistakes.

Coralee could be running out of time.

Why did I say those stupid things to her?

Coralee might be a liar, but she's out there in the storm. And she's all alone because of me.

She would never leave me alone like that.

I can't let anything happen to her.

I tiptoe back to my room and rifle through my closet until I find my snow boots, which have gone unused since we moved to Palm Knot. They're the closest things I have to rain boots, so I pull them on and grab my rain jacket, which I stuff under my arm.

When I crane my neck over the banister, the living room is empty. That's good. At least I won't have to climb out of my window.

I creep down the stairs, feeling oddly grateful for the noise of the storm.

When I reach the front door, I stop and listen. There are voices coming from the kitchen. Since the windows are all shuttered, no one will be able to see me once I'm outside.

The door creaks when I open it, but no one can hear it over the wind.

The instant I step out, I'm soaked. I throw my rain jacket on, but it makes no difference. The rain shoots down from the sky in diagonal sheets.

The wind blows so hard that I have to hold on to the banister to get down the porch steps. Once I'm out in the open, I walk like a sumo wrestler to keep my balance as I move toward the garage. After I I adopt this tactic, things don't seem so difficult.

But when I get to the garage, the door is locked.

My bike is in the garage.

If I want my bike, I'll have to go through the kitchen.

If I go through the kitchen, I'll get caught.

I curse out loud without worrying about being heard. I can hardly hear myself.

It's time to reconsider my options.

I could make a run for it, but I might never get there, battling against this wind. Even if I did, I might be too late by then. I glance down the driveway. I can barely see ten feet in front of me.

But what I *do* see is Grandpa Ike's truck. I guess there wasn't room in the garage for it.

I remember Grandpa Ike driving me home yesterday.

I remember him tucking his key under the windshield visor.

I have a new plan.

Ways I Could Fix Things (with Coralee) If I Could Time Travel

1. By actually listening to Coralee on the phone and talking her out of it.

2. By telling Mom and Dad right after I talked to her so they could tell Adina, who would stop her from leaving.

3. By calling Adina and telling her myself.

4. By going to Coralee's house and tearing down her satellite so she couldn't watch the news and never would have figured out who's at the cove.

5. By forcing Coralee to stay at my house yesterday so that I could stop her from leaving.

6. By not biting her head off when she came to see me yesterday. (Okay, maybe this wouldn't fix things, but I'd still take it back if I could.)

The Dare

〜

DRIVING BY MYSELF THROUGH the lashing rain is much harder than driving in the sunshine with Grandpa Ike riding shotgun. But it's still way faster than running against the wind.

Fortunately, I'm the only car on the road.

Unfortunately, the wind rocks the truck cab dangerously back and forth, and when I reach the strawberry farms, where there's almost no tree cover, I have to keep turning the wheel to the right to even stay on the pavement. I also have to keep slamming on the brakes and jerking the truck to avoid debris flying across the road: a yellow tricycle, a spinning plastic pot with a sapling planted in it, a birdhouse, two mailboxes.

The road is flooded. I don't know what I'm supposed to do, so I just push down on the gas harder, which seems to work okay, even though the truck groans every time.

I think I'm doing a pretty good job, and I start to feel almost confident. That is, until I approach the bridge over the inlet. The houses here are all shuttered up, and there are no cars in the driveways. No one is waiting the storm out this close to the water. On the other side of the bridge is the cove, and Coralee.

But there's a problem.

The water in the bay is coming in fast and high. So high that the bridge is flooded. My stomach twists in thorny knots. If the water is this high here, surely the storm drain tunnel is underwater by now.

I can't take the truck across the bridge.

But I can probably manage to get across on my own.

I veer into the closest driveway to the bridge and turn off the truck.

When I get out, the wind hits me ten times harder than it did back at home.

I assume my sumo wrestler stance again and bow my head into the gale, walking at a right angle. When I reach the bridge, I hold on to the pedestrian rail with both hands. The seawater laps at my knees so it's almost impossible to pick my feet up and walk. I turn and face the rail, step up onto the lower bar, and slide one foot forward, then the other. Left, then right.

Like Kacey on the tree branch.

Pain suddenly rips through me. I can't explain why, but it's enough to make me want to double over. It's enough to make me want to let go of the rail and float away on the surging waves.

I can't do this, says a voice in my head. *I can't make it across this bridge.*

My grip on the rail loosens.

But then there's another voice in my head. *Yes, you can.*

"I can't!" I cry aloud.

But it's like I can hear Kacey whispering in my ear. I know it's crazy, but I hear her voice all the same.

You can, Ethan. You can because I dare you. I dare you to make it across this bridge.

A dare. The one thing neither Kacey or I could ever turn down.

My grip tightens again, and I feel my legs pumping against the heavy water.

Through the deafening wind and beating rain, it's like I can feel Kacey pushing me forward.

And suddenly I know Coralee is alive. I *know* it.

I pump harder.

When I reach the end of the bridge, I find I can walk again. Main Street, protected by the rocky bay shore and the wall of sandbags, has only taken on a foot or so of water.

I hit the trail to the cove running and immediately slip in the mud, landing in the water. I grab hold of a small tree and use it to pull myself up. From there, I wade along the trail and through the tree grove. There's even less flooding here. The land rises higher than Main Street, and it's sheltered from the rain by the trees.

I feel a flutter of hope in my chest.

It takes me a minute to see her when I reach the opening in the trees. The first thing I notice is a splash in the water. Then I catch sight of one of Coralee's feet, kicking up through a white swell in the tide.

"Coralee!" I bellow. "Hold on, Coralee! I'm coming!"

I run into the wind, ignoring the sting of the rain and the sea spray on my face.

Coralee grips the rocks above the storm drain with one hand. Her other hand is pressed against the pocket of her hoodie. When the surge pulls out, only her legs flail in the water. When it pushes in, she's almost level with the rocks, her belly floating on the tide. Every time it pulls out, it tries to drag her with it.

She doesn't see me yet. Her eyes are shot with panic, her knuckles gray from holding on to the rock.

"Coralee!" I shout again.

The rocks above the drain are slippery. If I lose my footing, I'll fall into the water.

If I don't reach Coralee in time, her hand will let go, and she'll be pulled out to sea.

And she won't come back.

A second passes that feels like a lifetime. The cove and the bay and Coralee are whipped from my sight, and I'm watching Kacey edge out onto the branch once again.

"I can grab it, if I can just get a little farther out."

"Ethan!"

I'm sure it's Kacey's voice again, but when she calls my name, it's like a spell has been broken. I am back in the cove, and Coralee has finally seen me, and she's calling out my name, too, because she needs me.

"Ethan!"

I take a step forward.

Then another.

Then I'm navigating the rocks as quickly as I can. When I reach the edge, I lie down on my stomach.

"Grab my hand!" I shout, thrusting my arm toward her.

But she doesn't move the hand that's across her soaking hoodie pocket, and she can't let go of the rocks with her other hand.

"Coralee, grab it!"

"I can't!" she shouts.

I army-crawl closer to the edge and lean down even farther so that my hand can grasp her forearm.

"I'm going to pull you up!"

Coralee nods, sputtering through a mouthful of seawater.

I take hold of her arm and pull. She lets go of the rock and wraps her hand around my wrist.

Her full weight rests at the end of my arm. She doesn't weigh much, but she's drenched, and it takes all my force to pull her up. She is almost high enough to rest her elbow on the rock, which will allow me to grab her and haul her up the rest of the way.

That's when the biggest swell yet rushes through the inlet. It sucks the water out so powerfully that Coralee drops back down, and I'm only holding on to her three middle fingers.

"CORALEE!"

She's going to slip from my grasp. I'm going to lose her.

Suddenly, I feel a weight on my right side, and it's not just the wind or the rain. Another person is beside me, larger than I am, lying half on me and half on the rocks. The person shoots an arm out and grabs Coralee below her elbow.

"PULL!" yells a woman's voice.

We pull together. Coralee winces in pain as she struggles to raise herself up.

"Grab her waist!" the woman commands, but I've already taken hold of Coralee just below her rib cage. I feel something squirm next to my hand.

Together, we hoist her up onto the rocks, where she collapses and begins coughing out seawater.

"We have to move," the woman says to me. "This'll all be underwater in a minute."

I find a foothold between two rocks, and together we lift Coralee up underneath her arms. As we raise her, she murmurs something I can't hear. Together, the three of us lurch and stumble across the rocks and into the grove of trees, which has taken on more water in the past five minutes.

We pause to take a breath, and I look up to see who our mysterious rescuer is.

Even through the rain and the unnatural dark, I can tell it's her. The woman we saw in the Blackwood house. The thief.

"It's you," I say.

"Come on," the woman yells. "Let's get her to Mack's."

I hoist Coralee up again, grabbing her around the waist. Then I feel something wet lick my palm and pull it away instinctively.

That's when I look down and see the furry black nose poking out from Coralee's soaked hoodie pocket.

Saving Coralee

〜

THE NOSE IS QUICKLY followed by two still-shut eyes and two flopping triangle ears. Even though it can't see, the creature seems to realize that it's now on land, because it begins scrambling to free itself from Coralee's pocket. Coralee is too weak to stop it, and I grab the animal just as it slips out.

Sharp claws meet the skin on my forearm as I take hold of the wriggling wolf pup and try to stuff it in my pocket as quickly as possible. No sooner have I gotten it in and gotten my pocket zipped almost all the way up than I see another pup crawling from Coralee's hoodie, and I start the process over again.

Above the roar of the storm, I hear Coralee yell in my ear, "Don't let them go!"

"I won't!" I shout, zipping the second pup into my left pocket.

The mysterious woman watches me with bulging eyes, like she can't believe what she's seeing. But there's no time for her to ask me questions. Even in the past two minutes, the water level has risen, and it takes all my effort to wade through the grove while supporting half of Coralee's weight on my shoulder.

When we reach the edge of the road again, the wind coming off the bay hits us so fiercely that we instantly topple over into the water, Coralee on top of the woman, me on top of Coralee. I lift myself to a kneeling position and reach my hand out to Coralee to help her, too. She raises one hand, still keeping the other stubbornly over her pocket. There must be other pups still inside.

"Watch out!" I hear the woman scream.

I whip around just in time to see a street sign, pole and all, come flying straight toward me. I duck, and I feel it whisk through the air just above my head.

The woman yells something else, but I can't hear it. She points to Mack's, the closest building to us. It's less than half a block away, yet it seems impossibly far.

I try to stand and quickly realize that it's a bad idea. The wind will just knock me over again. The water is too deep to crawl. So I straighten my legs and hunch my back. I'm just low enough that I can still power through the wind.

Our rescuer helps Coralee adopt a similar position, and together we make our way slowly toward Mack's. When we reach the sidewalk, which is raised from the street, it's easier. Still, every couple of steps I wince as I feel something clawing at my stomach.

I actually shout with joy when we reach Mack's door. But then I try to open it.

It's locked.

I pound with my fists as hard as I can, thinking there's no way Mack will ever hear us. It'll just sound like another gust of wind or piece of debris caught in her doorway.

But miraculously, almost the second I start knocking, Mack appears on the other side and opens the door a crack. And almost the second it opens a crack, it flies open, knocking me off my feet again.

Mack stands in the doorway wearing rubber boots and overalls. The wind whips her dreadlocks back from her face. She moves to help me to my feet, but I point to Coralee, who looks like she's going to topple over again and float away any second. Together, Mack and the woman lift her into the store. Then the woman gets a strong grip under my shoulder and heaves me to my knees, allowing me to crawl across the doorway, which is flooding more with every second the door stays open.

I climb to my feet. Mack tries to close the door, but it's no use. One of the hinges is broken, and there's no way we can pull it shut in this gale.

I limp to the back of the dark store, past the lawn mowers

and weed killer and screwdrivers, to where I know Mack keeps the plywood. I drag two boards out to the door and then go back for nails and a hammer.

It takes the three of us, me and the woman pressing as hard as we can against the wood, and Mack hammering, to nail the plywood onto the frame, and even then, it's bowing like it's going to snap.

"Can you stay here, Ethan?" Mack yells. Even inside, it's almost too loud to hear each other. "Stand with your back against it, and press as hard as you can!"

I nod and watch as she and the other woman move to the metal shelf that holds the paints. Mack stands on one side, the woman on the other, and they slide it across the floor toward the doorway. I jump out of the way when they reach me and shift to the other side of the shelf to help them push it back against the plywood.

"It's the best we can do!" bellows Mack.

Then she points to the door that leads to the library. "It'll be safest!"

Coralee is slumped in a corner by the cash register, her eyes fluttering open and shut like butterfly wings trying to take flight for the last time.

I run to her. "Coralee? Are you all right?" She seemed okay when we were helping her through the grove. Weak, but okay. But maybe she's not. Maybe she has some internal injury I can't see.

284

Kneeling by her side, I grab her hand, and she opens her eyes and looks into mine. "Are you okay?" I ask again. "Does anything hurt?"

She opens her mouth to answer, but it turns into a limp smile. She puts her arms around my shoulders.

"You came," she croaks in my ear. "You saved my life."

The Library, Again

∾

I HOIST CORALEE UP. I want to carry her, but I can't crush the precious cargo in my rain jacket pockets, so I settle for wrapping my arms around her waist and limping together with her toward the library.

The woman grabs a milk crate from one of the shelves and follows us.

Mack shuts the door to the store behind us, and Coralee and I collapse on the couch beside each other. Mack hands us each a giant beach towel, which we wrap around our shoulders. The only light in the room comes from a few candles on the coffee table.

The woman places the milk crate at our feet. "Here," she says. "For the critters."

Mack takes a seat in the armchair across from us and

watches in awe as I unzip my pockets and pull the two wolf pups out, placing them gently in the crate. Coralee reaches into her pocket and pulls out two more, handing them to me. The pups' fur is soaked and matted, and their tiny paws tremble with fear.

I hear something hiss, and turn my head to see Zora and Zelda glaring out at us from under Mack's desk. Their sour faces, eyes narrowed and noses turned up, remind me of Suzanne and Maisie. They stare at the milk crate but don't move from their hideout.

Mack looks from the wolf pups to me and Coralee, and then to our rescuer, who has taken the other armchair.

"Your families have any idea where you are?" Mack says, settling her gaze on me and Coralee.

I move my head back and forth, and I know Coralee is doing the same.

Mack clucks her teeth. "Nothing we can do about it now," she says. "Phone lines have been down for about an hour. We just have to pray they don't keel over from worrying about y'all."

I suddenly wish I had thought to leave a note explaining where I was going. Would they discover I was gone, or would they just assume I was sleeping in my room? Would they try to follow me if they realized I wasn't there? No. They couldn't make it past the porch if they tried.

I look down. The pups are scratching against the plastic of

the milk crate unhappily. I unwind the towel from my shoulders and set it down in the crate.

All four pups climb onto it and begin scratching, burrowing, and walking in tiny clumsy circles over the fabric.

I glance up to see that everyone else in the room is transfixed by the pups too. When all four of them have settled into sleeping balls of wet fur, Mack slaps her knees.

"Well," she says, "I think everyone here has some explaining to do. Who wants to go first?"

An Explanation

❧

I TEAR MY EYES from the pups to glare at the strange woman.

"I'm not explaining anything until *she* tells us who she is and *you* tell us why you've been hiding her here," I say, crossing my arms in a show of defiance.

The woman exchanges a glance with Mack. Her hair coils in short wet curls, and in the candlelight her eyes look tired, like the weight of her long lashes is too heavy for them to hold up.

She returns my gaze but doesn't reply to me. Mack speaks first. "Coralee, do you know who this is?"

Coralee shakes her head. She stares down at the pups.

Mack purses her lips. "Do you think you have an idea who this *might* be?" she tries.

Coralee starts to shake her head again and hesitates. Then,

to my surprise, she gives a single sharp nod.

"You're my mother," she croaks, lifting her eyes to the woman in the armchair. "Aren't you?"

The woman's lips begin to tremble. She lifts a hand to her mouth and squeezes her eyes shut a couple of times. "That's right, Coralee," she says, her words thick. "I'm Nima. I'm your mama."

Coralee stares at her without blinking. I have a million questions, but I know that Coralee needs hers answered first. So I move my hand silently over and place it on her arm.

I want her to know that I'm here for her now; that no matter what lies she's told, I know she never meant to hurt me. I want her to know I'm sorry.

So I squeeze her arm. Then I look down at my knees, wreathed in scrapes and bruises, and I listen.

"I didn't even know if you were alive. I didn't think I'd ever see you again. Why are you here?" Coralee says.

"I—I wanted to meet you. I wanted to see my baby again. I wanted to make things right."

"By standing outside my window at night? By stealing a bunch of jewelry?"

"The jewelry—it's not what you think. I didn't steal it."

"Then where'd it come from?" Coralee presses.

"Do you remember that I used to work for Mrs. Blackwood?" asks Nima. "I took care of her, and I used to bring you with me when you were just a little thing. You used to play dress-up with Mrs. Blackwood's jewelry. You'd march around the house in her pearls like you were the queen of Palm Knot. She thought you were so funny."

Coralee shakes her head, her mouth slightly ajar in surprise. "I don't remember," she says. But at least that explains how she knew so much about the house.

"Well, one day Mrs. Blackwood told me she wanted to give me something. She handed me a velvet box with a few pieces of her jewelry inside. I told her there was no way I could accept it, but she wouldn't take no for an answer. She said she had all this stuff and no children of her own to give it to, so I should have it to give to you when you were older."

"But then you left," whispers Coralee.

Nima closes her eyes for a long second, and when she opens them, they shine with tears. "I was desperate," she says. "So unhappy in this town. I took the jewelry with me when I left, thinking I could sell it and use the money to make a new life for myself. But I couldn't. Every time I looked at that box, all I could see was you prancing around in those pearls, and I was so ashamed that I had taken them."

"Then what did you do?" asks Coralee.

"It wasn't easy. I didn't have a lot. But I finally got a job, and then a better one. And every night, I would come home, look at those jewels, and think about you."

Now Coralee's eyes are shining, too. "If you thought about me so much, why didn't you just come back?"

"I left you, Coralee," Nima says. "I left my baby. I hurt my family. And that was shameful. But I wasn't ready yet to be the mother you needed. And I knew I couldn't show my face here again until I was someone you could count on. Who could take care of you."

Coralee's shoulders tremble, and I give her arm another little squeeze.

"Why go to the Blackwood house first?" she says. "Why hide out here? Why not come straight to us?"

"Oh, Coralee." Nima sighs. "I have a lot of apologizing to do. I thought it would be easier to start with Mrs. Blackwood. I wanted to tell her I was sorry for leaving, show her the jewelry so she would know I had kept it for you. I didn't know she had died. When I knocked and no one answered, I used the spare key for the back door. It was in the same place Mrs. Blackwood always kept it. You walked in after I'd been there just five minutes.

"And when you saw me outside your window—I didn't mean for you to see me. I was trying to get up the courage to knock on the door, but I couldn't. So I hid here, with Mack."

"And you knew about this?" Coralee says, turning her gaze to Mack.

"Yes, baby, I knew," Mack replies, raising her voice over the noise of the storm. "Your mama was always a favorite student of mine. She had so much potential, so much spark. She showed up here on her first night back in town, and I told her she could stay with me until everything got sorted. I'm sorry I didn't tell you when you brought me that jewelry, but it wasn't my place to tell you what was going on. Not until your mama was ready."

Something heavy-sounding bangs into the wall outside, and everyone flinches. We listen for a few minutes with strained expressions as the wind picks up in a scream and seems to spiral round and round the building. One of the pups lifts its head up, its floppy ears moving forward in alarm.

I wonder if they miss their mother the way Coralee must have missed hers all these years.

I wonder if they know she won't be coming back for them again, like Kacey won't be coming back for me.

"Your turn," Mack yells over the wind. "Why were you out in the storm? And what are all these animals doing in my house?"

Coralee tries to clear her throat, but this sends her into another fit of coughing.

"It was on the news," I bellow. "About the red wolf that escaped from the preserve. They found her body by the Fish House, but they didn't find her pups. So Coralee figured out where they were and went to save them."

The steaks gnawed to the bone, the emptied foil knots. The mother wolf must have sniffed out the Fish House's Dumpster and brought the food back to the cove. She couldn't know there would be rat poison in them. And the holes on the beach weren't dug by someone looking for treasure. They were made by her, kicking up sand, trying to make a den.

What had Suzanne said in her presentation? Red wolves like to make their dens by a stream bank, or somewhere dark and confined.

Somewhere like the storm drain tunnel.

"That true?" Mack asks Coralee.

"Yes," Coralee says, struggling to speak loud enough to be heard. "I couldn't leave them out there on their own without a mother." From the corner of my eye, I see Nima flinch. "Somebody had to help them, and I knew no one else would."

"And you went to save Coralee?" Mack asks me.

I nod.

"But how did *you* know where we were?" I yell at Nima.

The wind and rain are indistinguishable now, like waves are crashing right against the wall, one after another.

"I was closing the shutters," she yells back. "And I could just barely make out the shape of a kid ducking into those trees, and I know that's where y'all like to play."

Nima jumps in alarm when we hear a deafening boom somewhere outside. Coralee grabs my hand and tries to sink deeper into the couch. Even Mack's forehead is pinched with worry, but she keeps her lips in a tightly controlled line.

It's too loud to speak anymore. It's even too loud to think.

And maybe that's a good thing.

I hold on to Coralee and keep my eyes on the little squirming pups that were almost swept out to sea.

Together, we wait for the storm to pass.

Each Other

❧

It's another hour, maybe two, before anyone speaks again. Coralee and I huddle together on the couch; Nima stays in her chair, her eyes mostly glued to Coralee; and Mack paces around the room. Zora and Zelda slink away from the desk and climb into the darkened stairwell that leads to Mack's apartment. The pups take turns trying to sleep and crawl about.

At one point, water begins seeping in from under the door between the store and the library, and I see Mack curse at it. There's nothing we can do but tuck our feet up on the couch and move the pup crate onto the table.

And then, suddenly, it's like some giant hand in the sky turns a tap, and the rain stops. The wind dies down, and I can hear the dull ringing left in my ears by the noise of the storm.

Mack moves to the window and puts her ear against the glass to listen.

"Storm's passing," she says with a sigh of relief.

"How do you know?" I ask. "Maybe it's just the eye."

"You only get the eye if you're in the center of the storm," Mack replies. "The center's out at sea. We got lucky."

"*Lucky?*" It's hard to imagine the storm being any worse.

"We'll stay here a spell to make sure it's passed," Mack says, "and then we'll figure out how to get you two home."

"Did you hear that?" I ask Coralee, who's balled up with her head against my shoulder. "The storm's almost over. We're going to be okay."

"I need water," she croaks. "Can I have some water?"

My own lips are dry and cracked with salt too. But when I start to get up, Nima gestures for me to sit back down. "I'll go," she says. "Mack has some in the bathtub upstairs."

She stands and sloshes toward the stairway, with Mack following behind her, grumbling about damage assessment.

"I'm sorry, Coralee," I say when we are alone. "I'm sorry I didn't listen to you when you called."

She sits up next to me and winces, rubbing her belly with her hand.

"Are you okay?"

"Yeah. The pups scratched me really hard."

"Me too." I pull up my shirt and examine the red blotchy patches on my stomach. "Some thanks for saving them."

"There were six," Coralee murmurs. "But I couldn't save the other two. They're probably dead now. But I had to try, Ethan. I couldn't leave them out there all alone to die."

"Of course not," I agree. "And you saved four lives today, which makes you pretty much the bravest person I know."

"You saved *my* life."

"Sort of. Me and Nima together."

We listen to the sounds of the floorboards creaking above us.

"Ethan?" Coralee says, turning to me, wiping her nose on her towel.

"Yeah?"

"I'm really, really sorry about Kacey. After Roddie took you inside, your mom came out and told me everything."

"You don't have to—"

"I'm sorry that I told Suzanne about it. I only did it because I heard her talking about some mean prank Daniel and Jonno were going to play on you, something about gym class and the flagpole. Daniel was mad about what you said about him being held back. So I told her they needed to quit doing stupid stuff like that. Then my big mouth just blurted it out. I thought it might make them stop. Suzanne used to be my friend, and I thought maybe she would just—"

"You and Suzanne actually used to be friends?" I interrupt.

Coralee nods. "Yeah. I was her best friend the summer her dad left. She hardly got out of bed in the morning, and then she spent the whole day eating cheese puffs in front of cartoon shows and crying. She wore the same onesie pajamas every day, and she wouldn't even shower. There was other stuff, too, but . . . anyway, it was pretty ugly. I came over to her trailer every morning, but then when school started—"

"Her trailer?" I ask.

"Yeah," says Coralee. "They moved into one for a while after her dad left. I was the only one who knew, and she swore me to secrecy."

I shake my head, thinking about how Suzanne made fun of Coralee's house to everybody, but Coralee hasn't said a word about Suzanne's to anyone. "So that's what she meant," I say. "She told me not to believe anything you told me about her. She must have been afraid you would say something."

"I think that's why she stopped being my friend," says Coralee. "She didn't want anyone around who had seen her at her worst."

"And you never told anyone."

"Except you. So you have to promise not to tell anyone either."

I feel an unexpected wave of sympathy for Suzanne, and a sudden rush of affection for Coralee, trying to protect Suzanne's secrets even though she's a bully.

"I promise," I say. "And I'm sorry for not giving you a chance to explain."

"It's okay. But just so you know, I never said that you killed anybody. I just told Suzanne what I thought had happened. I thought Kacey had died that day. From the way you talked about her."

We fall silent for a moment.

"At first, I made myself believe that she was going to be okay," I say finally. "I kept thinking that if I could get to her, I could convince her to come back. But then someone made me realize that she wasn't coming back. That she couldn't."

Coralee sniffles.

"Everyone just wanted me to move on, you know? So I tried. I tried to make myself believe that she was already gone. And it almost worked. Except that doesn't explain why—why it still hurts so much now."

Coralee considers this.

"Trying to destroy hope is like trying to clean sand out of your beach bag," she says. "There's always going to be a grain or two left."

I wonder how she knows so much about holding on to hope. Has she been hoping her mom will come back for her all this time?

"So . . . Nima?" I say, desperate for a change of subject.

Coralee shrugs. "I didn't recognize her. We don't keep any pictures of her in the house."

"Why did she leave? Why did you tell me Adina was your mom?" I want to ask Coralee about everything else, all the other lies. But not now.

Coralee puts her hands on her cheeks and lets her face rest in her palms. "Adina says it was really complicated," she says. "But I always kind of thought she just wanted something bigger for herself than a kid in a small town." And I never *said* that Adina was my mom. You just assumed she was, and I guess it was easier for me to let you think that than to explain the truth."

"Are you happy she's back?"

Coralee doesn't answer. She reaches a hand out to the box of pups and strokes one of them on the back with her pinkie. "Poor little guys," she says. "They're all alone in the world now."

"No they aren't," I say. "They're together. They have each other."

Home

CORALEE AND I GUZZLE down about four glasses of water each. We try to give the pups some too, but Mack says they're too small to drink from a bowl, and that they need milk, anyway. She turns on her battery radio and listens while the news anchors confirm that the storm is passing. She thinks we should wait for another half hour to make sure that things have settled down before we venture outside. While she and Nima rustle up an extra raincoat for Coralee and tall rubber boots for both of us (Mack says there's bound to be lots of snakes floating around), Coralee and I examine the pups.

Now that the wind and rain have let up, they don't seem as scared. They let us pick them up and ruffle their fur with the towel, and when I pet one of them along the ridge of its spine, it gives a contented sigh. Coralee snuggles one in the crook of her arm and rubs another behind the ears. When she's playing with them, she doesn't look like a girl who almost drowned, who has just seen her mother for the first time in years. She looks like a girl who just got a new puppy.

Mack even manages to find two eyedroppers. "So you can feed them when you get home."

"Home?" I ask.

"They may be cute, but those creatures can't stay here," Mack replies, wagging her finger at us. "It's going to be a while before anyone will be able to come get them, and I'll have enough to get on with trying to clean up this store. Plus, Zora and Zelda won't have it."

Coralee and I agree to take two pups each, and Nima finds canvas bags to carry them in. She hasn't said a word since she brought us the water, but now she unwraps a taffy and bites off half of it.

I raise an eyebrow at her.

"Low blood sugar," she says. "Do you want one?"

I guess that explains all the taffy wrappers we found last time we were here. It must be hereditary.

Mack opens the library window and unhooks the storm shutters. The light outside is weak and watery, but it still brightens the dark study.

"Oh, Lord," she sighs.

Coralee and I get up and walk to the window. My boots squelch on the wet carpet.

What we see through the windowpanes doesn't look like Palm Knot. It looks like a water park where someone accidentally left the taps on all night. Main Street is completely flooded, and tree branches and palm fronds are floating everywhere like green rafts. Across the street, a telephone pole has fallen on the roof of the Sand Pit like a giant wooden slide, leaving a starburst hole in the shingles. The trees that hide Coralee Cove lean at absurd angles, and what's left of their branches hangs down in defeat.

An old motorboat has drifted against the rocky wall of the bay shore. Each time the water pushes in, the boat collides violently with the rocks.

But the wind is only coming in sporadic, halfhearted gusts now, and the rain is a mere patter compared to what it was before. I crane my neck to look down toward the bridge. Waves no longer rollick over it.

Mack throws a rain jacket on over her overalls and pulls on her boots. She hoists herself out of the window and lands with a splash.

"How's the water?" Coralee says, the shadow of a grin flashing across her face.

Mack does not dignify this question with a response but wades out into the street and looks to the left, then the right. The water comes halfway up her calf.

"You live up by the Blackwood house, right, Ethan?" she asks.

"Yeah."

"Okay. About two miles. I don't like it, but we can manage. I don't want your folks going out of their minds. I'll take you, and Coralee can go with Nima. Once we get up on higher ground away from the sea, the flooding won't be so bad."

I turn to Coralee. "Is that okay?" I ask, my eyes flitting toward Nima.

"Yeah," Coralee says. "I'll be fine."

We squelch back to the coffee table, where Nima has laid out boots. I peel off my soaked snow boots and socks and pull the rubber boots on while Nima gingerly packs two pups and one eyedropper in each canvas bag. She hands the bags to us like a mom doling out school lunches. Coralee takes hers and lifts it over her shoulder, then marches toward the window.

"Thank you," I say, taking my pup bag.

"No, thank you," Nima says. "Thank you for caring so much about Coralee. You risked your own life to save her."

I shrug. "So did you." Nima may not have cared about Coralee enough to be a mom to her for a long time, but she cared enough about her daughter to help save her life today, and that has to count for something.

Mack helps Coralee and me out of the window and into the water. Nima follows us and closes the shutters behind her.

"Keep an eye out," Mack says. "Look for anything that might be dangerous. Snakes, gators, or downed power lines."

I do as Mack instructs, keeping my eyes trained on the water around us.

Mack takes the lead, and we file behind her with Nima in the rear. It's slow going. Every step takes ten times the effort a regular step would. It's hardest for Coralee, who is shortest by far and is up to her knees in water.

When we reach the bridge, she is out of breath already. I take the canvas bag from her shoulder. It's been hovering dangerously close to the surface of the water, and I know it's weighing her down. "I'll take them," I say.

To my surprise, she doesn't argue. I feel a tug on my shoulder and turn around. "Let me," Nima says. "You don't have to carry everything on your own."

Coralee shrugs and keeps on wading.

"Okay." I hand the bag to Nima. She's an inch or two taller than I am, so the pups are safely above water level, hanging from her shoulder.

Once we cross the bridge, we'll be able to walk in the yards of the houses farthest from the bay, where the flooding is less severe. That's what I tell myself as I drag my legs through the soupy water, stopping every few steps to disentangle them from debris.

"How did you get here?" Nima asks.

Just then, we crest the bridge, and I see Grandpa Ike's truck. Or what's left of it, anyway. A huge tree branch is skewering the windshield, and another pierces the cabin roof. My heart sinks.

I groan. "I'm going to be in So. Much. Trouble."

"What's that?" Nima asks.

"I drove," I say, pointing at the truck.

"Oh my."

Suddenly, I'm not looking forward to getting home at all.

Things We Pass in the Water

1. An ironing board
2. A doghouse
3. Two gardening rakes
4. A tricycle
5. Three tree saplings
6. A bird's nest
7. Two garden flamingos
8. A doorknob
9. Lots of roof shingles
10. The street sign that almost killed me getting to Mack's
11. A basketball
12. Two water moccasins
13. Lots and lots of fish

Reunited

❧

BY THE TIME WE reach the strawberry farms, the flooding barely slows us, and our main challenge becomes finding ways over and around all the debris on the road. When we reach the turn that will take me to my house, I promise Coralee to call her as soon as the phone lines are back up.

"Or come see me," she says. "Whichever one you can do first."

To my surprise, Nima catches me in a quick but firm embrace. "Thank you again," she whispers in my ear. "Thank you for being such a good friend to my Coralee."

Mack and I don't walk for long before I hear someone shouting my name.

"Ethan! Is that you?"

I squint up the road and see a white truck parked a quarter mile or so away from us.

"Roddie?" I yell back.

Two tiny figures emerge from the truck. One of them sprints toward us, while the other lopes behind. I clutch the bag with the pups close to my body and jog toward them.

"It's me!" I shout. "I'm fine."

Roddie reaches me first.

He glowers at me, raising his arms. I wince, ready for him to hit me, or push me. But the next second, he has enveloped me in an embrace so tight that I have to hold the pups in my arms and jut my elbows out so they won't be crushed.

"Um, Roddie?" I mutter. "You're kind of squashing me."

"Sorry," he says. "Sorry. You have no idea how worried we were." His voice sounds funny—it's all quiet and quivery.

When he finally lets me go, I see there are tears running down his cheeks. Grandpa Ike has caught up now and is standing to one side, his face drained of color. Neither he or Roddie are wearing their baseball caps, and it's weird seeing them like that. They must have left the house in a hurry.

Grandpa Ike takes an awkward step forward, like he can't decide whether to hug me.

"Are you all right?" he says. "You're not hurt?"

"I'm fine," I say. "We waited it out at Mack's place."

Roddie and Grandpa Ike cut their eyes toward Mack, like they've just noticed her.

"Hello, Ike," she says.

He reaches out to shake her hand. "Thank you," he says. "Thank you for taking care of our boy."

"Thanks for getting my brother home safe," Roddie says, pulling Mack into a hug.

I have to smile at the surprised O of Mack's lips as Roddie embraces her. I have to smile because I'm just as surprised as she is.

I had no idea Roddie cared so much.

"I would offer you a ride home," Grandpa Ike says, "but the truck can't get past the tree branch there in the road."

Mack shakes her head. "It's too flooded to drive back anyway," she says. "I'll be fine. Not my first hurricane. We're lucky the center missed us. This damage might look bad, but it's nothing compared to what it could have been. Ethan's a lucky boy."

"I guess we're a lucky family," Roddie says. "Thank you again."

"It's no problem. Ike, I'll still have your delivery in on time, storm or no storm," she says. "Oh, and . . . sorry about your truck."

Grandpa Ike looks from Mack to me, but before he can say anything, my bag begins to move and I look down to see one of the pups trying to climb out.

"Whoa," says Roddie. "What is *that?*"

"I'll tell you on the way home. Come on, let's go."

My Best Friends

❧

WHEN WE GET HOME, I see Mom and Dad climbing out of the Subaru. As they hear the truck turn into the driveway, they whip around and start running toward us. I hear Mom shriek. They're both drenched and caked in mud.

"They've been out searching too," says Roddie. "We split up to cover more ground."

Mom flings the passenger door of the truck open before Grandpa Ike can even put it in park. Dad is right on her heels.

"Oh my God!" she screams. "You're okay! You're okay!"

I slide out of the car and am immediately wrapped in their arms.

"Ethan!" says Dad. "We thought—we didn't know what to think."

"We went to check on you, and you were gone, and the truck was gone, and—"

"It's okay," I say. "I'm okay."

When Mom and Dad finally let me go, Roddie steps out of the truck behind me, and Grandpa Ike shuffles around.

"You two!" Mom cries. "You found him! You saved him!"

And before either of them can respond, Dad is hugging Roddie and Mom has flung her arms around Grandpa Ike. "Thank you, thank you, thank you!" Mom says, peppering his cheeks, which have gone bright red, with kisses.

Then she does the same thing to Roddie while Dad goes to shake Grandpa Ike's hand.

"Ugh, Mom, get off!" Roddie says. "You're all muddy."

But there's a big grin on his face.

When we get inside, the house is dark except for the glow of a camping lantern. But other than the power being out and some branches and loose shingles in the driveway, there doesn't seem to be any damage. Mom gives me a flashlight and sends me upstairs to change my clothes. I only make it up a few steps before she and Dad follow me.

"We need to change too," she says. But I know they want to stay close to me.

Five minutes later, Mom, Dad, Roddie, and Grandpa Ike sit in the living room as I tell them what happened. Mom lets out a little squeal when I get to the part about crossing the bridge, and Grandpa Ike says "Thatta boy" when I tell them

312

about saving Coralee. I tell them everything, except for the part where Kacey helped me over the bridge. I don't think they'd understand that part.

When I finish, no one says anything. Not even about the truck.

"That was a very brave thing you did, kid," Grandpa Ike says, stroking his beard.

"But also very foolish," Mom adds. "Why didn't you tell us you knew where Coralee was? We would have helped."

"I didn't want anyone else to be in danger."

"Next time, do us a favor and put us in danger, okay, bonehead?" Roddie says, ruffling my hair.

It's true that I wanted to keep everyone safe.

But I think maybe I went alone because I had to save Coralee. On my own. The way I couldn't save Kacey.

Dad shakes his head. "This wouldn't have happened if Coralee hadn't—"

"She risked her life to save those pups," I interrupt, feeling a defensive prickle run up my spine. "She went to save them because she knew no one else would care enough to do it. She's a hero. And she's my best friend. Just like Kacey is."

Dad's mouth is hanging open, but he doesn't say anything else.

"So," Roddie says finally. "Can I play with the wolf pups, or what?"

Moving On

❧

THE POWER DOESN'T COME back on that afternoon, or that night, either. Fortunately, Mom put a gallon of milk in a cooler of ice this morning, and she and I use Mack's eyedropper to feed it to the pups, who drink down so much, I'm worried their stomachs will explode. I wonder how long it's been since they've eaten.

Mom makes everyone peanut butter and jelly sandwiches for dinner, and we all eat them without complaint, even Grandpa Ike. I realize that I, too, am ravenous, and when I finish my first sandwich, I ask Mom for another.

"Of course," she says happily, jumping up from her chair.

She's been kind of hyper ever since we got home, following me from room to room and talking a lot about nothing in particular. I think she's worried that the strain of the past twenty-four hours is going to cause me to have a breakdown.

And that night, when the house is quiet and everyone else is asleep, I wonder the same thing. My thoughts keep drifting to Kacey in the nursing home. How much longer does she have before she goes? Will she be scared? Will she even know when it happens? Will I?

More than anything, I wish I could be there with her. But I know that's impossible. I know Mr. Reid still blames me. I know he won't let me see her.

When I wake up the next morning, my eyes dart straight to the pups where I settled them last night, in a box with some towels laid inside. They're curled up in a knot of soft tawny fur, their little black noses almost touching. It's like they know their mother is gone and that they will have to support each other now. One of them gives a small sigh, and the other extends its tiny pink tongue to lick its sibling's nose.

Seeing them snuggled together in the box reminds me of the way Coralee and I curled up together during the storm. But it also reminds me of how Kacey and I used to fall asleep in the back of the car on the way home from the pool when we were little, and how we used to sit close together when we watched horror movies in her basement.

There's a knock on my door.

"Can I come in?" says a sheepish voice. Roddie.

"Okay," I reply, sitting up and shifting over on the bed so he can sit next to me.

The bed frame squeaks as he sits down. He puffs up his cheeks and lets out a long sigh. I run my fingers over my hair.

"No school today," he says. "Too much debris in the road."

"Cool."

There's a long pause.

"Look, I'm really sorry," he says finally. "For what I said to you back in Boston."

"You don't need to—"

"At least I can explain. When I said those things to you, about Kacey being as good as dead, I was trying to help. I know it sounds weird, but I thought that maybe if I could get you to just face what had happened, then you might start to get over it. You weren't eating or sleeping. All you did was watch her window and talk about her. I thought the longer you went on like that, the worse you would take it when she really did, you know, die."

"And you also wanted me to get a grip so we wouldn't have to move."

Roddie's cheeks go pink. "Yeah," he says. "I didn't want to have to move."

"That's why you wouldn't speak to me for so long. You hated me because I'm the reason we had to leave Boston."

He shakes his head, his eyes widening. "No, no, you've got it wrong! I never hated you. If anything, I thought *you* probably hated me for the things I said to you. And I wouldn't blame you. I've been mad at a lot of people, Ethan. Mom and Dad and even you. But trust me. I've been angrier at myself than anyone. When Mom came down and said you had gone out into the storm, I thought—what if you never came back, and I never apologized for the things I said? What if I never told you how much I love you?"

"I love you too," I murmur. "I'm sorry you had to leave everything behind. Back in Boston, I just—I wasn't ready to move on yet. I couldn't."

"And maybe you still haven't," says Roddie. "And that's okay, I guess, as long as you get over it *sometime*. Otherwise you're going to end up like Grandpa Ike."

"Grandpa Ike?"

"I mean look at the guy. Grandma dies, and he gets so angry at the world that he shuts everyone else out, even his own family. It's been over thirty years, and he still spends all his time alone. You don't want to end up like that, do you?"

"No," says a voice in the doorway. "You don't."

Roddie and I look up in time to see Grandpa Ike disappear down the hall.

We stare at each other.

"I'll go after him," I say.

Roddie nods.

"And Roddie?" I add.

"Yeah?"

"I'm sorry that you and Grace broke up."

"What?" Roddie says, brows furrowing.

"I heard you guys talking yesterday, about how it was for the best."

"Oh," Roddie says. "We weren't talking about *us*, Ethan. We were talking about Kacey. How it's better for her not to be trapped in that hospital bed. She can be free now."

The Shrine

❧

I TRUDGE DOWN THE hall after Grandpa Ike.

Then I come to a sudden stop. Because his door is standing wide open, and he's sitting in a wicker rocking chair inside, like he's waiting for me.

Is Grandpa Ike really going to let me into his room?

"Well, don't just stand there," he calls.

I step through the doorframe.

Besides the rocking chair, the only pieces of furniture in the room are a quilted bed with a single pillow and a dresser that looks like Grandpa Ike might have made himself.

The dresser is covered with photos.

The walls are covered with photos.

Grandpa Ike clears his throat, and my gaze snaps back to him.

"I'm, um, I'm sorry," I say. "Roddie didn't mean—"

"Roddie's right," Grandpa Ike barks.

Neither of us says anything for a minute while I walk around, looking at the pictures. They are all of Grandma Betty. Pictures of their wedding, pictures of Grandma Betty dancing, even a painted portrait.

There's a little girl in a few of the photos, who must be Mom. Grandma Betty holding her as a baby in the hospital, Mom with Grandma Betty and Grandpa Ike building a sand castle on the beach, Mom dressed in some kind of animal costume, beaming from under Grandma Betty's arm. But there don't seem to be any photos after one of Mom blowing out the candles at her tenth birthday party. No middle school dances or high school sports teams or college graduations.

There's also not a speck of dust anywhere.

"So now you know why I don't want anyone in here messing around," he said.

"It's like a—like a shrine."

Grandpa Ike shrugs. "I guess you could call it that."

There's an empty spot on the wardrobe between a photo of Grandma Betty on a carousel and one of her with a black-and-white-spotted dog licking her face.

"You put one of your photos in my room," I said. "Before I came. The one of her on the bike."

"It's one of my favorites."

Grandpa Ike springs up suddenly, like a much younger

man. "There's something else," he says. "Something I want you to see. Let's go for a drive."

"But your truck," I say. "I ruined it."

"We'll take Roddie's." His face gives no clues if he's angry or not.

"I'm really sorry—about your truck, I mean."

He swipes a hand in front of his face like a bear swatting at a fly. "There are some things we lose, and it's a tragedy," he says. "Then there are other things. Things we probably should have gotten rid of a long time ago."

There's burned bacon downstairs in the kitchen, which must mean the power is back on, and bright rays of sunlight stream through the windows. It's almost like there never was any storm.

Almost.

Grandpa Ike waits while Mom and Dad watch me eat a few strips of bacon.

"The kid and I are going to take a drive," Grandpa Ike says to Mom. "If it's all right with you, that is."

Mom looks at me and back at Grandpa Ike. "I think that will be fine," she says.

I almost choke on my bacon. It might be the first time I've heard them agree on anything since we've been here.

"Can he drop me off at Coralee's afterward?" I say

hesitantly, unsure of whether whatever strange power that has swayed Mom to agree with Grandpa Ike will also convince her to grant my request. "I need to make sure she's okay," I add, just for good measure.

Dad raises an eyebrow, but Mom nods. "All right, but Ike will wait for you outside. And you do not set foot in the driver's seat of that truck, Ethan, or—"

Just then, the phone begins to ring.

Mom answers. She listens for a minute and chews on her lip. "Of course," she says. But her voice sounds uncertain. "Of course. Let me just see."

Then she puts her hand over the receiver.

"Ethan? It's Mr. Reid. He'd like to speak to you."

The Never Letting Go

An hour later, Grandpa Ike and I are in Roddie's pickup truck with the pups riding in their box on the seat between us.

I have to bring them to Coralee's, since as soon as I get home from visiting her, we'll be leaving Palm Knot.

Grandpa Ike drives in silence down roads I don't recognize, finally slowing and turning onto a driveway with huge wrought iron gates standing ajar.

Behind the gates, oaks drape over either side of the road and a brick wall runs alongside it.

He stops the truck and points to a fallen tree branch up ahead. "We'll have to walk," he says. "It's not far."

I lift the box out of the truck, where the pups will get too hot, and tuck it into a shady corner that Grandpa Ike says will be safe.

Then we walk beneath the shade of the trees, and with each step I take I become more confused. "Where are we?" I say.

"A place I spend a lot of time," he replies.

We climb over the tree branch, and on the other side I see a gate in the brick wall.

Next to the gate is a sign:

OLD PALM CEMETERY

"Oh," I say aloud. "Oh!"

Grandpa Ike leads me through the gate, and we weave between rows of headstones and angel statues until we come to a stop under a magnolia tree.

I read the headstone in front of us.

Betty Pomeroy, 1943–1983. Beloved mother and wife. Without you, all the light is gone.

Before I can stop it, a tear sneaks from the corner of my eye down my cheek, and I brush it away.

"Did you do all this?" I ask, pointing to the ground in front of my grandmother's headstone, which is covered in a bed of flowers. They're kind of bedraggled from the storm, but you can tell they were well taken care of before that.

"Yep."

I think about the dead and shriveling plants that were growing in Grandpa Ike's yard when we first arrived there.

It's hard to believe the same man who let that garden die a slow, brown death would have been cultivating this one the whole time.

"So this is where you come every day? When you aren't at home?"

"Yep."

"Oh. Wow."

"You asked me once," he says, "about why your mother and I don't get along. And the answer is complicated, so we better sit down." He gestures to a stone bench behind us.

"Your grandmother was the most beautiful person I ever met, inside and out. I'm not sure why she chose to marry me, to tell you the God's honest truth. And it—it broke me when she died."

"I'm sorry," I murmur, not knowing what else to say.

"It'll be thirty-four years next week," he muses. He looks lost in his own world. "Every year, Mack puts together a big wreath of white lilies for me to give to her on the anniversary. Those were her favorite flowers."

"So that's what you ordered from Mack!"

He cracks a small smile. "Like clockwork. Every year."

I stare at the letters carved into the tombstone. "Grandma Betty died of cancer, right?"

"That's right. Breast cancer. It was horrible. Months she lay in that bed before she was taken."

"That's awful," I say.

"When she died, she took the best part of me with her. There was your mama, just a kid, and me trying to outrun my pain, or trying to drink it away or fight it off. I'd leave for days at a time, not knowing where I was going, just knowing I needed to get away. I'd get picked up for bar fights and spend the night in the jail of a town I'd never even heard of before. If your mama was lucky, I'd remember to call to let her know where I was."

"So you just left Mom at home, by herself?"

"When Betty disappeared from your mama's life, I did too. I didn't want to feel anything for anybody anymore, because if I did—"

"You might lose them."

"That's right," Grandpa Ike says, running a hand over his silver beard. "And when I said I didn't want you here, what I meant was that I didn't like that I suddenly had people I cared about again, people I could lose. And I didn't like having your mama here to remind me that I did wrong. I remind myself of that every day. I know Betty would be ashamed of me."

His voice sounds foggy, and when I look at him, I see tears trailing down his cheeks. He takes off his hat and uses it to swipe them away.

I want to kick myself for being so thick. I had thought Grandpa Ike was just a grumpy old man when really, he was sad. Just like me. And I hadn't even seen it.

He puts his battered red hat back on his head, and for the

first time, I look at it and realize the faded stitching on it is the Red Sox logo.

Even though Grandpa Ike has never been to Boston.

I guess everyone has their own way of loving their family.

"Anyway," he goes on. "My point is that Roddie's right. You don't want to end up like me, hanging on to all your pain, your guilt."

"But it's different," I say, tapping my foot impatiently against the grass. "Grandma Betty died of cancer. It wasn't your fault. Kacey climbed that tree because I dared her."

"Just like I was the one who taught you to drive."

"What does that have to do with anything?"

"When we realized you had taken the truck, my first thought was that if anything happened to you, it would be my fault."

"But that's not—"

"I'm the reason you were out there in that storm. If you hadn't known how to drive, you never would have been able to go on your own. You have no idea how relieved I was when you turned up safe and sound. Your mama would have never forgiven me if anything had happened to you, and I would never have forgiven me either."

"But I was the one who decided to go," I say. "Not you."

"Just like your friend Kacey decided to go up in that tree. Nobody forced her."

We sit in silence for a minute, both of us staring at the

flower bed above Grandma Betty's grave. Then Grandpa Ike kneels down and kneads at the dirt around the plants that have been knocked sideways by the storm, trying to straighten them again. I kneel next to him and do as he does. Bumblebees waft in and out of the crooked blooms, which bob their heads at us in thanks when we right them.

"We never know where life is going to lead, Ethan. What so many small decisions are going to add up to."

"That's kind of what Mr. Reid said to me," I say quietly. "On the phone before. He said he doesn't blame me anymore. That I couldn't have known what would happen."

Grandpa Ike nods. "See? Nobody blames you."

I take a shuddering breath. "Then why do I still blame myself?"

He sighs. "Sometimes we hold on to guilt or grief because it's the last thing we have that ties us to the person we miss. We don't want to let them go because it feels like we'll have nothing left. But it's dangerous, Ethan. The never letting go. Because until you let go, you can't begin to remember. And if you don't cherish your memories of Kacey, then she really will be gone."

For a long moment, we sit listening to the hum of the bees.

"I don't want to say good-bye," I whisper to no one in particular.

Grandpa Ike pats a rough hand on my back. "You'll never have to say good-bye," he says. "Not so long as you remember."

Granny

∽

A FEW MINUTES LATER, we walk back to Roddie's truck.

It's hard to explain, but when we leave, I feel just a little lighter than I have in a long time. Like when you're carrying too many grocery bags and someone takes one of them off your hands.

Despite the huge puddles and scattered debris still on the roads, it only takes us five minutes to get to Coralee's. There's no visible damage, but the house seems to sit even lower to the ground than it did before. I guess it's survived its fair share of hurricanes.

"I'll wait out here," Grandpa Ike says. "Your mother's orders."

I smile at the thought of Grandpa Ike taking orders from Mom. "Hey, Grandpa Ike?"

"Mmm?"

"You were right," I say. "When you said that kids are stronger than people give them credit for. I think old people probably are too."

Grandpa Ike laughs. "I knew I liked you, kid."

I grab the box with the pups and stride up the driveway, but I'm extra careful going up the porch steps. They feel soggy beneath my feet. I almost reach the screen door before I see Granny.

"Are you Farmer Mitchell's boy?" she calls. "Did he send you with my eggs?"

"Um, what?"

Granny is seated in the rocking chair closest to the door. As I approach her, I can hear her ragged breathing, and I see an oxygen mask in her lap. Her milky eyes squint at me, as if trying to make out who I am.

"It's Ethan," I remind her gently. "I'm Coralee's friend."

"Coralee?" She tilts her head up and takes a labored breath. Then she rocks back in her chair. "Coralee. Of course. Sweet girl. Smart, too. She's sleeping. They all are. That's how I was able to sneak out here. They don't like me outta my bed, see."

She raises the oxygen mask to her mouth and sucks in a breath. Her arms are so thin that I can see the outline of her nubby wrist bones.

"Are you feeling okay, Granny? Can I take you inside?"

She waves a frail arm at me. "Have to enjoy this while I can," she says. "Ain't got much time left now."

Granny may be confused, but I believe her about not having much time left. Her face is ashen, and her flowered robe hangs like a tent over her. I should probably go inside and get Coralee or Adina, but something tells me that Granny is right. She should be allowed to enjoy the view from her rocking chair while she can.

"Is Nima here too?" I ask.

"Nima?" Granny echoes. A cloud passes over her face. But then light pierces her dusky eyes like the first stars peeking out after an evening storm, and she breaks into a grin. "My Nima. I knew she would come back for me. I knew she'd come 'fore the end."

Granny rocks forward, and something falls out of her lap. I place the pup box on the ground and reach down to pick it up for her. It's a book. A journal, rather, with a plain black cover.

"Is this yours?" I ask, holding it out to her.

But she shakes her head. "Just the stories," she says. "Coralee writes them down and then reads them to me. Helps me remember. Help her to remember when I'm gone, too."

My arm is still outstretched, but Granny doesn't take the book.

"Go on," she says. "Read. Read some to me."

I open the cover and flip through the pages, stopping

331

when something familiar catches my eye. The page is titled "Tiny the Gator."

I read aloud from Coralee's handwriting, which scrambles across the page as though it was written in a hurry.

That year the summer just refused to die, like a guest overstaying his welcome. I loved my Nima, but Lord, could she be a handful, and seemed like the hotter it was, the more energy she had for bouncing around, breaking things. So I sent her and her sister down to the county fair one day in September to get them out from under my feet. I had laundry to do, see.

Well, Nima had an arm on her like a quarterback, and she won first prize in one of those games, the ones where you throw a ball at a bottle to break it. And what was first prize but a live baby alligator, teeth and tail and scales and all. They gave it to her in a goldfish bowl. That's how small it was. She was holding that bowl like it was a prize hen when she came running down the road. She told us its name was Tiny. Tiny the Alligator! Can you imagine? Her daddy 'bout had a conniption fit, and I wouldn't go within arm's reach of that thing. But she cried and wailed and stamped her foot something awful, and that's how Tiny ended up in the bathtub. Any time one of us wanted to bathe, Nima had to come in and fish that scaly beast from the tub and take it to the yard till we was through.

Tiny stayed until he was too big to fit in that tub anymore. That's when my Chester took him out to the marsh in the middle of the night, and my, but I'll never forget the way that child screamed when she saw he was gone the next morning.

When I finish, Granny cackles merrily and slaps her palm against her knee.

"She liked that gator 'cause it was as feisty as she was, I tell you," she croaks. "She was heartbroken when Tiny got taken away."

So Coralee hadn't made Tiny up. He had been real. He just hadn't belonged to Coralee.

I flip through to the next page and read the title. "Nima

and Granny's Taffy Recipe."

"This recipe won the blue ribbon at the 1986 County Fair," I read, "and can always be relied upon in case of low blood sugar."

"Strawberry juice and sea salt. That's the key," nods Granny. "That's what makes it special from the others."

I flip through some more pages, scanning the familiar titles. "Nima and the Snake Bite." "Uncle Calvin's Story." "The Rolling Pin Rescue."

"These stories seem to be mostly about Nima," I say.

I shake my head as I flip through the book. "Nima's Slippery School Prank." Didn't Mom say she remembered something about someone turning a dance studio into a Slip'N Slide? Maybe that was because it had actually happened here in Palm Knot when she was a kid.

All the stories Coralee had told me were true. *They just weren't hers.*

"Coralee wanted to know her mama," Granny agrees. "My Adina didn't like it one bit, but that was Coralee's way of keeping her mama alive. They're real alike, those two. Adina is more like her brother Calvin."

"Calvin," I echo, remembering what Coralee told me about her "brother."

"He's a doctor. Graduated from medical school last year. Isn't that something?"

I jump when I hear the door creak open. "Ethan?"

Coralee stands in the doorway, looking from me to Granny to the book. "What are you doing out here?" she asks.

"Just talking with Granny," I say, closing the journal and placing it on the table next to Granny's rocking chair. "She was telling me about Calvin."

Coralee's face scrunches up like she's trying to decide whether to get angry. But she doesn't. She opens the door wider. "You better come in," she says. "Granny's not supposed to be out of bed."

Kacey's Song

∽

WHILE NIMA AND ADINA help Granny back to her bedroom, I follow Coralee upstairs.

"Calvin was my uncle," Coralee says. "Granny can't always remember things that have happened. He died in a car accident a long time ago, before I was born."

"Oh," I say, surprised to hear Coralee speak so matter-of-factly about the dead uncle she's been pretending is her own living brother. "That's too bad."

As we climb the squeaky steps, I still see Coralee's small handwriting scrawl across the pages of her journal.

Something about it reminds me of the tidy rows of flowers around Grandma Betty's grave.

Coralee opens a door, and I follow her through. Her two pups are on the floor, snuggled together in a pen she has made out of chicken wire and newspaper. I deposit my pups gently into the pen and look around. A little white desk stands in one corner of the room, with at least a hundred books stacked in crooked piles across its surface. Her bed has a pink bedspread with silhouettes of horses galloping across it.

"How is it with your mom back?" I ask.

Coralee wrinkles her nose. "She's not really my mom," she says. "Not yet, anyway. She and Adina talked almost the whole night long. She says she's moving back to Palm Knot. For me."

"Wow," I say. "That's really great."

"I guess," she murmurs, sitting down by the pen. "She's been running her own store. She wants to start one here, maybe inside Mack's. One of those places that sell cookies and ice cream and candy."

She says it casually, like it doesn't really matter, but I hear the faintest note of pride in her voice. "Like taffy?" I ask, smiling.

"How did you know?"

I shrug. "Lucky guess. What about the jewelry?"

"We're putting it away until I turn eighteen. Then Nima says I can decide what to do with it."

"That's cool."

There's a moment's pause before Coralee clears her throat and claps her hands together. "Anyway," she says. "I have news. We're going to be celebrities!"

"What?"

337

"The preserve just called before you got here," she says. "They're going to meet us at school tomorrow morning so we can hand over the pups. Maria Olivas from Channel Eight is going to be there and everything! They want to interview us for the news."

I shake my head, but I can't help smiling. Coralee will be telling this story for years to come. Only this one will be her own.

"You'll have to handle the paparazzi by yourself," I say. "I came to give you my pups. We're leaving today."

"Leaving?" asks Coralee, crestfallen.

"Kacey's dad called this morning. He said they wanted to wait for me before they took Kacey off her life support."

"Oh," says Coralee. "I thought—I mean, your mom told me he was kind of upset with you."

"He was," I say. "But he apologized. He said he thought Kacey would want me there. So we're leaving tonight. We're going to stay a few days, so Roddie and his girlfriend can do some college tours together."

It was me who suggested this to Dad. Maybe Boston College won't be sending scouts to Palm Knot, but that doesn't mean that Roddie can't still apply for a scholarship. He and Dad are going to work on making a recruiting video this summer.

"A few days?" Coralee asks. "And then you're coming back?"

I nod, then pretend not to notice when Coralee breathes a long sigh of relief.

"That's great," she says. "I mean, I'm glad you'll have a chance to see her again."

"Me too," I say. It's hard to hide the tremble in my voice. I suck in a deep breath of air and clear my throat. "Anyway, I'm sorry I won't get a chance to see the look on Suzanne's face when she realizes you're going to be on TV."

Coralee sucks her teeth and bugs her eyes out in an impression of an enraged Suzanne, which makes us both laugh.

"So, what else did Granny say to you?" she asks when our laughter has died away. Her voice has gone all light and casual.

"She thought I was someone else at first, but then she told me that she was trying to enjoy the time she has left."

Coralee looks down at the pups.

"She's dying," she says. "We've known for a while she wasn't going to get any better. That's why I left Atlanta. I was living with my dad there, but I told him I wanted to come back. To help Adina and to spend time with Granny while I can. But last week, they moved in all the hospice equipment. They only do that when they know someone doesn't have long. That's why I wasn't in school before."

"I'm sorry," I say, hanging my head. "I should have been there for you."

"How could you?" Coralee says. "You have Kacey to

think about. Granny's had a long life. I'll miss her when she's gone, but I know it's her time. Kacey was so young, like us. It's different."

I keep my gaze on two of the pups, who are resting so that their bodies come together to make the shape of a heart with a hole in the middle. As I watch, one of the pups snuggles closer to its sibling, closing the gap between them.

"I know I didn't know Kacey," Coralee continues. "But I really wish we could have been friends."

"She would have liked you," I say. "A lot."

"I want to play you something." Coralee pulls out a violin case from underneath her bed.

"You actually play?" I say before I can stop myself. "I thought—"

"You thought I made that up too?" Coralee finishes.

"Well, I just—I didn't—"

"It's okay, Ethan. What Suzanne told you is true. I do make stuff up sometimes. But it's not because—"

This time it's me who cuts Coralee off. "You don't need to explain yourself to me," I say. "Not to me or to anybody."

Because she doesn't. Because I get why Coralee lied. Like Granny said, it was her way of keeping her mother's memory alive. Of keeping her *mother* alive.

I understand Coralee now, and anybody who doesn't, well, that's their problem.

"Sometimes a story is all you have," she says. "Sometimes that can be enough."

I nod. "Maybe when I get back from Boston, I can tell you some stories about Kacey."

Coralee beams. "I would like that."

"Were you going to play me something?"

"Yeah," she says, pulling a violin and bow from her case, "I wanted to play you a song. I wanted to do something to help you remember her when she's gone. So I wrote this. It's Kacey's song."

Coralee rests her cheek against the violin and runs the bow across its strings. I can tell she's no musical prodigy by the way it whines every now and then, but she handles her bow skillfully. She plays a melody that is graceful and gentle one moment and carefree and bouncing the next. It's just like Kacey. Like Coralee has managed to capture everything that I loved—that I love—about her in this one song.

I want her to go on forever.

What I Know about Myself

1. My name is Ethan Truitt.

2. I have been in the car for one hour, forty-seven minutes, and five seconds.

3. I have a long way to go before I get where I am going.

4. Which is a nursing home, where I will see my best friend, Kacey, for the last time.

5. And when I see her, I will hold her hand until it's time to leave.

6. But I won't say good-bye.

7. I'll say this instead.

"We both have to let go now, Kacey. It's time for you to move on, to be free."

Then I will lean in close so only she can hear me.

And whisper, "I dare you."

Author's Note: The Red Wolf

Coralee might not have known it, but her determination to save the red wolf pups would have helped the whole species survive. In 2016, the US Fish & Wildlife Service estimated that there were only forty-five to sixty red wolves remaining in the wild, and two hundred living in captivity. That means that red wolves are even more endangered than other high-profile animals, such as giant pandas, mountain gorillas, and polar bears. Currently, the only wild population of red wolves can be found in northeastern North Carolina, with other wolves being kept and bred in captivity in sites around the United States.

But it wasn't always like this. Before Europeans colonized the United States, red wolves ranged as far north as Canada, as far west as Missouri, and as far south as central Texas. The red wolf had spiritual importance for many Cherokee peoples, who called it the *wa'ya*. But by the mid-1900s, red wolves teetered on the brink of extinction, due mostly to human interference.

The red wolf is now protected under the Endangered Species Act as a distinct species of canid, smaller than the gray wolf but larger than the coyote, with reddish brown fur that gives it its name. Like gray wolves, red wolves are shy and pose no threat to humans unless they feel threatened. They live and hunt in small packs, mate for life, and breed once a year between January and March, with an average of four to eight pups being born in the late spring. Mother wolves make their dens in well-hidden spots, such as in hollow trees, by stream banks, in burrows made by other animals, or even(!) in drainpipes.

Even though the red wolf is supposed to be protected, its survival in the wild, which helps to balance the ecosystem by controlling prey populations, is uncertain. Due to threats from illegal hunting, interbreeding with coyotes, and habitat destruction, the numbers of wild wolves left in North Carolina have fallen rapidly in the past five years. In 2016, the US Fish & Wildlife Service announced its plan to cut the wolves' recovery area drastically, meaning that most of the wild wolves would likely be removed and taken into captivity. Conservation groups are currently fighting for the right of the red wolf to remain and be protected in the wild.

Coralee is right: every animal should have someone

looking out for it, and you can help look out for red wolves! Here are a few ways to get involved.

- Contact your congressional representative. You can submit a letter in support of the Red Wolf Recovery Program here: http://www.pdza.org/contact-your-representative.

- Adopt a red wolf through the Endangered Wolf Center: http://www.endangeredwolfcenter.org/adopt/red-wolves/#.

- Stay informed and raise awareness among family and friends! Red wolves need people who are passionate about them to keep up the fight for their survival.

Acknowledgments

I owe thanks first and foremost to my entire family for supporting this dream of mine.

Especially to my grandparents, who always had a lap or a knee free and the time to tell me a tale, for first teaching me the art of spinning a great yarn. And to my uncle Bob, who remembers some of their stories and keeps them alive, for continuing my education. I hope this book does them all proud.

To my brother, Ed, for his strength in the face of hardship, and for his loyalty and love.

To Mom, who typed up my very first story and has read (and edited) almost everything I have written since (including these acknowledgments), for being my lifelong inspiration, for raising me to understand the power of words, and for teaching me how to wield them. To Dad, who didn't yell at me for taking Children's Literature instead of Econ 101 like I promised, for teaching me how to drive at nine, for showing me the courage it takes to follow your dreams, and for encouraging me to follow mine. I will always be grateful to them for being my first and forever fans.

To my agents, Polly Nolan and Sarah Davies, who welcomed me to Greenhouse with open arms, for having faith in me, and for loving this book as much as I do. I count myself very lucky to have had their guidance throughout the surreal and often befuddling experience of publishing my first novel.

To Alyson Day and her team at HarperCollins and Jessica Tarrant and the Orchard crew, for their staggering enthusiasm for *The Ethan I Was Before*. The hard work and passion they have poured into it have shaped this book into a better one than I ever knew I could write.

To my many early readers for their keen eyes and open hearts: Mom, Dad, Aki, Becca AbuRakia-Einhorn, Leah Henderson, Ritva Laakso, Kristin McDonnell, Molly Middaugh, and Sunita Stewart. To Katie McCabe, who went above and beyond to support a writer she had never met, to Han Nolan, who knew from reading three chapters exactly what this book was missing, and to my Hollins tutorial group, Amy Debevoise, Deanna Kubota, Anne McFatter Johe, and Andria Tran, whose unbelievably insightful critiques helped me transform a rough draft into an actual novel, I am especially grateful.

350

I have had the benefit of working with some incredible writing mentors along the way, from my summers at Duke Young Writers' Camp to my time as an undergraduate at Pomona College and Cambridge University, and throughout my graduate studies at Hollins University. I am indebted to these educators, who managed to build my confidence while showing me how to hone my craft. In particular, Barry Yeoman, Helen Macdonald, and Hillary Homzie have devoted much time and energy over the years to helping me on my way. I also owe especial thanks to Douglas Smith, my first writing teacher, for telling me at the tender age of sixteen that he would one day stand in a bookstore and read from one of my books. And to the extraordinary Claudia Mills, for providing more wisdom, support, and encouragement than I'd any right to ask for.

As a writer, I don't so much create stories as collect them with hopes that one day I may be able to repurpose or reinvent them. Just as Coralee borrows her stories from Nima, so I pinched a few from friends and family. I am grateful to Becca AbuRakia-Einhorn, to Inga Warrick, and to my grandmother Betty Standish (who really did have a pet alligator named Tiny) for sharing their stories with me and with Coralee.

Certainly, this book was also inspired by my experiences working with the students at Columbia Heights Educational Campus in Washington, DC. I was privileged to have worked with them, and I hope that Coralee and Ethan capture some of the perseverance, kindness, bravery, and resilience that they exuded.

Finally, there are two people whose support was indispensable in the writing of this book and without whom it would never have seen the light of day. From the first time she read the manuscript, Nancy Ruth Patterson has been *Ethan*'s biggest advocate and has cared for this story like her own. There aren't enough words to thank her for her unwavering passion for this book and for her enduring faith in my ability as a writer, which inspired and continues to inspire me to reach new heights.

Last and most importantly, my husband, Aki, supported me in every conceivable way through the writing of this novel and through all the manuscripts that came before it. Thank you for holding my hand every step of this journey, on good days and bad, and for your unshakable confidence in me, which in turn gave me the confidence to write *Ethan*. Without you, I would be lost.

Read an excerpt from Ali Standish's next novel,
AUGUST ISLE

1

Mom was going to leave me again.

I could tell by the warm flush on her cheek, the way her eyes darted eagerly around the house as if she were already gone, already seeing things Dad and I couldn't.

She never looked that happy anymore unless she'd gotten her next assignment.

Reluctantly, I paused *Baking Battles* and trudged into the kitchen, where steam coiled up from the pizza Dad had just picked up. Hawaiian. My favorite.

As I sat down in my usual spot, Mom draped herself into the opposite chair and tugged a piece of pizza free from the box. With her right hand, she began to eat. Her left fingers drummed lightly against the table.

"So," Dad said. He dropped down into his seat, but his shoulders stayed stiff. "There's something we need to talk about, kiddo. Well, something Mom needs to tell you."

Dad always carried a sigh in his voice when he had bad news. Mom pinned on a smile. She looked like a doll, like something made just to be perfect.

I looked more like Dad.

"I'm going on a trip, Miranda," Mom said.

A knot rose in my throat. Without realizing it, I must have been holding on to the tiniest bit of hope that I was wrong.

"You've only been home a week," I protested.

"I know," she said. "But this is a really good assignment. Documenting the effects of climate change in Argentina. The photographer they had lined up canceled, and the magazine asked me to step in."

Mom worked for lots of newspapers and magazines, going wherever they sent her, taking pictures of elections and earthquakes, festivals and floods. She traveled a *lot*.

Sometimes it felt like she just came home to sleep off the jet lag for a few days before chasing her next assignment.

"The story's for *Witness*," she added. I could hear the excitement in her voice, but I couldn't bear to see it glittering in her eyes, so I stared at my empty plate instead. *Witness* was a major magazine. If she did a good job, it would mean more commissions for more national magazines. More trips.

More time away from me.

"When do you leave?" I asked.

"A few days."

I looked up to see a glance pass between Mom and Dad. I wished I could reach up and snatch it from the air, unfold it, and read what was written inside, like a note passed from Kelsey Mays to Tiffany Rubald in the back of Mrs. Painswick's class.

"What?" I asked.

When Mom didn't answer, Dad ran his hand over his stubbly chin. "It's just that this assignment is going to be a little longer than most."

"Only a month," Mom added quickly. "I'll be back before you know it."

"A *month*?" I yelped. Mom's shoots usually didn't last more than a few days. "Can't we go with you?"

Mom's doll smile faded a little as she met my pleading gaze. Her eyes were a swirl of blue and gray, the color I've always imagined the wind would be if you could see it. The color of something you can never quite seem to catch.

"I'm sorry, kiddo," Dad said. "But I've got to be here for the Anderson case. And this isn't the kind of shoot where a kid can tag along."

Dad was a lawyer, and he had this big case about to go to trial. So big he was planning to stay over most nights in Chicago, where it was being tried.

"Then what am I supposed to do?" I asked. "Stay with Gram and Gramps?"

I didn't exactly like the idea of spending the whole month with Dad's parents in Ohio. Gram made brussels sprouts every night, and Gramps blasted the weather channel on high volume all day long. But they were my only grandparents, and I was their only grandchild, so they did spoil me a lot. Maybe spending the summer there wouldn't be too bad.

Mom reached over and smoothed a stray strand behind my ear. I wished she would keep brushing her fingers through my hair, but her hand returned to her lap.

"Grandma's still recovering from her hip surgery," she said. "They wish they could have you, but it just isn't a good time."

I felt my forehead wrinkling, my mind beginning to wander toward dark places. "You aren't sending me back to that camp, are you?"

Two summers ago, Mom and Dad had tried to send me to a summer camp—the kind with lakes and bugs and strangers.

I lasted approximately three and one-quarter days

before finally convincing my counselor that if she didn't call my parents to come pick me up, I would hitchhike home.

"No," Mom said. "Much better. We're sending you to stay with Aunt Clare. Remember? She brought her daughter, Sameera, to stay with us when you were eight. You loved them."

"Aunt" Clare was not actually my aunt—I didn't have any real aunts, or uncles, for that matter. She was Mom's best friend from childhood. She was really nice, I remembered, and Sameera was pretty cool, too, even though she had spent a lot of time showing off her gymnastics skills and also used all my toothpaste.

But that was four years ago, and Clare and Sameera lived all the way on August Isle, this little island off the coast of Florida.

"You're sending me to *Florida*?" I asked. "By myself? For a whole month?"

"I know it sounds like a long time," Dad said gently, "But before you know it—"

"—you'll be right back here in boring old Illinois," finished Mom.

Was that how Mom thought of where we lived? When you'd been to all the places she had, maybe it was a little boring. To me it was just home.

"It'll be fun, sweetie," she assured me.

Fun would have been spending the summer before

eighth grade watching *Baking Battle* marathons with Mom and cutting new recipes from magazines to add to my collection. I had actually thought this summer was going to be the one when we finally started trying some of them. Had hoped it so much I could almost taste them—the lavender-honey cupcakes with buttermilk frosting, and the mile-high peach pie with cinnamon streusel topping, and the brown-sugar pound cake with bittersweet chocolate glaze. Except I would substitute milk chocolate for the bittersweet chocolate, because who needed more bitter anyway?

"I know it's unexpected, kiddo," Dad said, his jaw twitching as he glanced again at Mom. "But can we try to make the best of it?"

I looked up to see that the flush was gone from Mom's cheeks. She bit softly at her lip. I had stolen the happiness right off her face.

Guilt swam in my stomach like a fish in a tank, nibbling away. Mom had gotten a big break, and instead of being excited for her, I was ruining the moment. All because I wanted her to stay in boring old Illinois and watch TV with me.

I took a deep breath and dragged a little smile onto my face. "Okay," I said. "Sure. Why not?"

I could only think of about a thousand reasons.

Later that night, I sat with my back against my bed, listening to the familiar muffled sounds of Mom packing. She and Dad were having a conversation that might have been an argument, but their voices were too low for me to tell. On my lap sat Bluey, the one-eyed stuffed dolphin I had slept with every night since forever. In front of me was a box of postcards.

Sometimes I felt like Mom had a million secrets she kept from me.

I only had the postcards from August Isle.

Until Aunt Clare came to visit, the Isle had just been one of Mom's secrets. It was Sameera who told me that August Isle was where my mom had spent all her summers as a kid.

I didn't want Sameera to know that she knew more about my own mom than I did, so I waited until she and Aunt Clare left to ask Mom about the Isle.

"It's very . . . hot," she said.

"That's it?" I asked.

"It was a long time ago, Miranda," she said. "I was just a kid."

"Did Grandma and Grandpa Crawford live there, too?"

"They spent summers there, like me."

Mom didn't exactly keep my other grandparents a secret, but she didn't talk about them much either. All I knew was that my grandmother had been a painter, and my grandfather had been some kind of business-man who spent most of his time in New York City. But they had died before I was born, in a car crash near the town where Mom grew up in Connecticut.

"Could we go visit August Isle sometime?" I asked.

"There's a whole wide world out there full of places to visit, Miranda," Mom said.

Which I chose to take as a maybe.

But in all the trips Mom had taken, she'd never invited me on a single one. The only place we'd ever been together—besides to Gram and Gramps's—was Disneyland on my tenth birthday.

It was my best birthday ever.

Anyway, after Aunt Clare and Sameera left, I tried to ask Mom about August Isle a couple more times, but she always just said she didn't remember much about it.

I wasn't surprised. There were so many things Mom didn't want to talk about. Like why she became a photographer, or why she and Dad argued some nights when they thought I was asleep, or why I was an only child.

Or why I sometimes caught her looking at me like I was a stranger who had wandered into her house.

So after a while I stopped asking about August Isle, and I didn't think much more about why she wouldn't talk about it. Not until the day I came home from school to find a postcard from Aunt Clare in the mail. Mom was traveling then, so I got a magnet and put it up on the fridge for her to see when she got back.

A few days after she came home, I spotted the postcard in the trash, underneath a banana peel.

I glanced up at the refrigerator, still sprinkled with a collection of last year's Christmas cards.

It was October.

I fished the postcard from the trash, wiped off the banana goo, and took it to my room. I stared at the street lined with colorful brick buildings and rows of palm trees, like it was one of those I-spy pictures, and if I looked long enough, I would find a reason for why Mom had thrown it away. Or why she'd never told me about the Isle in the first place.

When I didn't, I found a tin box and squirreled it away under my bed, next to the bulging binder of recipes I had never tried.

The next postcard arrived six months later and showed a Ferris wheel, looming bright over the ocean.

A few months after that one came my favorite, a card that showed a gigantic tree, light dappling through its lime-colored leaves.

I dug each one from the trash only days after it had arrived.

But none of the cards held any clues, and the messages Aunt Clare wrote were always short and cheerful.

Sending you our love from August Isle!
    —the Grover family

So eventually I stopped looking for answers in them.

Instead I found myself gazing at their pictures and imagining me and Mom into them.

In my imagination, we would ride bikes on the beach and stroll down the cheery street, maybe wearing floppy straw hats. I would point up to the canary-colored building with the white trim that looked like a slab of yellow butter cake piped with royal icing. "What's that place?" I would ask, and Mom would look up and laugh and say, "Well, it's a funny story, actually. . . ."

Now I set all eight postcards in front of me and stared at them once more.

It wasn't that I didn't want to go to August Isle. It was the only place in the world I actually really wanted to visit.

I had just never imagined going by myself.

But maybe I was looking at it all wrong. Maybe I should think about my trip as a chance to investigate. Just because I hadn't learned anything about Mom from the pictures of the Isle didn't mean I wouldn't find any clues about her on the Isle itself.

Maybe I could at least find out more about why she didn't like to talk about it.

And maybe, just maybe, I would find something that would help me understand why everything had changed between us.

3

I tried to stretch out the next few days the way the contestants on *Baking Battle* stretched their pastry dough thin. But before I knew it, we were pulling into a parking spot at the airport.

Mom looked up from her phone, brushing her hair back from her face. "Are we here already?" she asked. "Gosh, that was quick."

"So remember, Mom's going to be pretty out of touch," Dad said.

"I don't know how much service we'll have up in the Andes," Mom added.

"But she's not leaving until tomorrow, so call us when you get to Florida. And call me anytime, okay?"

Dad said, reaching back and squeezing my knee.

The three of us got out of the car and walked toward the airport. I carried my backpack while Dad took my rolly bag. Since she knew the airport like the back of her hand, Mom marched in front of us.

Inside, there were about a million people, including a lady with purple hair named Meg waiting to take me through security who I waved a shy hello to. Once we had watched my bag disappear behind the check-in desk, she stood to the side while I said goodbye to Mom and Dad.

"Well, this is it, kiddo," Dad said. I lunged forward and buried myself in his arms. If I burrowed deep enough, maybe I could still feel them around me when he left.

"Have fun," he whispered. "And remember to call, okay? I love you."

"I love you, too," I said. Then I turned to Mom.

She smiled at me as she unfolded her arms. For the first time all day, when she looked at me, I thought she actually saw me. For a second, I got a flash of the old Mom, the way things used to be. "Come here, sweetie."

Mom's grip wasn't as strong as Dad's. Her arms were light and slender, more like rays of sunlight you had to remember to feel. I wanted to let myself melt into them. "You're going to have a great time, okay?"

"Okay," I said. My heart was beating fast—too

fast—and I clutched at her back when I felt her start to pull away.

She gave a brittle laugh. "Don't worry, Miranda," she said. "Everything's going to be all right. You believe me?"

"Yes, Mom," I lied.

"Good," she said, letting go. I forced myself to let go, too. "And Miranda?"

"Mmm?"

She wore a funny expression, and for a second I thought I might have seen a shadow of worry cross her face. Then she gave her head a little shake and it was gone. "Just—have a good time, okay? Be safe. I love you."

Then she and Dad were walking away, and my heart shattered into a million shards that flew into my chest and legs and fingers and throat and made them all throb with loneliness.

And even though Mom couldn't hear me, I whispered something to her, the same thing I always whispered when she left on a trip.

I imagined my words carrying through the airport and landing on her purse or sticking to her blouse, where they would cling like burrs until she finally looked down and noticed them.

And then she would hear me calling to her.

Please don't forget me.

Please come home.

More books by
ALI STANDISH